# *BLOOD WAR*

## Blood Destiny Series, Book 8

### Connie Suttle

**SubtleDemon Publishing, LLC**

To Walter, Joe, Larry, Lee, Dianne, Sarah and Mark.
Thank you.

# Acknowledgements

As always, this book is the result of collaboration. If it weren't for the support of my editor, my cover artist and my beta readers, it would be less than it is. All mistakes, as usual, are mine and no other's.


## About the Author:

Connie Suttle lives in Oklahoma with her husband and a conglomerate of cats. They have finally banded together to make their demands, which has proven disconcerting to all humans involved.

You may find Connie in the following ways:
Facebook: Connie Suttle Author
Twitter: @subtledemon
Website and Blog: subtledemon.com


## Other books by Connie Suttle:

*Blood Destiny Series:*
Blood Wager
Blood Passage
Blood Sense
Blood Domination
Blood Royal
Blood Queen
Blood Rebellion
Blood War
Blood Redemption

# Blood War

Blood Reunion
* * *

*Legend of the Ir'Indicti Series:*
Bumble
Shadowed
Target
Vendetta
Destroyer
* * *

*High Demon Series:*
Demon Lost
Demon Revealed
Demon's King
Demon's Quest
Demon's Revenge
Demon's Dream
* * *

*God Wars Series:*
Blood Double
Blood Trouble
Blood Revolution
Blood Love
Blood Finale
* * *

*Saa Thalarr Series:*
Hope and Vengeance
Wyvern and Company
Observe and Protect*
* * *

*First Ordinance Series:*

Finder
Keeper
BlackWing
SpellBreaker
WhiteWing
* * *

*R-D Series:*
Cloud Dust
Cloud Invasion
Cloud Rebel
* * *

*Latter Day Demons Series:*
Hot Demon in the City
A Demon's Work is Never Done
A Demon's Due
* * *

*Seattle Elementals Series:*
Your Money's Worth
Worth Your While*
* * *

*BlackWing Pirates Series*
MindSighted
MindMage
MindRogue*
* * *

*Black Rose Sorceress Series*
The Rose Mark
Rose and Thorn*


*Other Titles from SubtleDemon Publishing:*

# Blood War

Malefactor
Transgressor*
by Joe Scholes

*Forthcoming

# Chapter 1

*yyld*

Ildevar Wyyld, founding member of the Reth Alliance, gazed out the window of his library, his hands held studiously behind his back as he examined the grounds around his palace. Three of the twenty members of the Grand Alliance Council, those who'd helped him create the Alliance in the beginning, sat inside his study. They'd all brought news and the news wasn't good.

"So. Solar Red has been in hiding all along. Do you think they remember what forced them from our Alliance to begin with?" Ildevar moved away from the window and sat behind his desk with a sigh.

"My spies tell me that many among them are long-lived, if not immortal. Of course they remember. We all know, too, that revenge is in their blood. Even if they'd been ousted three thousand years ago instead of three hundred, they'd still seek vengeance. My informants also tell me that Solar Red has created an offshoot of their religion, called The Red Hand. This is gaining a legitimate foothold on many worlds, some of them ours," Diedrick, First Grand Alliance Advisor, muttered angrily.

Farle, Nineteenth Grand Alliance Advisor, blinked at Diedrick. "You think they're torturing and killing already? Within the Alliance?"

"They can't help themselves. The more pain they can create before their victim dies, the greater pleasure they derive from the death." Nevarr, Fourth Advisor for the Grand Alliance Council observed. "Brother, what are we to do?" He turned to Ildevar.

"We cannot reveal ourselves. We are the last of our race as it once was, and we will die if we are discovered," Ildevar shook his head. "I fear that these murderers have allied with our enemy and they will recognize our hand if we intervene. Others must wage this war for us. If we die, the Alliance dies with us and the peace we have worked so hard to create and maintain will cease to exist."

"Who will wage our war, brother?" Diedrick asked. "Who among our Alliance holds the strength to defeat them?"

"The one who defeated them before, brother," Ildevar replied. "She is stronger, now."

"You have not heard my news," Nevarr sighed.

"What news do you bring?" Ildevar lifted an eyebrow at his Fourth Advisor.

"That Black Mist is conspiring with Solar Red. Therefore, they are also conspiring with The Red Hand and any other criminal faction that can put two murderers together. If Solar Red is seeking vengeance against the one who defeated them

# Chapter 1

before, then Black Mist is likely taking on their cause—for a fee, of course."

"Black Mist. Even we cannot find them, they are so cunning," Diedrick muttered angrily. "And they move about our Alliance at will. How many kings, queens and heads of state have they assassinated already?"

"Too many," Ildevar agreed. "Any death can be bought from Black Mist, including that of those who have paid them in the past. They have no care for any, it appears. They only care for the money that murdering brings."

"Is there anything we can do, then?" Farle asked. "We expect the Queen of Le-Ath Veronis to be our champion in this cause, but will we just sit on our hands while she protects us?"

"The Five-Year Conclave is swiftly approaching, too," Ildevar agreed. "This is the first she will attend, and that can offer an easy target for any would-be assassin."

"Find someone who can travel to Le-Ath Veronis soon. Someone who will be our eyes and ears there and report their findings to us. Admit it—even we do not know the full extent of her capabilities. We may be throwing an innocent before butchers if Black Mist is involved in this."

"Black Mist is involved, I swear it," Nevarr said. "Money has already changed hands. One of my trusted warlock spies handed the information to me yesterday."

"They'll have difficulty reaching her on Le-Ath Veronis."

"Not as much as you might think, brother."

* * *

*Vionn*

Tiearan Briar studied Corent River, who sat nearby, lost in melancholy. They'd chosen the riverbank beneath the willows for their meeting, and Corent was so immersed in thought he ignored the willow branch that brushed his shoulders as the wind stirred.

Corent was half-Green Fae, one of the rare half-Green, half-humanoids that lived in a secluded area on the planet of Vionn. The small race called themselves Green Birth, and they'd existed on Vionn for more than a thousand years.

The Green Birth Fae had been ousted from one world to the next throughout millennia, until they'd become increasingly hemmed in. Their particular sect did not kill; they existed solely upon a plant-based diet and were restricted to living upon worlds that held the precious crystal—Indis-Banuu—holder of the sun.

"We came here for the crystal, rare as it is," Tiearan sighed. Corent lifted the transparent crystal drop that hung about his neck and stared at it.

All Green Fae knew the sun's light and power gave them additional strength to do their work. The crystal they employed held the sun's light and the Green Fae's power, often for days, enabling them to work in the evenings or on cloudy days when the sun did not shine through.

"The Red Hand religion is an evil, Father Tiearan," Corent muttered. "They spread superstition and murder in the name of their god. They whisper the word magic as if it is a curse. How is this a curse?" He swept his hand toward the fertile fields about them.

"When we first came, we took what none wanted—the most undesirable portion of Farus," Tiearan said. "Nothing grew here except stunted trees and weeds. None challenged when we paid what we could for the land and began to farm. Now that it is a rich and fertile garden, they desire it. They cannot buy it back from us now—we do not wish to sell and Farus' new King is too poor. His people are on the verge of

# Chapter 1

revolt because he is taxing them too heavily. King Rindil, who has inherited a destitute country from his father, is now listening to the Pelipu in Ialus, who thinks of us as demons."

"They will not understand that it takes our power and Indis-Banuu to keep these fields, orchards and vineyards alive," Corent snorted. "Traders seek us out for the excess that we raise."

They wish to kill us anyway, because they have no understanding," Tiearan agreed. "We could leave—it is true— we have left many worlds for much the same reason. But no other world has given us the gift of children, as this one has," Tiearan sighed. "We did not know that mingling with the Vionnu who have come to live and work beside us would produce children. You and the others like you are a joy to us. Yes, we could Flash away from this world and start again elsewhere, but we would be forced to leave our half-Fae children behind. Your bodies will never survive the Flashing, my child. You would be left behind with the peaceful Vionnu and would become a target for a vengeful religion and a greedy King."

"I know it is against our code to kill, Father Tiearan, but many among our Vionnu allies have offered to take up weapons, although their hearts are not in it."

"They have no training for such," Tiearan huffed. "It would be as slaughtering innocent children. The Pelipu has spread his lies and now his followers believe it is our intent to bed their virgin daughters and produce demon children until all of Vionn is consumed."

"They will torture us, before we die by their hand," Corent's voice held sadness.

"Rindil has accepted money from the Temple already, and has begun building an army. The Pelipu will send seasoned troops to add to Rindil's. What do they think we will do against so many? We have no weapons and no desire to use them, should we have any." Tiearan focused on Corent's face. "I am grieved that things have come to this, child," he said.

Corent gazed back at Tiearan. Tiearan was quite old, although he looked very young. Tiearan had the long, pale-gold hair of the Briar clan; Corent's hair was a light blue-green, which often turned a deep blue if he stood in the sun long enough. His mother always told him that his hair reflected water and sky, depending on whether he was in sun or shade.

"What shall we do, then, father Tiearan?" Corent and every half-Fae child had grown up with their Green Fae mothers teaching them to call the older males father. And the older males treated the children as if they were theirs, teaching them small things, smiling often and handing out praise when it was deserved. Corent had known that love from the beginning. He was now in danger of losing that, in addition to his life.

"Child," Tiearan sighed, "we are sick inside our hearts. We wish to leave, but we cannot take our half-Fae children off this world with us."

"Do you regret our births?" Corent asked, studying Tiearan's expression.

"We do not regret our children, only what may happen to them."

"Shall we merely sit back while they take us, then?"

Tiearan watched Corent. Corent's face reflected his mother's—Rain of the River clan. She was worried for her half-Fae son. Rain was the one who'd offered a suggestion and now most of the elders were considering it. They had gone as far as to approach a Karathian Warlock on a nearby world, but he

# Chapter 1

was one of the mercenaries who traveled beyond Karathia's orbit and asked an exorbitant price, which Green Birth couldn't pay.

The Green Fae seldom dealt in gold or precious gems; they dealt mostly in trade—for metal objects and other goods—which they did not manufacture and had little desire to do so.

What little they had in the way of riches (as calculated by the Vionnu) was garnered through trading. They traded away what others considered wealth for nails, hinges, glass bottles, corks, and other items that were needed. Most of the gold they received was paid to the crown as taxes.

"We have come up with an idea," Tiearan finally said. Corent's attention was immediate. "I have not told you before, child, about some of the worlds outside our own. A world lies a few Flashings away where there are real magic wielders," Tiearan snorted. "And the Pelipu worries about us."

* * *

*Earth*
*Gryphon Manor*
*Lissa*
Winkler was having a second helping of ribs and grinning at me. "Do I have a bedroom at the palace, now?" he teased.

"Honey, I think you can have just about anything you want," I replied, smiling like an idiot at my wolf. We'd been talking nonstop ever since he'd folded in. The wolf I'd seen in a carved box at his funeral had been made to look and smell exactly like him. It just hadn't been him, and he'd smiled and kissed me—several times—as I wiped tears away and described the service.

I saw so much in his eyes, so many years that he'd experienced that I had no part in. We had catching up to do—

and time enough, now, to do it. Even Gavin and Tony were having a decent conversation with Winkler—they'd seen him now and then while he'd still been the Dallas Packmaster.

"Lissa, I'd like to ask a favor," Kiarra sat nearby, with Merrill and Adam right behind her.

"What do you need?" I asked, watching as she brushed nearly white hair back from her face and smiled tentatively at me.

"We might want to borrow Gavin and Tony sometimes, if that's okay. They have good experience with things like this, and we might need their help."

"Help with what?" Gavin and Tony were both interested, but Tony was the one to ask.

"With Ra'Ak spawn. These rogue Ra'Ak won't be following the rules and it's a sure bet they'll be making spawn as quickly as possible. The vampires we have can scent them just as well as the werewolves, so it's easy for them to locate spawn. With their enhanced speed, vampires have the easiest time killing them, too. If Gavin and Tony consent to freelance for us, we'll give them Folding and Looking capability."

"You can do that?" Tony was very interested now.

"We can do that, but you have to follow the rules as far as using those gifts go," Kiarra smiled at him.

"I'm in," Tony declared.

"If Lissa agrees." Gavin's response was more circumspect.

"I agree, if you want to," I nodded at both of them. "I don't have a problem with it."

"I'll come next week, then, and we'll take care of it." Kiarra was happy, I could tell. We folded home not long after that, Winkler pulled me into my bedroom and proceeded to lock everybody else out.

# Chapter 1

"I've waited forever for this, and the good news is that I won't poison you if I nip a little," he grinned at me just before he lowered his head and gave me the best kiss ever.

A woman told me long ago that werewolves were possessive in bed. I thought she was only talking about her werewolf. She wasn't. Winkler not only had me clawing on his back and moaning his name, he had me tucked against him and was nipping my shoulder if I tried to move while he napped afterward.

* * *

"So, what's the big brouhaha Council meeting about this morning?" Winkler asked. I was watching him dress the following morning and keeping my mouth shut while I did it—it's never attractive for the Queen to drool. Yeah, I would have watched Winkler all day. If I could have. Muscles rippled in his arms as he pulled on a dress shirt.

"Oh, I'm supposed to talk now," I mentally pulled myself away from Winkler's physique.

"Yeah," he grinned.

"Well, we're pulling in all the vamps who have female vampire mates, just to make sure the female mate in question wants to be with the vampire and isn't under compulsion or duress. The idea is to make sure the mates aren't being mistreated."

"I thought the bond had to be renewed every hundred years."

"It was like that on Earth. Other worlds have less or more time, depending on their Council. However, if you think that Wlodek actually checked to see if the female—or male if that was the case—actually wasn't under compulsion, then you can likely think again. Most of those vampires on Earth belonged to the Aristocracy, and it was prestigious to have a female vampire among your many possessions. I don't believe for a minute they'd let that get away if they could help it. Part of today's meeting will be about making it unlawful to place compulsion of any kind on your mate. There's no need to hide anymore, so there shouldn't be any reason for it."

"If you'd been susceptible to compulsion like everybody thought, you'd be stuck with Gavin only, wouldn't you?" he asked. I stood and went to help button his shirt. Winkler pulled me against him and kissed my forehead.

"Yeah." I leaned my head against his chest and listened to his heartbeat for a moment. "I missed you."

"I tore down your house."

"I don't care. I won't ever get to live there, anyway."

"I get that." He tilted my chin up and rubbed my nose with his before kissing me. "I'm getting mindspeech from Tony. He says all hands and the cook need to go to the Council meeting, in case we meet with resistance on the no-compulsion-on-your-mate thing."

"Cheedas doesn't need to be anywhere near the Council meeting, so tell Tony to leave the cook out of it."

"Will do." Winkler kissed me again before leading me from my suite and toward the dining hall.

* * *

The usual crowd was there at the table, plus a few extras. I was coming to accept it as normal—that people would just show up. What surprised me, though, was Dragon's presence. He was sitting beside Gavin, having sausage and eggs with my irascible vampire mate. Dragon stayed and motioned for me to sit down again after the others left, including Winkler, Drake and Drew. Gavin and Tony probably wanted to go over procedure in case the Council meeting wasn't a peaceful one. Dragon moved to the chair next to mine.

# Chapter 1

I watched his face—dark eyes examined my expression carefully while he wore his usual, inscrutable scowl. I waited for him to speak. "Lissa," he began, "I haven't failed to notice that you're not speaking to me." He looked away, as if that troubled him.

He was right—I hadn't really spoken to him since we'd come back from Falchan after getting rid of the REHs there—the Ra'Ak-enhanced humanoids. He'd gotten upset when I interrupted him while he was laying down the law—in a Warlordy sort of way.

He'd done some yelling at me afterward, about following the orders of a superior officer (or an approximation, anyway). Dragon was the leader of our little army of thirteen, although I hadn't officially signed up. I guess that made me a draftee—and a low-ranking one, to boot. He'd yelled at Drake and Drew, too, since they hadn't properly explained the chain of command thing.

"You gonna yell about that, too?" I asked.

Dragon sighed as he turned and focused eyes so dark they were almost black on me again. His boys—all three of them, had gotten his genes and good looks. All had dark eyes, black hair they kept braided down their backs and all wore dragon tattoos.

"Lissa, we're family," Dragon sighed. "Your family. We pulled you out of here too fast, so you wouldn't have the opportunity to argue or turn us down. Belen said it was important to take you with us and we didn't have time to explain that."

"Well, why don't you have a talk with Merrill and Wlodek about sending Lissa in to do the dirty work without any information." Yeah, it pissed me off whenever I was asked to do something with little or no instruction or information.

"I did have a talk with them, and they explained how much you hate that. I also know that you hold yourself back from them—like there's a barrier between you that they may never be able to tear down. They regret that reserve you have with them. They want to count you as family so bad they can taste it."

"Yeah? Too bad they didn't see things that way before," I grumped. "With them, their objective was to send Lissa here or there and get her to do this or that, they just wouldn't tell her anything, because heaven forbid she might learn big, bad, vampire secrets or something."

"You were a young vampire, and they generally don't give out important information to vampire young. You might have been given more after the five years was up."

"Well, gee, too bad that sort of turned to shit, then, huh? I've never finished my five years of instruction. Feel free to tell Merrill that if he thinks he and Gavin are going to start teaching me again, to forget that idea right now."

"I didn't come to stir up old wounds and grievances," Dragon looked down at his hands. A tattoo of one of Grace's Lace-feathered Eagle feathers was at the base of one of his thumbs. "I came to make things right between you and me," he went on, looking at me again. "This way family dinners and vacations will go a lot smoother."

"What family vacations and dinners?"

"The ones Devin and Grace are asking for."

"Dragon, you came just to see if you could give me a headache, didn't you?" The migraine was coming on—I had a knot between my eyes, now. I was worried enough about the Council meeting; it was beginning to make my skin itch. Now, Dragon wanted to clear the air. It's funny that clearing the air always involves clouding it up, first.

# Chapter 1

"No, little vampire." He reached out toward my forehead with his fingers. I jerked back, but he already had the back of my neck cupped in his other hand, soothing the headache while light formed around his fingers. "I am First among the Saa Thalarr, Second before that and Warlord on Falchan before that. I am used to giving orders and demanding the full attention of my underlings. I failed to remember that the Queen of Le-Ath Veronis is not an underling. I also failed to let her know that in order for us to appear as an ordinary band of warriors, that one had to lead and the others follow without question or interruption. Things might have gone better if that information had been passed along first thing. I allowed my temper to stand in the way of more prudent judgment. I'll try not to let it happen again. And just so you know, Caylon Black says he should never have been fool enough to spar with you to begin with."

"I'm not upset with Caylon."

"Just with me, is that right?"

"You told me once that you would have slept better while you were Warlord if I'd been guarding the nights," I said. "That's what I do, Dragon. I try to keep the people I care about safe. Sometimes I open my mouth before I think, but that isn't a sign of disrespect. Not for you or your brother or Caylon. I'm still waiting for people to accept what I am. While I was human, and as a vampire." I snorted at my human comment. I'd never been human; I just hadn't realized it before.

"When I went to see Howard Graham," I went on, "he still felt it necessary to point out that I wasn't his—like I hadn't gotten that message long ago while he was beating it into me."

"Lissa, these people aren't Howard Graham. They're waiting for you to accept their love. I think you're holding yourself in reserve with all of them so the pain won't be so bad when they betray you. Gabron betrayed you, I know. That has dealt a blow. I wish there was some way to make you trust us. Some way that you might be able to listen to me have my little fit after you interrupted my instruction and know that underneath it, I still love you. I think I loved you the minute you dropped several Solar Red priests and their van in the street from fifty feet above their temple. If there was ever any way to get those fuckers' attention, that was the way to do it."

"They were about to go into a house where a couple and their five children lived. They had guns, Dragon. No way was I going to let them kill any babies if I could help it."

"I know. I'm asking you now not to measure all of us against Howard Graham. I might yell at you, but if you think I would ever lay a hand on you, then you need to think again. Merrill says that one of the biggest mistakes he and Wlodek ever made was the decision to hand out a beating as punishment. I think he would stand naked on the dome of your palace and scream an apology if it would make any difference."

"Interesting visual, but I don't think that'll help," I muttered, leaning my head into my arms on the table.

"For now, I'm asking you to forgive me. I want things to be better between us when Grace and Devin ask you to dinner. I owe you my life, Lissa. I just forgot that for a while. Tell me you don't regret saving me—and Refizan—all those years ago."

"I don't regret it, Dragon," I straightened and looked at him. "And I'd do it again, even if I do feel a little grumpy at you."

"Good. I don't like needing my ass saved, but if it needs saving, I'd prefer that you did it." He grinned before standing and stretching.

# Chapter 1

"Anytime," I said, smiling back. When I stood, Dragon pulled me into a bone-crushing embrace. "Just don't forget we love you," he whispered and disappeared.

* * *

"Where is the Raona?" Roff asked when Flavio led him into the Council chamber. Gardevik Rath, Lissa's High Demon mate, was currently presiding over the Council, logging names of attendees as they arrived. He was Prime Minister on Kifirin, under his brother Jayd's rule. Of all Lissa's mates, he had the greatest amount of experience in governing.

"The Raona is on her way; I just received mindspeech from Gavin and Winkler," Flavio explained as Roff took a seat next to his vampire sire. "Both are escorting the Queen to today's meeting."

"Is she well?" Roff asked.

"She is quite well. Winkler returned to her and I believe they spent the night together."

"Someone else spent the night with my Queen?"

Flavio lifted an eyebrow at Roff's statement—he'd made my Queen a proprietary statement. "Child, are you trying to tell me something?" he asked.

"I wish to spend the night with the Queen. I see all the others with her and I want to be one of them."

"Are your memories returning?" Flavio asked gently.

"No. I still cannot remember," Roff frowned at the admission. "But I want her, father. I want to know her better. Is that wrong?" Roff searched Flavio's face for approval.

"It is not wrong. Perhaps you should court her. I hear women love to be courted. Do you have your comp-vid with you? Order flowers and use my account."

Roff immediately thumbed through many arrangements, looking for something he thought the Queen would like. "What about this one?" He held up the comp-vid.

"Lilies are always nice, but ask them to add roses. Roses are generally the accepted gift."

"Ah. It says when you wish to say I love you on these red roses. That seems appropriate. I will send roses and lilies." Roff set about placing the order. "What is the Council meeting about today?"

"Today, we are discussing something that is unprecedented. Lissa wishes to see all the female vampires and their mates. We will learn if any of the twenty-seven are trapped in compulsion."

"How will we know that?" Roff asked.

"The Queen will know, child. And since this has never been done before, we will have extra guards coming in case any of the males object to their compulsion being removed at the Queen's command."

"Some of the females may not want the males they are with, but may be forced to stay with them anyway? That doesn't seem right."

"It isn't." Radomir settled into a seat beside Roff.

"Hello, Uncle Radomir," Roff beamed. He'd come to like Flavio's vampire sibling very much, even if he was a bit different and a member of a very secret race. Flavio had explained about the Saa Thalarr shortly after Roff's turning, and introduced Radomir as a vampire brother.

"Roff," Radomir offered a smile.

"Radomir has come, in case the Queen needs help," Flavio explained.

"What will you do, Uncle Radomir?"

# Chapter 1

"Make sure they don't get out of hand. Some of these vampires may be very possessive." Radomir was fourteen hundred years old, didn't look more than twenty-five and was darkly handsome, with black eyes and dark hair. He offered a grin and a nod to Roff, who seemed baffled that anyone would force a female to stay with them—especially if the female had no love for the male involved.

"Here she is," Flavio tapped Roff's hand. Roff jerked his head toward the door. Lissa entered the Council chamber, Gavin on one side, a male he didn't recognize on the other. She was dressed tastefully in a green silk tunic and slacks.

"Is that her new mate?" Roff asked, nodding toward Winkler.

"He is a mate we thought was lost. He has now returned to the Queen."

"Was he lost, as I was lost to her?"

"No, child. Everyone thought him dead. You were wounded and turned vampire. Only your memories have vanished. You have always been here." Flavio smiled encouragingly at Roff.

"I cannot say how frustrating it is to not remember her from before. Or many others. And I do not understand why Giff weeps when she sees me."

"We will explain that in time. Meanwhile, we will work to get your memories back."

* * *

*Lissa*

My skin tingled as I walked inside the Council chamber, although only Council members were inside, waiting. The mated vampires had been ushered into my library and would be brought to the Council chamber when their item was called on the agenda. Flanked by Winkler and Gavin (Winkler insisted, displacing Tony) I took my place on the high seat at the front.

"All members are present, my Queen." Garde, who'd arrived early to tick off names, nodded formally to me. *Remember this meeting is being fed live to the Alliance*, he cautioned mentally. *We do not wish to alarm the Alliance if they see you turn to mist. Do you recall our security meeting, Avilepha? We've had to explain some of your actions as swift movement by a vampire. We have no desire to explain away other anomalies.*

He was right—we'd had a security meeting shortly after we'd allowed Bryan's cameras inside the Council meetings—they not only fed images of the meetings to the local vampire population but to the Reth Alliance as a whole. Everybody was allowed to see vampires in action.

The only meetings that weren't fed to the general population were executions, and it was better that nobody was allowed to see those. Only the Council and any involved parties invited by the Council viewed executions. Le-Ath Veronis was one of the few worlds belonging to the Alliance that executed certain offenders. The difference was that Le-Ath Veronis' justice was swift, as any vampire was more than aware.

*I won't turn to mist or do anything else unbecoming*, I promised Garde. He breathed an audible sigh of relief.

"What is the first item on the agenda?" I called out. Heathe, who'd come to do the agenda, made the announcement.

"The unlawful placement of compulsion against a mate," Heathe called out. Kyler would normally have made the announcement, but Flavio asked Kyler to stay home. I didn't blame him—the prospect of forcing a female vampire to stay

# Chapter 1

with her mate upset her as much as it did me. Heathe volunteered to make announcements; Grant and Davan wanted no part of it, either.

Honestly, I'd have stayed in bed with Winkler if I could have. This wasn't going to be pretty, no matter how you looked at it. We were about to find out how many female vampires had unfair compulsion placed, just so a male could have a (potentially unwilling) trophy wife. "Bring in our guests," I said, working to keep the worried sigh from escaping. My uneasiness was growing, even with a Council full of vampires with me.

Twenty-seven vampires and their female mates were led inside the Chamber. Chairs had been set out for all of them, and I watched the women as they followed their male mates inside.

All of them. All of them had some sort of compulsion placed. I didn't take time to sort through it—it could have been anything from you can't go shopping, to you will give me blowjobs until the end of time. It no longer mattered—all compulsion would be removed before they left the Council chamber.

If the women needed a place to stay afterward, I'd already made arrangements for them at a halfway house. The youngest female before me was more than four hundred years old, so it was possible they hadn't been outside or on their own in a very long time.

"My Queen, I wish to make a statement," one of the male vampires stepped forward. Yes, I probably should have seen it coming. I didn't. All twenty-seven males had claws out and all twenty-seven females had their throats cut before the war inside the Council chamber commenced.

# Chapter 2

*L*issa

We were only able to save eleven of the twenty-seven females. We might have saved more if forty-three members of the Council hadn't joined the male vampires who'd just committed murder or attempted murder against their mates.

Someday, somebody was going to have to explain this to me—why some men feel obligated to kill their wives if they refuse to stay in an unhealthy relationship. Somehow, these vampires had managed to get together with forty-three members of the Council, devise a plan and then make their murderous statements.

* * *

"Lissa, if you will hold still, I will heal this gash." Karzac was at his grumpy best as he worked to heal the wound on my thigh. That's all my attacker had been able to touch before

Gavin sliced him to shreds. He'd only reached me to begin with because I'd tried to get to one of the women before she died.

"How's Roff," I asked, instead of grumbling back at Karzac. Roff, Flavio and Radomir had been surrounded by rogue Council members. Flavio and Radomir had no trouble fending off attackers, but Roff had been knocked down and deeply clawed.

Without even thinking about it, Radomir had dropped to his knees, given permission and then offered Roff blood. Roff was now sleeping the eight hours it would take for Radomir's Saa Thalarr blood to bring the changes to his vampire body. I'd wanted to offer blood to Roff if he ever returned to me. Radomir had done it instead. I sighed.

"Roff is very well. I believe Franklin is with him, checking for additional wounds."

"Do you think Radomir's blood will bring back his memories?"

"Lissa, you are wounded, sixty-four vampires are dead including sixteen females, your Council chambers are in shambles and you're worrying about Roff's memories?"

"Thanks for the wake up, honey," I muttered sarcastically. "I was trying not to think of what the media is going to make of this. This makes the riot on Serendaan look like a schoolyard brawl."

"Serendaan's King deserved the blow he took. And the fight that came after." Light formed around Karzac's fingers as he touched my thigh. I didn't want to look while he worked—I'd done it once and the flaps of skin hanging from the wound made me want to blow chunks. "I trust you've canceled Council meetings until tempers are calmed and the chambers can be repaired?"

# Chapter 2

"I'll take care of it," I sighed. "I want to take a look at our prisoners, too. We'll move the trials up to the next Council meeting. Gavin, Aryn and Aurelius are questioning all of them now."

"Your Falchani and your wolf are also in the dungeons, and your wolf is, well, a wolf. I believe he's growling at the prisoners, too."

"You don't think he should?"

"As long as he removes no vital body parts until judgment is passed, I think I can live with it," Karzac replied. He knew, as did I, that Winkler had taken down at least two vampires inside my Council chamber. As a Spawn Hunter, he no longer had to undress to become wolf. He'd gone to his wolf and that wolf had snapped heads off two vampires who'd just murdered their wives.

"I can't believe they all went crazy like that," I tossed up a hand.

"Lissa, please stop moving about. It makes it difficult to heal shredded skin."

"Fine," I mumbled. "Did I take you away from something? You don't usually dress in a suit." I focused on what Karzac was wearing for a moment.

"Devin, Grace and I took Kevis to Refizan for his naming ceremony."

"Oh, Karzac, why didn't you stay there? Somebody else could patch me up." I reached out to touch his cheek—his head was bent over my wound as I lay on the bed inside my suite.

"Dragon has promised to bend time to get me back for the ceremony. I will miss nothing."

"That doesn't make this right. Call Frankie or Shane. They can fix me up. Go on, shoo." I was moving my hand again, making Karzac's frown deeper as he worked.

"What in the name of the first Warlock happened?" Erland strode into my bedroom and he didn't look particularly happy. That was unusual—Erland didn't anger easily.

"A bunch of wife-killing vampires plus a few of their closest collaborators, that's what happened. Erland, will you call another healer so Karzac can go back to Kevis' naming ceremony?" I begged Erland to do something. Karzac wasn't happy. Actually, I'd settle for not happy. Karzac was seriously grumpy.

"Healer, she is more upset than she sounds." Kifirin had arrived. "You are not helping. I will deal with the wound."

Karzac looked up and raked Kifirin with green-gold eyes that weighed and measured before he nodded and folded away. It was a relief, actually.

Erland stepped away but stayed inside my suite, preferring to remain silent as Kifirin touched my thigh with gentle fingers, healing in a blink what Karzac had struggled to cure. "Lissa, you and I know that you could have done nothing other than what you did inside the Council chamber," Kifirin admonished. Well, he knew if the others didn't. "If you are not energy, you cannot prevent things such as this. Trying while in your corporeal body would have destroyed it."

"And bending time to bring back the dead is interference. I know," I sighed.

"We must have permission for those things," Kifirin agreed, brushing hair back from my face. I brought my eyes to his, knowing I would see stars in their dark depths. I wasn't wrong.

I existed in a paradox. If I turned to energy and left my corporeal body behind, I held a great deal of power. When my spirit was stuffed inside a corporeal body, I had a corporeal body's limitations. Did it irritate me? Irritate is much too tame

# Chapter 2

a word. At times, it infuriated me. And the knowledge that Kifirin was the only mate I could keep if I left my corporeal body behind had me holding onto it—dearly.

Yes, I carried my body as mist at times when I went to energy, but if I wanted to expend any of that energy, I had to set my body down somewhere and concentrate on what I wanted to do. I sure didn't need an unconscious body lying on the floor of my Council chamber while I took care of business. Bryan's cameras had recorded the whole incident anyway. The entire Alliance didn't need to know that my body was vulnerable at times.

"Wc lost sixteen female vampires." Those were precious and rare lives—all wasted.

"My love, do not allow this to worry you. These lives will return."

"Kifirin, they deserved justice in this life. Not the next," I grumped, wiping away the first tear. I'd forced myself not to cry.

Until now.

* * *

"How are you feeling, child?" Flavio sat on the edge of Roff's bed.

After Roff was knocked down and clawed by a rogue vampire, Radomir removed the attacker's head and then quickly offered his blood to heal Roff. Roff wasn't sure what it meant when Radomir gave formal permission for him to take blood, but the blood had been the best he'd tasted.

Roff had been extremely sleepy afterward, even amid the battle raging inside the Council chambers. Once it was over and the brief rebellion quelled, Radomir helped put Roff to bed, explaining that he'd sleep for eight hours. Now, Roff was waking and his sire was asking how he felt.

"I feel very well, father," Roff politely covered a yawn. "Perhaps a little hungry."

"Good. Come with me; we'll see if you can eat solid food, now."

"Father?" Roff was confused. As a vampire, he'd learned that solid food made him ill.

"Radomir's blood may have brought about changes, child. We'll see." Flavio urged him to get out of bed. Roff rose, slipped into a shirt and pants, then folded wings tightly against his body and followed his vampire sire to the kitchen. Flavio's comesula cook was there, preparing breakfast.

"Try this," Flavio handed a plate of pancakes to Roff. Roff recognized them; thick, sweet syrup would go over the pancakes. He remembered the sweet taste from before, but he doubted they'd taste good now.

"Go ahead, try them," Flavio coaxed. Roff poured warmed syrup over his pancakes and cut off a small bite. The sweetness hit him immediately and he moaned in pleasure.

"Father, these are excellent," Roff sat down at the small kitchen table and dug in. Flavio got a plate for himself and joined his youngest at breakfast.

* * *

*Lissa*

"Lissa, wake, my darling." Only one of my mates woke me like that—Erland had spent the night. *After* Kifirin placed me in a healing sleep. The schmuck.

"Erland, please tell me I can fold away and not come back for months," I mumbled as he kissed and stroked my hair.

"Sadly, you cannot. I have received mindspeech from Gavin and Anthony. Your prisoners are demanding to see you."

# Chapter 2

"Great." I forced my eyes open. "They think they still have rights, don't they? Has the entire Alliance seen what happened inside my Council chambers yesterday?" I blinked up at Erland's handsome face. I still didn't understand how he managed to look so good after a full night's sleep. I looked like a rumpled mess every morning.

"And most worlds outside the Alliance have witnessed your debacle. Certainly those with any sort of signal-receiving technology. Your grandfather has already offered to send warlocks if you want your prisoners to suffer before their beheading. He found the murders of those poor women appalling."

"Tell Em-pah to hold off, although it's tempting." Erland leaned back to allow me to sit up in bed. "But those murderous assholes can wait until after we've had breakfast."

"They will undoubtedly wait until after breakfast," Erland agreed and insisted on carrying me to the shower.

* * *

"If you will bathe and dress, we will visit the Queen this morning," Flavio informed Roff. "I believe the flowers you sent her should arrive before we do."

"I sent the Queen flowers? Father, why would I do that?" Roff's brow furrowed in puzzlement.

"Child, do you not remember her—again?"

"Did I remember her?"

"Oh, my child, she will be horribly disappointed," Flavio sighed.

* * *

*Lissa*

"My Queen, these came for you." Grant placed a vase of flowers on the table beside my plate.

27

# Blood War

*Lissa, have you received flowers?* Mindspeech came from Flavio as I was admiring the arrangement of roses and lilies.

*Just now,* I returned. *Did you send them?*

*No. Roff sent them yesterday. When he still recalled who you were. Now he has no memory of you again.*

"Fuck," I muttered, causing everyone at the breakfast table to look up.

"What's wrong?" Winkler asked.

"Radomir's blood didn't help Roff's memory. He's back where he was when he first woke as vampire. He has no idea who I am. Again." I tossed my napkin onto half-eaten food. Rolfe had kept Giff away from breakfast with all of us—she'd been very upset over Roff's wounding the day before.

The baby would come soon, too; her baby pouch was getting larger every day. I was glad she didn't have this information to add to the stress she was already experiencing. As for me—I wanted to weep. Roff had sent me flowers the day before, which might have meant something. Today, he didn't know me again.

"Grant, where's Toff?" I asked. Giff didn't need to worry about Toff right now.

"He's in my office—Heathe and Davan are babysitting until I get back. Rolfe dropped him off this morning after Giff fed him. Why?"

"I'm going to adopt Toff, that's why," I rose from the table. "Roff may never remember either of us, and it's already done enough damage to Giff. Get the paperwork started. We'll work this out."

"Lissa, before you go," Erland held out a hand and a thick, creamy white envelope appeared in it. "Your grandfather sends this, with his regards."

# Chapter 2

"What is it?" I asked. Erland floated the envelope to me—it bore the crest of the King of Karathia—my grandfather, Wylend Arden. I slipped the note from the envelope to read. It was an invitation to the hundred-year ball at Wylend's palace, held, of course, every hundred years.

Well, that beat the vampires' annual meeting all to heck. Only having to get dressed up every hundred years? That sounded great. I was invited to attend—with Erland, of course. Only those with Karathian blood, plus their mates and young children were allowed.

"It's not an invitation, it's more of a demand," Erland was now smiling over my shoulder as he read it.

"You're saying it's a hostage situation?" I asked.

"Well, everything but," Erland let his chin drop to my shoulder, and he kissed it while he was there. "The children are expected, too, you know."

"So Daddy and Amara will bring Wyatt?"

"I think so," Erland said, allowing his mouth to travel to my neck.

"Erland, do not give me a hickey," I tried to swat him away. The ball was to be held in three weeks.

"I'll find something for you to wear, my darling, and we'll dance in your grandfather's ballroom." Erland tilted my chin up and gave me a blinding smile. I realized he was doing his best to take my mind off Roff.

"Want to come to the dungeon with me to visit my prisoners?" I asked. Yeah, I was blaming Roff's second memory loss on those assholes. It probably wasn't good to see them while I was so angry, but I was determined to go anyway.

"Nothing would make me happier, my love," Erland assured me.

* * *

# Blood War

Gavin, Tony, Erland, Winkler, Drake, Drew and Aryn were in the dungeon with me as I stood outside a cell that held three vampires. While most dungeons might be dark, leaky pits filled with rats and other vermin, mine was clean, well-lit and held cells strong enough to imprison vampires.

The three vampires held inside this cell were former Council members, AKA the ringleader assholes—the ones who'd volunteered to recruit others Council members to help the twenty-seven married assholes. They'd been more than happy to cause murder and mayhem. Already the Alliance media was calling the brief uprising The Fang Rebellion, and the increase in tourist requests to visit the palace (to see the Council chambers) had quadrupled.

"Did you really think you'd get out alive?" I stared at the three.

"Did you think to force us to part with our possessions?" one of them hissed.

"Possessions? What the fuck are you saying?" I stared at him incredulously. "You're only three hundred years old, for Pete's sake, and you didn't have a mate in all that. Slavery was outlawed long ago. I know you're from Driskilhin," I held up a hand before he could protest. "Even though your papers say you're from Trell," I added.

"I spent some time on Trell," he insisted. He was proud of his vampirism, I could tell, and flaunted his appearance as well as he could. Well, a nice face and fancy clothes weren't going to help him now.

"I don't care if you spent time on a pig's ass," I snapped. "You'll die, just like your friends, there." I nodded to the other two, who were older and knew to shut the hell up.

"Without a trial?" he sneered.

"Oh, you'll have a trial," I assured him. "I have messages from more than ninety percent of the remaining Council members, asking for your immediate execution. I assured them that we'd put you on trial, first." The most vehement message had come from Susila, our only female Council member. She and Oluwa had fought off a couple of rogues. I'm sure the rogues would be impressed with Susila's fighting skills—if they were still alive.

"You only have sixty-two Council members left," he laughed.

"Yeah. Those still alive are the ones with the most fighting experience. Too bad you thought they were all soft." Suffice to say, all of Earth's former Council members had sailed through the fray with flying colors, and with Radomir and Winkler helping, it hadn't taken long to take down the brief rebellion.

Sadly, Roff had no fighting experience and he'd suffered. He needed to get his fighting lessons from Gavin and Tony, and he needed to get them soon. I never wanted to see my winged vampire bleeding again. Not ever. I didn't care whether he remembered me or not—I still loved him.

"I wanted to see you die," the vampire interrupted my silence. "A King belongs on the throne of Le-Ath Veronis. Not some weak female."

"Aaand the misogyny comes out," I muttered.

"I can dispatch him now," Erland offered. He'd stood beside me, listening to the exchange in silence until now. Well, he probably had a spell or two up his sleeve and was itching to exercise a little power. "You'll be a pile of ash this big when I'm finished with you," Erland formed a small circle with his hands.

"Fucking Warlock," the vampire hurled his body against the bars of his cell. Erland didn't even flinch. Damn, that Warlock wasn't just a handsome face after all.

"Do that again and you'll be less than ash," Erland snapped. "You've had your say. I'll enjoy watching you die."

"You," the vampire hissed at me between the bars of his cage, "will die. I'm sorry I couldn't hand that death to you myself, but Solar Red will come for you, I promise. You are marked for death, bitch."

Well, those words, marked or not, were his last—both his companions sliced him to death before he could turn to fight them. They hadn't intended for the information concerning Solar Red to get out—I could see it in their faces.

Gavin and Aryn took over after that, but the sketchy information we got from the remaining two ringleaders only told me one thing—that the one who'd died was right. They'd been contacted by Solar Red and the payment they'd received was for something they wanted to do anyway—come after me eventually. I hadn't approved any of these to come to Le-Ath Veronis, and I felt overwhelmed. It was a chore to examine every request, and many had been approved by others in my absence.

"Fuck," I muttered when the questioning came to an end. Gavin and Aryn wisely advised that we keep the Solar Red conspiracy out of the charges brought against the remaining vampires.

It was enough that they'd committed treason against the crown, in addition to murdering other vampires. Their deaths were assured once they were put on trial during the next Council meeting. I nodded in silent agreement at the suggestion. The Alliance didn't need to know that Solar Red wanted me gone.

# Chapter 2

"Come, Lissa, we have more important things to attend."
I accepted Erland's offered arm and we stalked away from the
prisoners. After the first one died at the hands of his fellow
conspirators, the vampires in other cells no longer wished to
talk. Just as well—I wasn't in the mood to listen.

* * *

"What's this?" I asked. Grant had handed a comp-vid to
me the moment I arrived in my private study.

"The summons to attend the Five-Year Conclave,
complete with a list of more than three hundred agenda
items," Grant said, hauling Toff into his arms. Toff had been
running around my desk and laughing as Davan struggled to
pick up the string of papers, envelopes and office supplies that
Toff dropped in his wake. Grant had just curtailed Toff's race.

"Come here, baby boy," I lifted Toff from Grant's arms
and settled him on my hip. He grinned at me and swiped at
the comp-vid in my other hand.

"No, you don't want to go to a meeting with a bunch of
dried-up politicians," I held the comp-vid away from Toff's
tiny fists. He giggled. I tossed the comp-vid onto my desk. The
Conclave agenda could wait—the meeting was two months
away and I had more pressing personal business.

The rest of the day was spent putting the application
together for Toff's adoption. I held the baby on my lap while
Davan patiently filled out legal papers. He smiled often as we
went through the required forms—Toff would be a member of
his family, too, once the application was approved.

Uncle Davan was good with paperwork and he and Grant
made suggestions on what to write in as the reason I'd be
adopting Toff. When we were finished, there was only one
thing to do—I had to call Giff into my study and ask her
permission.

33

# Blood War

Rolfe ushered her into my office only a few minutes after I sent for her. She'd grown her hair longer and had taken to wearing women's clothing, even though she was young and far from making the turn. I'd added a stipend to her salary for clothing, and Rolfe generously added to that amount.

"Raona?" Giff nodded to me. I could tell she'd been crying.

"Giff, I've asked you here to get your permission to adopt Toff," I said. "Your father's memory has worsened, it seems, and I worry that you'll have your hands full with your own child very soon. This will ensure that Toff will be cared for. He'll still be your brother, of course."

"Raona, I appreciate your offer. Rolfe said you might suggest this, and we think it is a good thing," Giff sniffled. Grant held out a box of tissues. Giff accepted it with a tearful nod of thanks.

"Good," I breathed a relieved sigh. "I'll present the application to the committee that handles the surrogate sire applications—this won't be much different. It may take a month or so, but I'm sure it will be approved."

Toff chose that moment to giggle while he patted my cheek.

"You want to be a prince?" I smiled at him.

"Mmm-mmm," Toff laughed.

* * *

Gavin found his way into my bed.

"Honey, we hardly ever have time to talk," I grumped as he settled my head on his shoulder.

"Cara, I miss the days when we sat upon rooftops and discussed the rules, or any other thing that came along," he kissed my forehead and brushed hair away from my face.

# Chapter 2

"Me, too," I sighed. I ran a finger down the center of his chest. Gavin is all muscle, and just as broad across the chest and shoulders as the Falchani twins, who'd been working out with blades for around a hundred years. His skin was clear, though—no marks or tattoos. "Have you had time to visit with Aurelius? How's he doing?"

"My father is fine," Gavin was doing more nuzzling and kissing. "He likes you very much. You know he wishes to sit in on all the Council meetings."

"I want to add him to the Council, then, if he wants it. I don't care if he's a Spawn Hunter. Anybody who is such a good parent and taught you and René, well, I think I'd like his advice, now and then. I get good advice from Garde, too, and he can even run the meetings if I'm not there and Kifirin doesn't want to."

"Anthony has been asking how old Gardevik is," I felt the smile in Gavin's words.

"Well, Garde is over a million years old—those High Demons don't kid around about immortality."

"You are joking with me, cara mia, surely." Gavin tipped my face up so I could look into his beautiful, brown eyes.

"No, honey. Kifirin verified it. Garde even remembered seeing Kifirin a few times when he was younger, before Kifirin slept."

"That is astonishing," Gavin took the opportunity, while our faces were so close, to give me a proper kiss. "How old is his brother, Jaydevik?"

"Jayd's a little younger—apparently he was number-three son. They had a brother in between, but he threw himself into the volcano in his humanoid form and that was it for him."

"I see you have had some talks with Gardevik, then."

"Yeah, he doesn't mind answering questions for me. He's pretty patient, actually."

"I like him. He and I agree on most things."

"I can see how that might be." I ran fingers over Gavin's mouth. He kissed them and then got down to business.

* * *

*Black Mist Headquarters*
"These things take time."

Tetsurna Prylvis, High Lord of Solar Red, wasn't satisfied with Viregruz's answer, but he knew better than to argue with the creator of the assassin's league known as Black Mist. Viregruz had killed for lesser offenses. Viregruz's appearance, too, belied his talent and ability. He looked sixteen. Prylvis' sources said that Viregruz was well over three thousand.

The Tetsurna had no idea what might halt time for anyone, even the founder of Black Mist, but he depended upon the assassin and his contacts to kill the Queen of Le-Ath Veronis. If she hadn't interfered years earlier on Refizan, Solar Red would not only be entrenched in the Reth Alliance, they'd have taken it over.

"Will it be soon, then, Master?" Prylvis didn't like groveling, but if it gained the death of his target sooner, he'd do it. He would never admit it, either, but he had a network of spies, just as Viregruz did, and they were working toward the same goal—to find a way to kill the Queen of Le-Ath Veronis.

After all, if Prylvis obtained the objective through his own people, there was no need to pay Viregruz's exorbitant price. Sadly, the vampires he'd hired on Le-Ath Veronis had been defeated and captured before they could kill the Queen, but this was only his first volley. Many more were scheduled.

"It will be when I say it will be," Viregruz's temper was running short. "My Blood Captains have hired spies to search for weaknesses in the walls surrounding her city, and for entrances into the palace that are poorly guarded. Once we have this information, our plans will be made and the Queen will die. I'll have my payment and you'll have your dearest wish. Leave me, now. I must feed."

"Please, may I stay to watch?" Prylvis had only seen it once, and he ached to see it again.

"Oh, very well. Captain," Viregruz nodded to one of his commanders. "Bring my meal."

"Immediately, my lord." The Captain bowed and left the room swiftly, returning with a young girl in a matter of minutes. Her eyes betrayed her terror as she was hauled before Black Mist's founder.

"I always enjoy their screams," Prylvis found a seat and made himself comfortable as he prepared to watch Viregruz consume his meal.

* * *

*Karathia*

"Lissa's adopting Roff's child." Griffin sat at the breakfast table with his father, Wylend Arden, King of Karathia.

"My granddaughter is adopting?" Wylend gazed at his son, whose given name was Brenten. Wylend knew that Narissa, Griffin's half-Elemaiyan mother, had given him that name. It wasn't one he'd have picked for a child, but Narissa had stolen the child away and he hadn't been able to find the boy. Wylend had to contend with things as they were, and a son not only grown but older than his father. "What does Toff's father say?"

"Roff's memory has worsened after he was wounded in the Vampire Council chaos," Griffin admitted. "I don't believe he'll object to the adoption, do you? Especially since he cannot recall that he has children." Griffin busied himself with the food on his plate.

"Then have her bring the child to the ball. I wish to meet any relation, adopted or not. All children are to be brought to the palace to determine the strength of their gift."

"Toff is a comesula. He has no gift, Father."

"I know this, my son. I wish to meet the child anyway. He will have a favored place in the family as my youngest great-grandchild."

"Then I will inform Lissa and Lord Morphis that Toff's presence is requested by the crown." Griffin smiled as he buttered a roll.

* * *

*Le-Ath Veronis*
*Lissa*

"What? He wants us to bring Toff, just because I plan to adopt him?"

"That is one of the functions of the ball—to meet the children. They are inspected by Wylend and his Council, to see if any hold special promise. That's how Erland was sorted out and trained at court. Amara and I will be bringing Wyatt."

Griffin was trying to make me see the reason in all of this. I just wasn't. Toff was comesula; would one day be a beautiful, winged vampire like his father if I had anything to say about it. He would never be a warlock or anything close.

"Lissa, do you wish to disappoint your grandfather? He wants to see the child—asked to see him, in fact."

"Fine," my shoulders slumped. We sat at the breakfast table in my palace. Griffin had come just as we were finishing our meal, asking to talk for a few minutes. I needed to return to my suite to change clothing for the day; we had a postponed

# Chapter 2

Council meeting to make up, a trial to conduct and executions to perform.

I also intended to announce that Aurelius would be the first to join my Second Circle, as a Special Advisor. He would not be one of my mates but would be treated with the same respect and wear a silver Claw Crown ring, denoting his service as an advisor to the Queen.

Cheedas, the old comesula cook, was scheduled to receive a silver ring, too. I often went to him for advice in matters concerning the comesuli. The vampires from Earth had heartily agreed to Aurelius' selection already, and none had objections where Cheedas was concerned.

Aurelius and Garde were going to be my private advisors, either one capable of taking over Council meetings if needed. Garde still acted as Jayd's Prime Minister on Kifirin, but things there were now running smoothly. Garde had two assistants, one from the House of Weth and the other from Foth—High Demons that he trusted. Jayd was getting their kingdom and their treasury back in order with Garde's help and a sizable loan from the Crown on Le-Ath Veronis.

Only Jayd, Garde, Kifirin and I knew about that loan. Kifirin had nearly emptied a vein of gold under the southern ice cap in order for me to extend that loan, but then it was supposed to be mine anyway.

The casinos twenty miles away, as well as the ones near the ocean on the light side, were making profits and taxes were going into a general fund to run everything except the palace itself. It was a point of pride not to accept money to do so.

The taxes collected from exports helped with the everyday costs of running my palace. Oxberry wine, produced by Roff's winery, constituted a large portion of Le-Ath Veronis' exports. Merrill and Adam had gotten upset that the crown was paying for some expenses for the gambling cities, without taking anything from the taxes collected. Therefore, taxes from the exports, combined with taxes from the fruit, vegetables and meats sold to the gambling cities, went toward the crown's expenses.

"They wish to run more water lines down the easement," Aurelius cautioned me as he and I walked into the large Council chamber. We now had fifteen cities represented. Once the application was approved for an Alliance vampire to relocate to Le-Ath Veronis, there were six cities available for them to choose from for their new home.

The banks on Le-Ath Veronis were doing well, also—the vampires inevitably moved their liquid assets here. Adam, Merrill, Flavio and Charles were all on the Bank board. If there were any wrongdoing, I would hear about it quickly.

"They keep trying to wiggle their way into that ten-mile buffer," I grumbled.

Aurelius smiled. "Forbidden fruit," he agreed and led me to my seat.

"We need more wall patrols," an Alliance vampire stood to make his request after the other business was concluded. "We have at least twenty a day, if not more, Casino City visitors attempting to scale the wall and get inside Lissia. If they could find vehicles, there would be more attempting to find their way into the other cities. As it is, we arrest them and hand them to the city guard, but we can't keep up with the growing number of wall climbers."

"What is their excuse?" I asked.

"They want to mingle with vampires. As if the vampires working in or visiting Casino City aren't enough for them to gawk at. I have no idea what the fools think they will find, once they get inside a vampire city."

# Chapter 2

"They love the feel of danger," Flavio said, standing. "Many still think we kill with the bite. They want to feel the thrill, I think, of associating with creatures stronger and wilder than themselves."

"Perhaps we should have a few High Demons run through the streets, then," I muttered. If a High Demon went Full Thifilathi, you sure as hell didn't want to stand in their way.

"Lissa, that, of course, would be highly unlikely and extremely dangerous," Aurelius brought me back to the present.

"You're right," I nodded to him. "I have some with experience in the field of security who have expressed an interest in working for the crown. I will entertain applications for additional city guards. Send them to me in the next two days and we'll get this sorted out."

"Thank you, Raona," the Alliance vampire sat down.

* * *

"That only took three hours longer than it should have," Aurelius noted as we made our way toward the kitchen and a much-needed meal. There'd been no debate on the executions, but they'd still taken longer than expected. Every remaining Council member voted guilty, and Trevor and Gavin took turns beheading guilty vampires.

We'd worked right past dinner, with blood substitute passed among the vampires to keep us going. Our late dinner was quiet, with hardly anyone speaking. Drake and Drew tried to take me to my suite afterward, but I fended them off and Aurelius and I went to my private study instead.

Once there, I sent mindspeech to Radomir, asking him to bring Lisster and Rush, two of his co-mates. Lisster was a shapeshifting leopard and Rush was a black lion; both were members of the Saa Thalarr and mates to Devin and Grace. Lisster, Radomir and Rush arrived moments after I'd sent mindspeech to Radomir.

"We're having security problems with fence-climbers," I said, once they were seated and comfortable. "The city Councils are supposed to be in charge of that, but they're overwhelmed with people sneaking in from Casino City and trying to hobnob with vampires. Would you three like to take that problem on? I'll be hiring vampires from the cities as guards, but I need somebody to oversee them and make sure they don't kill anybody. We've been in the media too much already."

"I can knock heads," Radomir grinned.

"Sounds like fun," Rush offered a perfect smile. He was tall, dark-skinned and had muscles that impressed even vampires. Most people (vampires included) would be foolish to take on the black lion.

"Love to," Lisster snickered. Honestly, I wouldn't want to be any vampire that pissed Lisster off. He was a shapeshifter by birth—a leopard. He even had spots on his back, legs and neck while in humanoid form. Yeah, I wouldn't want to get in his way, either.

"Come to me; I will parcel out assignments," Aurelius said. "You will be working closely with Gavin, Anthony, Drake and Drew." We offered our three new Crown Investigators a drink, and they accepted.

# Chapter 3

*L*issa

We'd hired our new guards and Crown Investigators just in time, it seemed. Three wall climbers stood before me inside my study. They'd not only climbed over the wall, they'd managed somehow to paint insults on the wall and a few nearby businesses before Lisster and Rush hauled them in.

Drake and Drew took them into custody at that point and brought them to me. They all looked to be in their twenties or early thirties—two men, one woman. From Rorda.

"You signed the agreement to honor the laws of Le-Ath Veronis before you came, did you not?" I gave them an angry gaze.

"Yes, Raona." They were contrite. *Now.*

"And you did this anyway, even though you knew you could be caught, sent off-planet and never allowed back?" I

43

was pacing, now. Something about these three bothered me. Drake and Drew didn't normally bring me fence-climbers.

They must have thought something was up with these, only they couldn't use their *Looking* abilities to interfere. Those were the rules they had to abide by, being Spawn Hunters for the Saa Thalarr. My head jerked around after I'd passed them. "Grant, check their bank accounts. See if they've gotten any large deposits lately, or whether their recent spending is supported by the jobs they have."

Grant, standing behind me, started tapping on his handheld computer. He already had their records pulled up. "No deposits, but they've been throwing Alliance credits around like they were among the wealthy, and I see that all three work in prison detail on Rorda."

"Find out if any Solar Red suspects are imprisoned there." The three that stood before me began to sweat. I'd hit the proverbial nail on the head with these. The Solar Red fuckers, now trying to come back to power, wanted me dead since I'd brought them down last time. Three vampires in my Council had failed to exact revenge.

These three, playing at being pranksters, were trying to scope out a way to get to me. Well, they were going to be mind-wiped by compulsion and sent home. The Rordans were also going to be notified, and that notification was going to be copied to the Alliance.

Aryn had come to the palace to help; he was with us, watching our prisoners carefully. "I will be happy to place compulsion, Raona," he said. Aryn always dressed impeccably, like many of the older vampires. He was old, too, I could tell by the scent.

"Go ahead. Before you do, though, find out if they've gathered or sent any information off world. Drake and Drew

# Chapter 3

are already searching their rooms at the casino." They'd had the temerity to stay at the Chessman.

"Is this going to hurt?" The female asked timidly.

"Why are you worried about that now?" I wasn't pleased with any of them and I think they knew it. "You risked your life doing this. Why weren't you worried about it before you signed up?"

"Ari, shhh," one of the males tried to hush her.

"You got her into this, didn't you?" I had my arms crossed and went to stand in front of him.

"Do not stand too closely to this filth," Garde skipped in and glared at all three, smoke pouring from his nostrils.

"Are you a vampire?" Ari asked Garde. I'm sure the information provided by Solar Red had given her a description of vampires in general, and breathing smoke wasn't anywhere in that description.

"I am High Demon," Garde growled. "You are threatening my mate. Do not threaten her further, or I shall allow the Thifilathi to come."

"Garde, honey, back up a little, okay?" I misted to his side and grabbed his arm. We didn't need heads twisted from bodies. That wouldn't be good, especially since their apparent crime didn't warrant a death sentence. Not yet, anyway.

"How did you get?" One of the males asked, but he didn't get a chance to finish the question. Aryn took over immediately.

"You will forget what you just saw. Now, let's see what you know," Aryn placed compulsion, so I pulled Garde from the room. The farther away from the interrogation room we went, the calmer he became until his eyes cleared and his skin lightened. He was still blowing smoke, though, as he turned me in his arms and gave me a possessive kiss. The Thifilathi was still not far from the surface.

"We found a few things, and asked the hotel staff to pack up the rest," Drake and Drew appeared beside us. Garde pulled back and accepted what Drew handed him. They'd found a portable computer in the hotel room, with information on the space station orbiting Le-Ath Veronis, plus specs for the shuttles, the landing area and the casinos.

I'd have to call in Adam and Merrill. We were being scoped out and I was worried that Solar Red might be planning an invasion. Garde, Drake and Drew thought so, too.

"They're not on any Alliance worlds, not in any numbers, anyway," Drake growled, looking at the images of the space station's interior. "That means Solar Red is based on a non-Alliance world and able to grow as fast as they can recruit thugs and criminals."

"And they want to take us out," I muttered, staring at the images of the casinos. They'd only gotten one or two interior shots—casino security was pretty tight.

"You, at least," Drew looked grim. "Erland showed us the old footage from Refizan."

"How fast is that army coming along?" Garde asked my twins.

"We're in good shape, but we need to know what kind of weapons they have, so we can prepare for that."

"Yeah? I hadn't thought about that." It made me rub my forehead.

"Baby, don't worry, all right?" Drake pulled my head against his shoulder.

"I'm not worried so much about me; I'm worried about my vampires and my comesuli, not to mention the guests."

# Chapter 3

"We'll take that into consideration," Drew said, rubbing my back while his brother pulled me tighter against him.

"They aren't organized enough, yet; these are only scouting parties," Kifirin folded in. I hadn't seen him for days. "Come, Avilepha, you have not been energy for a while. We will take care of that now." Kifirin folded me away before I had time to argue with him.

* * *

"Solar Red is scouting Le-Ath Veronis?" Dragon scowled as his sons gave him information they'd gotten from the three spies.

"Aryn wiped the information from their minds and we put them on a ship back to Rorda under guard shortly after that. We kept their computer and everything else they had, but they'd managed to send out some information before we caught them. We transmitted our records to the authorities on Rorda and to Alliance headquarters. The Alliance isn't happy with Solar Red, right now; I think they blew up White Light temples on Oblerik. That means they're scouting other worlds, too."

"I fail to understand how they keep recruiting," Dragon snorted.

* * *

*Lissa*

"Erland, what have you done?" I had my hands on my hips, now, staring with distaste at the dress he'd laid across my bed.

"You should wear this to the Century Ball," Erland flashed a smile that could melt hearts and cause general swooning. "It will go perfectly with my suit."

That meant, of course, that Erland was wearing white to my grandfather's shindig. I liked white okay, but this dress

47

was a blinding white, with crystal beading. Just the reflection of light off it could cause blindness. "Honey, I'll look like a chandelier," I said as tactfully as I could.

Shadow, who'd come in to pick up oxberry wine for Grey House, was gazing speculatively at the dress, too. He snickered and nodded at my chandelier comment.

"Will you settle for white satin, then?" Erland was being patient with me.

"I think I'll need to see it, first," I offered dryly.

"Very well," Erland sighed dramatically. "I had no idea I had such a demanding mate."

That caused me to blink at him in shock. He turned his smile on me. "I was merely teasing you, my beautiful Queen." He came to kiss me, waving one hand while he did so. When he pulled away, a second dress was on the bed. It was white satin, just as he said, and much more suitable than the other.

"I'll wear that," I sighed in resignation. The second dress was still going to draw moths, it was so bright, but not as many as the first one.

"You'll be beautiful," Erland kissed me again.

"Not as beautiful as you," I poked at him when he let me go.

"Few are," he tossed back his black hair and laughed.

"And he's not insufferable or anything," I smiled at Shadow. "I'll wear my Tiralian crystal with this." Shadow had made a complete set of Tiralian crystal jewelry for me, and all of it held protection spells. He was a real honey, all right.

"When is this blow-up?" Shadow grinned at Erland.

"The Ball is tomorrow evening. My mate had best not be late. The King of Karathia is not noted for his patience."

"What will Toff wear?" I asked. We had to take him; Wylend had requested it.

# Chapter 3

"I have provided the outfit already," Erland sniffed. I'd hired two comesuli nannies to care for Toff when Grant, Davan, Giff and I weren't available. "How well do you dance, my love?" Erland gave me a skeptical look.

"Merrill and Franklin taught me the foxtrot and the waltz. Anything outside that and you may get your toes stepped on."

"Just follow my lead," Erland was trying not to laugh.

"You're leading? In this century?" I went after him. Few ever realized that the Karathian witches and warlocks switched attraction from males to females and vice-versa every hundred years or so. Erland was on the downside of a female cycle; anyway, that's what he called it.

"Isn't this rather undignified?" Gavin walked in while I was chasing Erland around the bedroom.

"I can chase you," I offered, stopping by the padded bench at the end of my bed.

"I will not run, I prefer to be caught," he smiled. I stepped up on the bench and Gavin came to get me. I wrapped my arms around his neck, my legs around his waist and started kissing him.

"Don't wrinkle the dress," Erland herded everybody else from the bedroom and shut the door.

* * *

"I hope it's not after Labor Day," I said as I slipped into white heels.

"Are you going over those human holidays again?" Erland was already dressed in a white tux with a red rose on his lapel.

"Are you knocking my holidays?" I teased.

"Of course. Belittling them. Ridiculing them."

"Honey, was tact not part of your lessons at court?" I smiled as sweetly at him as I could.

"I passed all those tests and promptly forgot everything I learned."

"I can see that. Let's get Toff; his nanny should have him ready now." I placed the Tiralian crystal bracelet on my wrist.

"Look at our little man," I laughed when the nanny handed Toff over—he wore a tiny blue suit.

"Mmmm-mmm," Toff grinned at me. Erland took him from my arms and folded us to Karathia.

The children were placed in a nursery when their parents arrived—Wylend and members of his Council would test them once all the guests were there. Pronouncements would be made over which children held exceptional talent and would be taught at court. The babies couldn't be brought past the age of four. If they hadn't been selected by that age, they wouldn't be.

Several babysitters were there to care for the children, and each child was given a wristband to identify them. Each wristband was fastened on with power, so the child couldn't slip it off. Toff had a small green band with Erland's rune placed on it. The fathers' runes identified the children at court.

"Just a formality," Erland took my hand. I waved at Toff while being led away.

Griffin and Amara caught up with us a few minutes later, and both kissed me on the cheek. "How's Wyatt?" I asked.

"A bundle of energy," Amara smiled. "Wylend says he already shows promise."

"That's great," I said, and gave Amara a hug. Wyatt would likely be King of Karathia, one day. That day was probably a long way off—Karathians were nearly immortal.

# Chapter 3

Servants were passing out wine, sparkling wine and other drinks, and Erland pulled two glasses off a tray and handed one to me. We were sipping sparkling wine and making small talk until Wylend chose to make his entrance, and that meant I wasn't expecting what happened. In fact, it was the last thing I'd thought might come to pass, given where we were and whose palace this was.

Every light in the place went dark. The darkness was so thick; even I had a hard time seeing through it, which worried me. Many there thought Wylend had done this as a way to make a grand entrance, because the lights shone again after bare seconds.

It wasn't until the screaming began that we knew something was wrong. One of the babysitters ran into the ballroom, shouting in terror. "A child is missing!" she shrieked. "A child is missing!"

The shouted announcement caused a general stampede, with every parent inside the ballroom rushing toward the nursery. Erland and I, followed by Griffin and Amara, joined the crowd.

Toff wouldn't be a target—he wasn't Karathian. While we struggled to get near the nursery, however, the mystery of who might accomplish something like this ran through my mind—who could get past what I was sure were shields placed by the strongest warlocks?

Guards had been stationed around the nursery and children were being handed off as runes were announced, one by one. Crying toddlers were given to frightened parents as each father's name was called.

The crowd thinned before us and I was beginning to feel frightened. Wyatt, the King's heir, hadn't been handed over, yet. If someone had an ax to grind or wanted something from Wylend, this might be the way to do it.

The guards were down to the last four children when Erland's name was called. He and I stepped forward, half-breathing a relieved sigh, to take Toff. Amara was in tears by that time. The child was handed over, but he was much too small and wore a tiny, green jumpsuit. Wyatt had been handed to me.

"This isn't Toff," I stared at Erland in alarm. He examined the bracelet carefully—it was his rune. "Amara," I turned to hand Wyatt to her. She blinked at me in shock before pulling Wyatt against her and weeping tears of joy.

"Where's Toff?" I demanded, misting past the guards to examine three remaining children. None of them was Toff. That's when I started screaming.

* * *

"Lissa, we have this." Wylend had come and was now handing a note to me. Erland took it; I was too numb to move. He read it aloud so I would know what it said.

*King Warlock*, the letter read, *we have your grandchild and heir. We are in desperate need of the services of one of your kind, and have not the money to pay. A battle comes our way and as you know, we do not engage in violence. Nevertheless, our own children will die if we do not receive assistance. According to our divinations, we will need the presence of one of yours in one month's time. Fail to come and your child will die as one of us—those who come for us intend to kill us all.* The note was signed *Tiearan of the Briar, Chief of the Green Birth.*

"How the fuck did this happen?" I muttered. Amara sat nearby, soothing Wyatt. He'd been fed earlier and was a bit fussy, refusing sleep.

# Chapter 3

Griffin was looking at his son, more than likely thanking whatever mistake had spared him. I wasn't thankful. Not in the least. Somebody had Toff. Somebody who would likely not understand what he was, or what his needs were.

"The Green Birth are peaceful Fae; they must truly be desperate," Wylend paced. We were all inside my grandfather's private study—had been ushered there as soon as I'd realized Toff was the child taken. "The only way they could accomplish this is if every member of their clan, which could include thousands, pooled their talent and drained the sun crystals they use. They couldn't have gotten past our shields, otherwise."

Wylend was angry. I couldn't tell if he were angrier that Green Birth had gotten past the spells around his palace or that a comesuli child had been taken. He certainly wasn't angry that Wyatt had been spared. I could see the relief he and the others felt concerning that bit of salvation. Erland was trying to soothe me, but that wasn't a possibility.

"And what will they do, if they discover that they do not hold my heir?" Wylend asked, turning his eyes on me. That question made my blood run cold. Everyone was saying Green Birth Fae didn't kill, but nothing stopped them from handing Toff to the ones who would.

"Lissa, this is complicated," Belen folded in. "None of mine can interfere with this."

"If I send any of mine, I have no idea what will happen," Wylend ran a hand through his hair. "My warlocks have a tendency to kill first and then request an explanation. And if the Green Birth discover the child is not my heir, he could still die in any number of ways."

"Don't you worry, I'll go myself," I stood up angrily. It was clear to me that nobody else was worried about a tiny comesula. "I'll go to Vionn and figure out what's going on. I'm warning you now, if I don't find anyone worth saving there, I'll take the planet apart. I don't care who it is. And if they've hurt Toff, well, so much the worse for them."

I jerked the skirt of my dress away—Erland had stepped on a part of it. Erland tried to stop me, but he had no hold over me. Nobody did, when I went to mist and then to energy and pulled even more power from the planet itself before rocketing toward the world its inhabitants called Vionn.

* * *

*Le-Ath Veronis*

"Her leathers, blades and boots are missing." Drew was angry. Nobody had thought to tell any of them until the following day. Erland slunk in and passed along the information. Garde was furious, as was Gavin. Connegar and Reemagar folded in and they didn't look happy, either.

"At least the Green Birth will not harm the child themselves," Reemagar sighed. Aurelius had arrived to calm Gavin, who looked angry enough to dismantle the palace—with Garde's help.

"Belen won't let us help; he says this is outside our abilities, according to the rules," Drake grumbled. He'd already had a talk with Dragon. His father informed him that unless Lissa's life was in danger, he couldn't go.

* * *

*Vionn*
*Kingdom of Farus*
*Lissa*

I had my clothing, my blades and a few extras rolled up in a large duffle bag I'd brought with me. The line I stood in stretched fifty people long as sunlight bore down on the flagstone-covered courtyard of King Rindil's castle. I'd done

# Chapter 3

some *Looking*—Rindil had allied himself (and Farus, his country) with the Temple of the Red Hand on Vionn.

The Red Hand was very close to what Solar Red had been in the beginning—only Solar Red had perfected their maiming and killing techniques over the centuries. Red Hand's temple was on the nearby continent of Ialus, two days away by ship from the shores of Farus, where Rindil ruled as King.

The Pelipu, Head of The Red Hand on Vionn, had somehow convinced Rindil that killing off the Green Birth Fae was a good idea. He would rid Vionn of the Fae (who were demons, in his estimation) and Rindil and his nobles could get their hands on the richest farmland on the planet. Rindil was currently recruiting soldiers for his half of the army—he and the Pelipu were sending armed troops to kill a race that wouldn't lift a weapon to fight back.

Citizens of Farus stood in a line, signing up for the army. Most of them looked poor and were dressed in rags. A few I saw didn't have shoes. It was obvious that Farus was going through hard times, which explained why money from the Pelipu and his temple had tempted the new King of Farus.

It didn't matter that many from Farus coexisted with the Green Birth Fae, and that the half-Fae children would die with their Fae parents. The whole thing made we want to curse. Instead, I was about to join the army, just to determine whether anyone involved in this one-sided war deserved to live.

The army took males or females, which was a good thing. At least they weren't backward about that and honestly; I think the newly crowned King would be happy to get anyone he could.

Most waiting in line to join the King's army didn't have any experience at all. It didn't matter—what experience did they need to go after someone that didn't kill? Whenever I thought about Toff, who was stuck somewhere in the middle of it all, I felt sick.

"Name?" The Sergeant was tired and grumpy; he barely bothered to look at me when I reached his table. A scribe sat next to him, making out the records.

"Liss," I said. I had my doubts that many of these could pronounce more than one-syllable words, so I shortened my name.

"From?"

"Seaport."

"Have your own clothing, or do we need to provide?" the Sergeant gruffed. He was middle-aged, bald, had two teeth missing in front and looked as tough as shoe leather.

"I have my own," I said.

"I have need of a runner and bodyguard," someone walked up behind the Sergeant. "What is the name?"

"Says Liss," the Sergeant didn't sound complimentary as he looked up at the newcomer. The one who stood behind him was tall—nearly as tall as Tony—and was handsome, even with the scar that ran down the left side of his face. He was dressed in black, head to heel, and was clean and didn't smell, like everyone else.

"Liss," the tall man said, "do you stay this clean most of the time?"

"Yes, sir. As often as possible. If water is available, I will most certainly be clean."

"Good. You're with me. Mark it down, scribe."

That was how I came to be hired into King Rindil's army as Captain Solis' runner and bodyguard. He'd hired me sight unseen, just because I was clean. I also discovered by *Looking* that he preferred men and was in a long-term relationship.

# Chapter 3

He stood on unstable ground, however, and he knew it. Farus didn't mind same-sex relationships, but the Pelipu didn't see things the same way. The Pelipu and The Temple of the Red Hand were causing rumblings, and soon all of Vionn might hold the same prejudiced outlook that the Pelipu did.

Solis was protecting himself by hiring a female as his bodyguard. Most might think he'd hired me for obvious reasons and not look past that.

I trotted along behind Solis, whose legs were longer. Not that it bothered me; I could outwalk him anytime. I just didn't want to draw attention to myself. If the Pelipu didn't like gays, he sure wasn't going to like what I was.

"Do you have weapons, Liss?" Solis asked as we walked toward a sea of tents below the castle.

"I have weapons. Sir."

"You don't have to call me that unless we are around others. Then it is proper."

"Of course."

"I had no idea that anyone from Seaport was so polite," Solis observed.

"Generally, I'm not polite," I said. "I just didn't want to frighten you right away." That made him laugh. I was speaking the local language—I'd had that talent for a while, now. Pheligar had given me all languages except High Demon, and that one I'd learned with difficulty and on my own.

Turning away from those thoughts, I focused on Solis again. I wanted to ask him what he thought about the war. I wanted to ask when the army would head out to conquer the Green Birth and the citizens of Farus who coexisted with them. That would be overstepping my bounds, so I kept my mouth closed and those questions to myself.

I also wondered what everyone was doing on Le-Ath Veronis and what they'd done with the increasing number of wall climbers with connections to Solar Red. Those thoughts were a nagging problem at the back of my mind, but Toff had to come first.

I had no idea how organized Solar Red was or what their intentions were where Le-Ath Veronis or I was concerned. Nobody else seemed to be worried about Toff at all. That pissed me off.

In a royal way.

How the hell had the bracelets gotten mixed up? Had Green Birth done it? I couldn't imagine that they'd trade the real heir for someone else who didn't make a bit of difference to the Karathian population. That worry chased itself around in my mind, so I had to let it go for the moment. I was going to see what there was to be seen, and then make a decision at the end of the road, here.

"What's that following at your heel, Solis?" A fellow officer fell in step with Solis.

"My bodyguard and runner," Solis replied, not bothering to stop and chat with the newcomer. The other, also a Captain, decided to stay in step with us and insult me at the same time. Well, he could multitask; I'll give him that.

"That's not tall enough to take a good swing from regular army, even."

"You think I'll let regular army insult me in that way?" Solis' hand fell to the hilt of his sword.

"Not at all," the other one held his hands up in a placating gesture. I wanted to tell him that I'd take him on and he'd be dead in a blink, but I kept the words behind my teeth.

"I'll bet she doesn't know how to take care of your blade," the other one said.

# Chapter 3

"Liss, do you know how to care for a blade?" Solis flung behind him.

"Yes, sir." I did—Drake and Drew made sure of that. I could clean, sharpen and polish, even though my blades, made by Grey House, didn't need sharpening. Drake and Drew had brought old blades to me and watched carefully while I did it, until I'd passed inspection. Falchani are funny that way. You don't mistreat a blade around them—they get downright serious about it.

"See?" Solis wasn't even looking at the Captain at his side. "Desmun, if you don't have anything constructive to say, I have other things more pressing."

"I'll trade my runner for her." Desmun had a motive and it just became clear.

"No, the assignment has already been recorded and I don't have the patience to go back and change it now. You're stuck, Desmun. Besides, I don't expect Liss would welcome you in her bedroll. Good-bye, Desmun." Desmun stopped walking and Solis and I soon left him behind. I released a breath I hadn't realized I was holding.

"This is our tent, and will be for the next three days," Solis announced as I dumped my duffle inside. "After that, we'll pack up and move out. Regulars set up the officer's tents, and the tents with a single green stripe are the Sergeant's tents. Two green stripes are Lieutenants, and three green stripes are the Captains' tents. General's tent is all green. Got it?" Solis pulled me through the tent flap into sunlight again, and swept out an arm. Five more Captains' tents surrounded ours, all with the designated three green stripes. Beyond them lay eight tents with two green stripes, and twelve with a single green stripe. A sea of plain canvas tents surrounded us past that point.

"Yes, sir." I nodded at Solis' gesture. He led me inside the tent, again, which was divided into two sections by a canvas drape. He pointed out his portion; it was the section at the back of the tent. "I use this space as my sleeping quarters and office. Understand?" I nodded again.

"Good. The space inside the flap is yours, and it's your job to guard me while I sleep. Regulars are supposed to keep watch during the night, but you need to at least trip anyone coming in without permission."

"Oh, I'll do more than that, sir."

Solis smiled briefly. "Good," he nodded. "Stow your gear and we'll go watch the exercises. Wear your blade."

Solis was waiting outside the tent when I walked out of it, wearing black leathers with both blades strapped to my back.

"You use both of those?" Solis lifted an eyebrow.

"When I have to," I said. The hilts of my blades lay conveniently over my shoulders so I could put my hands on them quickly if needed. The Falchani knew what they were doing when they designed those sheaths and leather harnesses.

"The Pelipu's troops will be arriving by sea this afternoon, and will march from the port to meet us tomorrow. I expect trouble when they arrive. Some are mercenaries, although they wear the uniform of the Temple. Don't ever let that fool you, Liss."

"Don't you worry, sir." I was back to walking slightly behind him, down a trampled grass trail between tents. We were into the tents for the Regulars, and eight Regulars slept in a single tent slightly larger than Captain Solis'. We passed the Regular mess tents on the way to the sparring grounds.

"The officers' mess is on the other side of the officers' tents," Solis said, as sounds of metal blades clanging and

# Chapter 3

wooden blades clacking against each other grew louder. "You'll either be eating with me there, as my bodyguard, or bringing both our meals back to the tent if I have work to do while I'm eating," Solis said. I nodded mutely.

His eyes, just like mine, were now on the practice ground and the sparring that was taking place there. Some of the men barely knew how to hold a blade, and if they did, they held it badly. Dragon and Crane would have scowled before wading into that mess and yelling at all of them.

Dragon always said if you didn't have enough strength to hold a sword with one hand, then you'd best use two hands and be faster than your opponent. These guys would have washed out of the Warlord's army, I think.

"I hope the enemy either gives up or dies laughing," Solis muttered sarcastically as we watched. Desmun caught up with us as we stood and watched.

"Pitiful," he grumbled. "Are they taking civilians off the street?"

"I believe so," Solis replied.

Desmun stared at the hilts over my shoulder. "Steal those blades?" he asked.

"They were a gift," I said. "Sir."

"Of course they were." Desmun turned back to the sparring. One particularly clumsy young man dropped his wooden practice blade and got thumped when he stooped to retrieve it. A Sergeant, standing nearby and watching, yelled at him, causing the boy to flush to the roots of his light-brown hair. If he'd done that in a real battle, his head would have been missing when he straightened up. I didn't understand what had motivated him to join the army to begin with, without benefit of any training.

"Lack of money," Solis commented, as if he were reading my mind. I'd been shaking my head; I realized it after a moment. Desmun turned to watch the clouds gathering behind us.

"Messy night, tonight, and messier day tomorrow," he complained. Great. Rain was coming. "I hear those Green bastards can make it rain anytime they want," Desmun went on.

"Sounds like you're jealous," Solis replied indifferently. "I hear the locals who've joined the Green Fae once practiced a different version of the same religion the Pelipu practices," he added. "They rejected it in favor of living a peaceful existence."

"I wouldn't repeat that rumor near the Pelipu's troops," Desmun snorted. "They think religious deserters ought to be boiled in oil."

"What do you think, Liss?" Solis asked, his dark eyes studying my face.

"I'm still trying to find something worthwhile in this whole, sorry mess," I answered truthfully. If Toff weren't somewhere on this planet, I wouldn't have bothered.

"Mind if I see what your bodyguard is made of?" Desmun asked.

"You want an excuse to take your shirt off?" Solis wasn't looking at Desmun.

"I won't whack her around too much," Desmun replied.

"Use wood blades," Solis didn't sound as if he cared. Desmun took off to find some wooden practice blades. I started to follow him. "Liss," Solis said softly, catching me by the shoulder, "If you don't know what you're doing, now's the time to say. If you do, don't let him hurt you. If you're better than he is, best not to let him know. Not right away, anyway. He'll warm up to you after a while." Solis jerked his head

# Chapter 3

toward the practice ground, where Desmun had claimed two wood practice blades.

"Fuck," I muttered, causing Solis to snicker.

Desmun only fought with one blade, and only handed me one. I let him whack me lightly after about a minute, and then let him whack me again a couple of minutes later. In between, I settled for blocking his blows with the flat of my blade, just as I'd been trained. Honestly, one of my twins could have knocked him senseless wearing a blindfold and armed only with a knife. I let him get one last blow in—he was satisfied with that—and I walked away, rubbing my wrist. That's where Desmun's last blow had landed. Desmun challenged a Sergeant afterward. I had no desire to stay and watch. Solis was ready to go, too.

"Someday," he said, as we walked toward his tent, "I want to see you fight with both those blades."

# Chapter 4

*L*issa

It was late spring in Farus, and the thunderstorm that came through drenched everything, in addition to making the footpath between tents look like a river as night fell. I was grateful the tents had some sort of waterproofing in the cloth; otherwise, we'd have been dripped on all night.

I took the small shovel that Solis handed me and dug a trench around the tent, with a channel on each corner to divert the rainwater into the pathways in front of and behind the tent.

The footpaths were the lowest ground we had around us, which meant everybody walked through water up to their ankles to get anywhere in camp. We walked in the rain to get to dinner and walked in the rain back from dinner.

# Blood War

I helped hang up Solis' clothing after he undressed, in a useless attempt to dry it out. I think he and I would settle for extreme dampness at that moment; we were both soaked.

Solis, sitting on a campstool in his underwear, wrote out two messages by candlelight as darkness fell around us. I heard plenty of cursing going on outside the tent—there wasn't any way to keep a fire going during the storm.

"Take this one to the General," Solis handed a message to me with a wax seal. "Take this one to Captain Cordus; his tent is just this side of the General's." Cordus' message didn't have a seal. "Use this bag," I was given a waterproof courier's bag. After stuffing both messages inside the bag, I nodded to Solis, walked from the tent and headed into a driving rain.

"Message, General," the General's bodyguard announced when I showed up at the green tent. I pulled out the sealed message and handed it to the General.

"You are?" he asked, examining the wax seal.

"Liss, Captain Solis' bodyguard and runner, sir," I replied. I hadn't seen anyone saluting, so I was thankful for that.

"Wait for a reply," he growled and opened the message, reading it swiftly. I stood near the tent flap while the General wrote out a reply, rolled it up and sealed it with wax from a candle. I took it, slipped it inside the waterproof bag and walked into the rain again.

Captain Cordus came next, and he didn't ask me to wait for a reply. I handed off his message and left, carrying the General's reply to Captain Solis. Solis gave me thanks in a distracted sort of way, so I left him in his half of the tent and went to dry myself off as best I could.

* * *

# Chapter 4

The General read Solis' message again before committing it to his candle flame. *If something happens to your bodyguard*, the note read, *ask for Liss.*

* * *

I'm sure the Pelipu's troops would have looked much more dashing if they hadn't been soaked to the bone when they rode up the following morning. As it was, they looked somewhat bedraggled in wet gray tunics beneath chain mail.

A tabard was worn over the chain mail bearing a large, red hand across the chest. That red hand was supposed to be the hand of their god and according to them, it ran with blood when the god was angry.

Well, if Red Hand was anything like Solar Red, the god's hand probably ran with blood when he was happy or even feeling so-so, too. The chain mail these troops wore had to be a bitch in a rainstorm, I figured. I wanted to snicker at their obvious discomfort, but held myself back as Solis and I watched the Pelipu's troops ride past. Their horses weren't happy either; their manes and tails hung in wet clumps as they clopped along, their heads down in the rain.

"What do you think, Liss?" Solis asked after the last Red Hand mercenary went past.

"You're right," I nodded. "Trouble just arrived." Solis offered a humorless chuckle.

* * *

In addition to my blades, I now had a knife clipped to the back waistband of my leather pants—Connegar had sent a note wrapped around the knife. I'd found it inside my duffle while looking for a bar of soap to clean up after dinner the night before.

"Glinda insisted that you take this—just in case," the note read. The knife was a good one, with a black steel blade.

# Blood War

A long, sharp knife was Glinda's weapon of choice, apparently, and I wasn't about to argue with her. Before she joined the Saa Thalarr and Jayd had inadvertently found her, Glinda worked as Erland's bodyguard on Campiaa for more than twenty years.

I clipped the sheathed knife to my waistband and practiced drawing it a few times. Since I couldn't use claws without giving myself away, the knife might come in handy.

I'd left my body behind to turn to energy sometime before dawn; I'd know whether anybody tried to wake me and could get back in less than a blink if necessary. I'd also written a quick message to Connegar and *Sent* the note back to Le-Ath Veronis using Power. All I'd written was a quick thanks—to him and to Glinda.

*  *  *

I wasn't interested, but Solis wanted to watch the Pelipu's troops finish setting up their camp after breakfast, so we went to observe. They'd only erected tents the night before and many of them slept on wet ground since they hadn't dug trenches around the tents.

Rain still fell around us, with the occasional rumble of thunder. Quite a few Red Hand troops decided to change the location of their tents, so Solis and I watched as they struggled in the downpour.

Higher ground was at a premium and Red Hand's officers had most of that already covered with their tents, leaving the Regulars to scramble for better placement.

Putting up tents in the rain was a tedious task, I discovered, and tent stakes don't hold well in rain-soaked ground. More than a few tents were blown over by occasional high winds. Red Hand's commanders had red striped tents,

# Chapter 4

with the High Commander's tent a solid red. Everybody else had plain canvas, just as Farus' army did.

"Message, Captain Solis," a runner, not more than sixteen or seventeen—I knew by the scent—splashed up beside us, handing a folded note to Solis.

"Commander's meeting in a mark," Solis sighed, stuffing the note in a pocket. "Let's go dry off a bit before we have to show up and decide the pecking order." I trailed behind him, rain dripping off both of us as we went.

* * *

"Take the knife, leave the blades," Solis instructed, just before we left his tent. I'm ashamed to admit I used a little Power to dry off. I was sick of being wet, already.

I put my blades, sheaths and harness inside my duffle before splashing after Solis toward the General's tent. His was much larger than any of the others, and he'd been inside the first room, (if you can call something with four cloth walls a room) when I'd delivered Solis' message and then waited for the General's reply.

We walked into the main body of the tent; Solis and the other Captains got a campstool, Sergeants and Lieutenants stood at the back. The High Commander of the Pelipu's troops sat opposite the General, with only a small table between them.

Only Captains and Generals got bodyguards, and I and the other bodyguards present knelt next to our Captain's seat. The other officers used a pool of runners to get messages around and depended on the Regulars for safety—they didn't get personal runners, either.

I was the only female in the room, too. Was I surprised? Of course not. I'd seen a few women in the Regulars, and only one female Sergeant so far. She looked as if she could take on a charging bull all by herself. She'd been assigned to keep order among the troops while the meeting was held.

"The Pelipu's instructions are quite clear," the High Commander huffed after lengthy introductions and much posturing took place. "He has placed me in charge. All others answer to me."

"My men will answer to me, first," the General said quietly. "I will discuss orders with you but I will not be taken out of the chain of command. I answer to my King, after all, not yours. This is our country and I am familiar with it. I hold the maps and am able to read them. I know where the enemy is located and can lead you there."

"Very well, but I expect full notification for all significant orders." The High Commander wasn't happy; we all knew that, but the General did have a point—this was his country and he knew where the enemy, such as they were, lived. I was holding off *Looking*, to be honest. This would be a slaughter unless I did something about it.

There was more discussion, followed by questions and answers afterward, and one of those questions was what would be done if fights and squabbles broke out between the troops. It wasn't difficult to determine that Red Hand might be spoiling for a fight with Farus' army, whom they obviously held in contempt.

"I suggest a joint judgment, with officers from both sides to hear and decide the punishment," Solis offered. That recommendation was eventually agreed upon, with two from each side to be appointed by the General and the High Commander. This march was going to take about a month. How much trouble were they expecting?

The trouble started that afternoon. Two Red Hand troops wanted to cut in line at the mess tent. The Regulars shoved

# Chapter 4

them out. Knives were pulled and three men were cut up—all of them Farus Regulars. Solis was called to the judgment afterward, which meant I was by his side the entire time.

The Red Hand Captains wanted to dismiss it as high spirits. Solis didn't say anything; he chose to allow Captain Cordus to do all the arguing for some sort of punishment instead.

Finally, it was decided that the two who'd caused the trouble had to pull night guard duty for a week. Night guard duty consisted of one or two nights before falling to someone else, so a week wasn't such a stretch. I thought that was rather light punishment for slicing up your allies, but I wasn't in charge and wasn't going to be. Not of this rabble.

The rain had finally stopped when we set out the following morning, but we were going to be traveling over extremely wet ground, which meant the wagons would likely be stuck within the first hour or two. They were in the middle of the marching army, since they carried supplies. I'm not sure whom they expected to attack for what we had—the food was terrible.

Our combined army consisted of three thousand Farus troops, twenty-five hundred Red Hand soldiers and a contingent of teamsters, coopers and blacksmiths. I wasn't counting the small group of camp followers that trailed along behind, both male and female. Honestly, we might have been better off with only a few hundred troops since we were going to a massacre, but some people tend to go for overkill.

Solis and I rode along the south side of the marching army, with other officers scattered up and down the line. My poor horse was dubbed Brownie, and he was quite patient with me since I hadn't ridden anything after my short stint on

Falchan. Yes, the ass was sore at the end of the day. I mentally told it to get used to this and went on.

There wasn't much chance for the Regulars and Red Hand to get into altercations while we were on the march, but they found a way once we stopped for the day.

"Come on, let's watch blade practice while we wait for dinner," Solis turned our horses over to the Regulars assigned to picket duty. I'd been about to take care of the horses myself, but that didn't seem to be my job. Instead, I gave Brownie a pat and followed Solis.

The evenings were the time to get in blade practice, or in many cases, blade lessons. We watched some clacking away with wood blades, out on the muddy ground. The new grass on the practice ground was wet and slippery, too, and the heavy boots of sparring troops had mud churned up in no time. If the soldiers weren't careful, they'd lose their footing and fall right into the muck.

I drew in a deep breath and almost went around Solis when I saw one of The Red Hand troops challenging the boy who'd dropped his practice sword in the dirt the first day.

I didn't think he'd improved much in the four days since then, and The Red Hand soldier was comfortable with a blade, I saw that right off. Solis grabbed my arm and pulled me back. I gave him a swift glance; his face was set.

Perhaps I should have done something other than stand there and watch The Red Hand mercenary give the boy a beating. And when the young man slipped in the mud, the mercenary deliberately delivered a hard blow to the head. I don't know whether the others heard it but I did—the boy's neck snapped and he collapsed like a sack of spilled grain.

Solis didn't stop me this time; in fact, he was striding angrily beside me as we watched the mercenary deliver a kick

# Chapter 4

to the already dead teen. Solis' shout had the mercenary backing up, however, and one of The Red Hand Captains was coming in—he was probably worried there'd be trouble. He was right.

"The boy's dead," Solis knelt beside the body.

"I wasn't expecting him to fall," the mercenary whined his excuse. I wanted to kill him, right then and there. It was all I could do to keep my eyes and fangs under control.

"Take the boy and call the General," Solis snapped to the Regulars that came running up at his shout.

That's how we ended up at another judgment that night, with the General and the High Commander weighing in. All the Captains had come as well, from both sides. Apparently, the mercenary was the High Commander's prized blademaster. His malevolent nature had led him straight to the most inexperienced youth in Farus' army.

"If your man was as experienced as you say, then he should have been expecting the fall—the others were falling in the muck," Cordus complained to a Red Hand Captain.

"But no one can predict when the fall might occur," The Red Hand Captain defended his position and the mercenary. We had set up the judgment in a clear spot outside the camp, far enough away that prying eyes and ears wouldn't be privy to the proceedings.

The entire Farus army was angry over the incident, although they hadn't treated the youth very well, either. Red Hand had overstepped their bounds and I was beginning to wonder if it wasn't intentional. After all, the new King of Farus had sent the bulk of the army his country could afford on an errand, when a fourth that number might have sufficed. However, his advisors might have been worried over the number of well-trained troops the Pelipu was sending, and that, in my opinion, was a legitimate concern.

"Your soldier knew the boy had no training; how could he not? He should have asked someone with more experience to spar with him," Cordus snorted.

"He merely wished to teach the boy."

"He was not teaching; I have many witnesses to that."

"All the witnesses are your own troops." The Red Hand Captain sounded bored.

"This is getting us nowhere," the High Commander stood. "I suggest one of our own traditions to decide this. Our man, with a blade, against the best you have. The one that survives, wins."

"That is not how we handle things," the General rumbled.

"It's the quickest way to settle this. We could be at this for days," the High Commander yawned to get his point across.

"Let me," I said softly to Solis. He turned to give me a concerned look as I knelt in my accustomed place next to his campstool.

"You're good, but not that good," Desmun muttered to me from his seat beside Solis.

"I like this," the High Commander grinned maliciously. "Your smallest female, against my most experienced blademaster? That's a joke."

"Are you sure you can do this?" Solis asked me quietly.

"If I wasn't, I wouldn't volunteer. Who would go otherwise?" I asked.

"I would," Solis answered. I'd already guessed at that and wondered then if this whole incident wasn't a set-up.

The High Commander wanted command of the entire army—had from the beginning. What better way to assert his

# Chapter 4

authority and prove that he should be in charge, since his were the better troops and all?

What better way to discredit the General's leadership as well? Prove to all that he was weak and worthy only to be second-in-command, if that? Yeah, I was extremely distrustful of the Pelipu, who seemed to have his own best interests and ideologies at heart. Too bad he wasn't here to be scrutinized.

"I want the female to go against Mardis." The High Commander was pushing his agenda, now.

"Liss, are you sure?" Solis asked again.

"Most definitely," I nodded. Mardis deserved to die. He wasn't expecting to do anything other than kill whoever came against him and then hand total control of both armies to the High Commander. He had his sights set on Solis, who was the General's best swordsman.

"Bring Mardis," the High Commander smiled. Torches were brought, as was Mardis, and a fighting square was set by placing a torch in each corner. We had to stay in that area to fight. I was learning the High Commander's rules—if you stepped outside the square, you were declared the loser and beheaded as a coward. He had some fucked up rules, all right.

Solis, Cordus and Desmun all pulled me aside to talk to the General. "I'm not familiar with your skills, Liss, and I am placing my trust in you over this," he said softly. "If you are able, take him down swiftly."

"How fast do you want this to be?" I asked.

"As fast as possible." The General wasn't comfortable with this, I could tell. I could see the concern in his face, and that surprised me. The concern wasn't for what this might do to his command if I lost—the concern was for me.

# Blood War

"I'll make it fast," I nodded. Solis walked with me to the edge of the square. Mardis, wearing trousers only, was already inside the fighting square. He made quite a show of flexing bare arms and shoulders. Well, if there was a bigger asshole on Vionn, I hadn't met him yet.

I drew both my blades and checked them over, just to have something to do. "Think you to frighten me with two?" Mardis snorted. I didn't answer him. I was tempted to launch into a diatribe over what filth and scum he was, and that wouldn't do. Dragon and the other Falchani let their blades do the talking. Mine were about to sing.

"On my signal," the High Commander stood on the perimeter of the fighting square, as did the General and the Captains from both sides. I watched Mardis. There was no way I wanted any surprises from this asshole.

I watched his left hand (which was gloved and clenched), and then noted where he was standing, extrapolating the movement he'd have to make if he threw something in my eyes. Yeah—he was a jerk on top of being an asshole. A deadly jerk.

The High Commander shouted and Mardis moved swiftly to fling his handful of pepper flakes, but not swiftly enough. I had enough time to close my eyes against the pepper he'd tossed in my face, but his head was already severed. I stood there, sneezing violently as our audience watched Mardis go to his knees and then topple over, his head rolling out of the fighting square.

I was led away between Solis and Desmun, still sneezing, my eyes watering from the pepper flakes that clung to my skin. I'd sheathed my blades, but I'd have to clean them when I could see properly again.

# Chapter 4

"Here," Solis handed a small towel that he'd drenched in water to me.

"The calf-brained idiot planned this," Desmun swore and paced along one wall of Solis' tent.

"More than likely with the High Commander's blessing," Solis agreed quietly. "Keep your voice down, Desmun. Do you want the spies to hear?" Solis watched me as I blinked; I was finally seeing better after washing my face twice. The sneezing had stopped, thankfully.

"Who taught you how to fight with blades?" Solis asked when things settled down and Desmun's curses had softened.

"My father-in-law," I answered honestly. If I'd done things my way, I'd have gone to mist, those pepper flakes would have gone right through and my claws would have severed Mardis' head.

"You're married." Solis said it flatly.

"Yes. Is that a problem?" My answer caused Solis to look up at Desmun.

"I'll never tell," Desmun muttered. "I've never seen anything like that. Those skills don't need to be hidden away in the home."

"Were you not aware that married females aren't supposed to join the army?" Solis was grinning at me, now.

"Had no idea. If it becomes a problem, though, just let me know. There are other things I can do." I could go to the opposition, to sit and wait for everybody to clash together before I made my final decision.

"I don't think I want you anywhere except right where you are," Desmun said. Solis nodded in agreement.

"We may move you over to the General, though," Solis said. "Warn, his bodyguard is good, but he's not the best. I can trade off and take Warn for mine. Shouldn't be a problem."

"Message for Captain Solis," a runner stood outside our tent. Desmun went to pull back the tent flap, inviting the young man inside. He handed the rolled-up scroll to Solis, who broke the seal.

"The General is thinking the same thing," Solis said, standing up and stretching. He and I had been sitting on the two campstools he had inside the tent. "Come on, Liss, you'll be guarding the General from now on. Mind you, if he isn't kept safe, you'll answer to me." I gathered up my things and followed Solis and Desmun from the tent, the nearly forgotten runner trailing behind us.

"Warn, I trust you don't mind acting as bodyguard to Captain Solis," the General said.

"Of course not, sir," Warn dipped his head to the General.

"Take your things to my tent," Solis said, and Warn nodded to him as well before leaving to gather his belongings.

"Desmun, go out and see what the Regulars are saying about Mardis' death. I want to know if there are any rumors we need to dampen," the General ordered. Desmun nodded and left the tent.

"I'd like to know what Red Hand is saying as well, but they've tightened their perimeters and we can't get a single spy through right now," the General raked a hand through his hair with a sigh. "Now, young woman, I want to know where it is you learned to fight like that."

"Her father-in-law taught her," Solis grinned.

"Laws were made to be ignored, eh?" The General laughed.

"I think I might be able to sneak over, if you really want to know what Red Hand is saying," I told Solis and the General.

# Chapter 4

"Liss, that could cost you your life and I wouldn't be able to stop them if they caught you," the General said. "Maybe in a night or two, when things have settled down. They have spies, I have spies. It's a terrible world when you can't trust your allies, isn't it?"

"Allies," Solis snorted. "This is the cat inviting the tiger to help him hunt the mouse. It's not just the mouse in danger, here."

I felt the same way, but I wasn't about to voice my opinion and I wondered why these two were suddenly discussing everything so freely in front of me.

"We have a weapon against you, should you turn against us," the General smiled grimly. "You can be put to death for enlisting as a married woman."

"Oh, that's just lovely," I muttered. Well, if they tried to kill me, they might have some angry Larentii to contend with, not to mention an angry Lissa.

"You'll be all right, Liss," Solis patted me on the back and stood up. "I'm not looking forward to Warn's snoring." He yawned as he walked out of the tent.

"Get some sleep, Liss. We'll be up early tomorrow." The General stood as well.

I nodded and left his portion of the tent, going out to my front section. At least it was bigger than what I'd had with Solis, but I didn't have very much to fill it, anyway.

That night, I placed a larger shield around us and included the officers' tents, after checking all of them for any sign of taint. One bodyguard was missing when he should have been inside the tent, but after *Looking*, I found him with one of the camp followers, having a good time. I withdrew quickly—didn't want to see more of that than I had to.

* * *

# Blood War

If the High Commander was surprised by my sudden appearance at the General's elbow at breakfast the next morning, he didn't show it. He just kept eating at his table with two of his Captains. I tasted my morning tea and grimaced.

"Something wrong?" The General had laugh lines around his eyes. He looked to be in his mid-forties, with slightly graying brown hair and green eyes. He was straight and fit, though, and I figured he'd earned his rank.

"This tastes like mud," I grimaced again. I don't know what kind of tea the General liked—they'd served me the same thing and expected me to like it. Solis liked his tea lighter and it was palatable, at least.

"The stronger the better," the General smiled wider and sipped his tea.

"Whatever you say, sir," I shuddered and set my cup down with a thump. He laughed. Solis, Desmun and Captain Nord came in to sit with us and they were served better tea, I just knew it. Warn was with Solis, Desmun's bodyguard, Maks, was right behind him, and Nord's bodyguard, Ander, was at his elbow.

"I think you grew two heads and four arms after last night," Desmun said, looking at me. I was trying to chew the bacon I'd been served—I think the pig was at least a hundred years old before he died and then they didn't butcher him for days after that. It was the toughest bacon I'd ever had.

"I don't think my blades would cut this stuff," I set the slice of bacon on my wooden plate with a sigh.

"You'll get terrible food for a few days; I had to send the cooks back to the castle in chains last night," Cordus came over and sat down, his bodyguard, Gus, with him. "They'd been paid off by Red Hand spies."

# Chapter 4

I wondered what Red Hand had paid them to do, other than listen to the General's conversations with his Captains over breakfast, but like the other bodyguards, I kept my mouth shut.

All the bodyguards were kept out of the General's tent later while he had a private conference with the Captains. The other two Captains, Blade and Grip, had shown up, finally. They could be excused for being late, though—they'd been up part of the night with the Sergeants, quelling a disturbance or two among the Regulars.

"I hope I don't have to tell you not to let him down," Warn was in front of me suddenly while I was watching The Red Hand troops, who were camped just north of us.

The High Commander was sending a couple of men away on horseback. That made me frown. "Look at me when I'm talking to you," Warn demanded, jabbing a finger in my chest.

"I don't have any argument with you," I pushed his hand away. "And whatever the General wants, he'll probably get unless he asks for sex. Why is the High Commander sending two men toward Phergis?"

Phergis was the capital city of Farus, where Rindle's castle stood. It was also the nearest city to Seaport, where the Pelipu's troops had landed on Farus.

"He's sending two back?" Warn whirled to look. The two racing horses were all that could be seen, now. That caused him to snort. "Fucking spies," he muttered.

"Probably on their way to deliver a message to the Pelipu," Gus said. "It'll take a day and a half to ride back to Seaport, and then another two days to cross the channel, and a day beyond that to get the message to The Red Hand himself."

"So, we have ten days or so, before a message comes back?"

"Sounds about right," Ander agreed. "And who knows what was in that message to begin with? Could just be that the commander didn't like his breakfast this morning." The others laughed.

If I were free to go and wasn't worried over my discovery, I'd go right then, place compulsion on the High Commander and find out things for myself. Meanwhile, I was forcing myself to play by the rules.

The Captains came out after a while, ordered everybody to saddle up and we were on our way half an hour later, after the General's tent was taken down and packed away.

We were still traveling over wet ground—the wagons got stuck as usual, which held everything up and we went about half as far as the General wanted to go.

He was frustrated by our lack of progress and grumbled when we were forced by darkness to camp for the night. The High Commander was giving us the cold shoulder, too, choosing to show up for meals only.

"This bread is disgusting," Desmun tossed the dry lump onto his plate. "Is it too much to ask to get decent bread, at least?"

He was right—the bread was disgusting, but I had a feeling that the people in the cooking tents were the ones being punished for infractions, since the regular cooks had been arrested and sent back to Phergis. What could you expect except a lousy meal?

"With your permission, General, I'll go out and find better cooks," I volunteered.

"Can you get me a good breakfast tomorrow morning?" The General asked.

# Chapter 4

"I can try," I nodded. He gave permission, Warn offered to watch the General and Captain Solis, so I went looking for cooks among the Regulars.

"Who can cook? Show me your hands," I said to the first tent filled with Regulars, all of whom were trying to eat what we'd been served. Two hands went up. "Do you like to cook?" I asked my second question. Both hands stayed up. "Good. Meet me at the cooking tents tomorrow morning, two hours before sunrise."

I went to the next tent and asked my questions again. Before it was over, I had thirty-five willing hands, and they all showed up at the cooking tents very early the following morning.

I kept my shield up around the General's and the officers' tents—I'd have an early warning in case anything happened while we all went over basic biscuit and bread making.

The bread dough had to be set to rise in special pots hauled in the cookwagons. We sliced the bacon thin enough that it would cook quickly and wouldn't be so tough we couldn't chew it.

We made gravy to go with the biscuits and fried potatoes—we had plenty of flour and potatoes. Few eggs, though; those were as precious as gold until we reached a town to the north and east. I learned we were hoping to get more salted beef and pork, there, and perhaps a fresh meal or two.

"Well, this is certainly an improvement," Solis said as I sat between him and the General with my plate of food. I'd taught the new cooking staff that one of the perks of cooking was getting extra rations. It was only fair.

"You get to decide how to punish the ones we took off cooking detail," I said, biting into a decent piece of bacon.

"Take my advice and don't let them anywhere near the cooking tents from now on."

It was a better day all the way around; the wagons barely got stuck once, and only three fights broke out.

"Feel like doing a little sparring?" The General had taken his green coat off and dropped it onto a campstool as soon as a handful of Regulars got his tent up.

"If you want," I nodded. Actually, I wasn't looking forward to it. I figured we'd have an audience, and I wasn't wrong.

"You won't upset me if you give me a thrashing," he grinned and lifted his blade. At least the ground was firmer, here, and the new grass was taller.

I was happy with the smell of spring in the air, but I wasn't crazy about the horse poop and the trenches that were dug every night. They were far enough away that they didn't bother the others, but if the wind was right, it carried the stench straight to my supersensitive nose.

The General and I had a good exercise but I didn't go on the attack, I just blocked his blows as I usually did when sparring. He was good, I'll give him that. Our audience seemed disappointed, though.

"You think she's going to upstage the General?" Solis barked at them when they started grumbling. That got everybody's attention, and they turned back to their bladework.

"Here, you're holding that wrong," I went to correct a young man, who was struggling with his opponent. This one was around nineteen; I'd gotten his age from his scent. I placed his hand in the correct position. "And there's no shame in holding it with both hands, if it'll save your life," I told him. "If it came down to holding it with both hands or losing my

# Chapter 4

life, I think I'd hold it with both hands. If your wrist gets whacked, let the other hand help out." He was nodding at me, his eyes wide. I watched him clack his wooden blade against his opponent's, who was more experienced, I could tell.

"Parry with the flat of your blade," I added after a while. "If you nick your blade, it could break, or at least cause you problems getting a good edge back on it," I suggested. He nodded and whacked away, conscious now of using the flat as opposed to the edge.

"Let's clean up before dinner," the General pulled me away. I nodded and went with him.

# Chapter 5

*L*issa
"Do you remember when you offered to sneak into the enemy camp and do some spying?" I listened as the general washed himself in a bucket of water a Regular had brought to the tent. I nodded. I'd get my own bucket, as soon as the General was done.

"I'd like for you to do some spying tonight, after everyone else is bedded down. Head for the trenches first, then sneak into their camp from there, if you can. Just remember, I'll punish you myself if you get caught."

"I understand, sir," I nodded.

Using a bucket to wash and cold water to do it isn't the best way to take a bath, but it could have been worse. I had soap tucked inside my duffle, and I managed to get my hair clean, combed out and braided before we went off to dinner.

# Blood War

Meals were a definite improvement with the new crew in the cooking tents. The High Commander came over to our table, too, and ate with the General while pointedly ignoring me.

That was fine; I thought he was a shithead anyway, and I'd killed his star mercenary. He could be grumpy if he wanted.

"How long until we reach the town?" he asked around a mouthful of food. Yeah, not only was he a shithead, he had bad manners, too.

"Two days; we lost time with the wet ground and the wagons getting stuck and moving slowly," the General answered. "We should have been there, or close, already."

"What will we find there?" The High Commander asked. I decided I was going to call him HC, for short.

"It is a large, bustling village, surrounded by farmland and herds," the General replied.

"No vineyards?"

"No, the soil isn't good for that," the General dipped into his bowl of stew.

"We need wine for a ceremony," the HC complained.

"They'll have some there, but I warn you, it may have been made by the enemy."

"I don't care where it comes from, only that it's available," the HC grumbled. Well, he wasn't getting a star or a happy face on his homework today.

I waited until just after lights out to make my sojourn away from the tent, heading toward the trenches, just as I'd been told. They smelled awful. I took a quick turn around them, making sure nobody else was there to notice I didn't use them, and on the way back I slipped between Blade and Grip's tents, turning to mist in the process. It only took a few seconds

# Chapter 5

to get to The Red Hand camp. I buzzed into the HC's tent while he was talking with two of his Captains.

"We'll find some excuse to hole up in that town until our messengers return with the Pelipu's directive on the matter," HC tapped a cylindrical case, which was nearly four inches in diameter and probably sixteen inches in length. "I know what my feelings are on the matter, but I won't act until I receive his orders."

"What about the others?" One of the Captains asked.

"The Pelipu will tell us what to do. Go to bed; we have an early ride in the morning."

The General was still up and waiting for me when I returned. I told him what I heard and saw. He seemed surprised that I'd seen the cylindrical case. "That's their holy writ—at least part of it," he sighed. "They'll make an excuse to stay in Windle until their messengers arrive. I can't say I like the sound of this, but what else can we do? Right now they hold the money purse and it will do us no good to go on without them."

I wanted to ask him what his true feelings were on all this, but I held off. There wasn't any reason why he should tell me anything of the sort.

"What sort of ceremony requires wine?" I asked instead. "I know little about this religion."

"They use wine in many, so there's no way to tell for sure," the General replied. "Go to bed, Liss. We have an early morning ahead of us."

Since I couldn't sleep anyway, I left my body behind and went to energy, traveling far away under twinkling stars. I slept easier, once I returned.

* * *

"We're still a good three weeks away, and it looks like rain again," Solis rode up next to the General the following morning, with Warn right behind him.

"You may not have to worry about the rain," the General said, and proceeded to tell Solis what I'd overheard the evening before.

"We'll have to quarter the bulk of the army on the northeastern edge, I think," Solis said thoughtfully. "Windle is where the ground starts to rise at the foot of the mountains. It'll be a steady climb once we get past it."

* * *

*Le-Ath Veronis*
"Where is the Raona?" Roff walked beside Flavio after the Council meeting. Aurelius and Garde had come to handle it in Lissa's absence. Flavio studied his youngest vampire child and wondered what to tell him.

"Child, she had something important to do. She should be back in three weeks or so," Flavio sighed. "Her mates did not receive any notification of her absence."

"Is that why Gavin seems so angry?"

"More than likely," Flavio nodded at Roff's observation. "He is not angry with you." Gavin and Tony had begun to teach Roff how to fight. Flavio felt it necessary after Roff's wounding.

"Is he angry with Lissa?"

"In a way. He worries about her. He wants to keep her safe always, and she sometimes prevents him from protecting her as he wants."

"Is she in danger?" Roff was worried now and his wings tightened against his back.

"No more than usual, I think," Flavio soothed Roff. "Lissa has talents that the rest of us lack."

# Chapter 5

"We're having a security meeting tonight," Tony walked up beside them.

"May I come?" Roff asked.

"You may come, but you may not speak of what you hear," Flavio placed compulsion. Roff nodded in silent acceptance.

* * *

*Karathia*

"Brenten, you've been moping around since the ball," Wylend glanced at his son. Griffin had a standing invitation to have breakfast with his father, and usually took advantage of it. Griffin studied his father's face. They looked very much alike, he and his father. "I'm sure Lissa will be fine—I understand she holds a great deal of power, although she seldom uses any of it," Wylend added.

"It's what she is," Griffin sighed. "She doesn't *Look*, because she doesn't want to pry most of the time. She refuses to push anyone unless they are committing a great wrong. There are times when she should speak up and she doesn't. And times when she should remain silent, and she doesn't."

"If you had raised her, perhaps you could have taught her those things."

"I wasn't allowed. Considering what happened after, perhaps it's for the best."

"Are you saying that the pain was less, this way? Erland has told me what happened. All of it." Wylend sipped his tea.

"She hasn't been wrong about me. Most of the time," Griffin muttered. "She shouldn't be on Vionn, now."

"I don't believe anyone could have stopped her," Wylend observed.

"No, father. I mean what I say. She shouldn't be there now. I switched the bracelets. I knew Green Birth was coming, and that they wouldn't give up until they had my son. Every future I saw showed Wyatt living with the Green Fae until he was grown. The only way to stop it was to provide a substitute. I did what I had to do to make sure they didn't take Wyatt."

* * *

*Vionn*

*Lissa*

I was glad to come to Windle. The General took rooms in town on the northeast end, not far from where the army camped. I'm sure he did it to keep an eye on the HC, who took rooms at a nearby inn. Solis, his unspoken second-in-command, took the adjoining set of rooms. He and Warn helped watch over the General.

"Where are you going?" Solis stood on the steps leading into the inn—I'd met up with him as I walked out the door, slinging on my leather jacket. Evenings were quite cool in the foothills so I took the jacket, although I didn't feel the cold as much as the others did.

I could easily have gone without a coat, but everybody else with us was shivering and wearing warmer clothing. Solis wanted to know what I was doing; he was just returning from a short conference with the other Captains.

"Out for a little air; those rooms can get stuffy," I said. "I'll be back." Solis gave me a curt nod and walked through the door, leaving me to my business. I'd waited for a week and a half to deliver this message, but it had to be delivered—in a way that left no doubt with the ones who'd snatched Toff.

I'd gone *Looking* for him twice, now, but there was some sort of buzz around him and I couldn't get a clear picture. Most likely, whatever power they'd used to snatch him to begin with was now clouding any images of him.

I had horrible visions of Toff being turned over to The Red Hand if Green Birth didn't get exactly what they wanted.

# Chapter 5

Green Birth, Red Hand. What a joke. If I didn't do something there at the end, Toff could be killed anyway, right along with Green Birth and their half-Fae children. I walked into a stand of trees, made sure there wasn't anyone to see and went to mist.

Green Birth was scattered in a series of valleys beyond the mountain range we would cross as soon as the HC decided to move—if he decided to move. I had my own worries concerning the message he expected from the Pelipu. It couldn't be anything good, in my opinion.

Spring was barely beginning in the valleys as I flew over them, with trees starting to bud and a hint of green grass on the valley floors. A river ran through the place and there were orchards and fields already planted with early crops.

A vineyard filled an entire valley. I selected an apple orchard, the early spring blossoms white and waving in the breeze, casting their sweet smell toward the river. I knew Tiearan Briar lived nearby; he was the one who'd left the note behind when they'd taken Toff.

I was silent as I used claws to sever branches, carefully laying them out on the cleared ground north of the apple orchard. Those trees might not bear fruit this season. I didn't kill the trees, but I needed their limbs to send my message. Once everything was laid out as I wanted it, I misted back to Windle.

* * *

"Tiearan, you must come." Rain, dressed in her working woolens, stood in Tiearan's doorway as he prepared to go out on his errands for the day.

"What is it, Rain?" Tiearan knew it wasn't the army; they were still more than two weeks away.

"We have a message."

"Then why didn't you bring it with you?"

"That would be difficult," Rain looked frightened, and that was beginning to concern Tiearan.

"Lead the way," Tiearan gestured with his hands, and Rain led him toward the apple orchard.

"How do they know our sun-runes?" Tiearan stared at the apple tree branches, sliced expertly and placed carefully to spell out the words. They never taught the sun-runes to anyone—they used those to enhance their power.

"I would have expected a different message—perhaps a threat," Rain muttered. Spelled out in apple tree branches across a clear space of ground were the words, *a child is not a bargaining token.*

"This frightens me," Tiearan sighed.

* * *

*Karathia*

Erland stared at Wylend. "He knew? He switched the bracelets? Wylend, this is bad. Very, very bad. If Lissa learns of this, things could definitely turn against us. Do you know how long it took, and how difficult it was, to convince her to be my mate? I will be tossed off Le-Ath Veronis in a blink if she discovers I knew before she did and didn't tell her. What am I supposed to do about that? I don't want to tell her, because of what will happen. And if she finds out I know, things will be worse."

"For both of us," Wylend nodded. He sat in his private study, Erland sitting in a chair before his desk. Absently Wylend brought power to him, changing the whorls in the wood pattern on the surface of his desk.

"This makes everything more vulnerable. Solar Red is forming on three worlds outside Alliance territory," Erland continued. "They've spread their command base, thinking

# Chapter 5

they can't be destroyed simultaneously on three separate worlds. They may be right. They are gaining popularity with Black Mist and The Red Hand. You know how widespread both of them are. If those two decide to throw in their lot with Solar Red, then we'll have an epidemic on our hands. We need Lissa's help with this, but she's one of their main targets."

Wylend blew out a frustrated breath. "The Red Hand enjoys torturing their victims to obtain confessions and admissions of adherence to their own faith—before they kill them. Their excuse is that at least the victims go to the Red Hand god when they die."

"Black Mist just kills. Or tortures and dismembers, before killing. They have no god, other than the pleasure of inflicting pain. I still can't believe they're hired as assassins on non-Alliance worlds." Erland shook his head. "They'd kill the ones who hired them as easily as the ones they're hired to kill—and have done it, many times."

"Well, Solar Red has their eye on Lissa, now, and she's off by herself, haring after a kidnapped comesula." Wylend stood and stretched.

"She was planning to adopt him, that's why he was brought here, remember?" Erland felt a bit of anger.

"I realize that. I know she loves the child—enough to make him her own. Brenten was the one who told me she was considering adoption, and that's why I asked her to bring him to the Ball. Even then, Brenten knew and was manipulating things. I'm not sure how I would have felt, or how I might have reacted, if I knew what was coming. My Council is meeting shortly. Do you wish to attend?" Wylend headed for the door. Erland stood and followed him out.

* * *

*Vionn*

# Blood War



*Lissa*

"They're as tight-lipped as anything I've ever seen," the General grumbled. He, Solis, Warn and I were having our evening meal. I listened carefully as the General complained about our current situation with Red Hand. "My spies have nothing to report, except the usual altercations. Two of ours were beaten and left for dead this morning. Windle's healer is tending them now. The High Commander will be here for breakfast in the morning, trying to explain all this away."

"So they haven't caught the perpetrators?" Solis asked.

"No." The General wasn't happy about that, I could tell. We'd sat in a deserted corner of the inn, eating roasted chicken and talking when four Red Hand troops walked in and sat at a nearby table. We had to stop talking, then.

The innkeeper's daughter, a girl of sixteen, came out to serve them. They all ordered a meal with wine. Their wine came first, followed by platters of roasted chicken with potatoes; just what we'd had.

One of the men reached out for the girl when she dropped off their food, causing her father to appear immediately. He told them, quite loudly, that his inn was respectable and he didn't allow anyone to touch his daughter.

I was right with him on that one. The Red Hand troops proceeded to grumble loudly the whole time they ate and left after hurling more insults at the innkeeper and his daughter.

"Stupid filth," the wife, who cooked for the inn, muttered under her breath as she came out to help her daughter clear the table. The others didn't hear her words, but I did.

After we finished eating, we walked to the healer's home to check on the two wounded men—they'd been beaten badly and were still unconscious. I had my doubts that one would

# Chapter 5

wake at all and the other probably had brain damage from a severe head wound.

The General was angry, I could tell—these men had been on late watch and had likely been accosted by their attackers while everyone else was asleep. The early morning watch had found the wounded night guards on the edge of camp when they arrived for their shift. Neither of the unconscious men had awakened since then.

"We'll check on the Regulars," the General said after we left the healer's home. We walked—the army was less than half a mile away and I figured the walk would serve to clear away some of the General's anger. We met up with Desmun, Nord and Cordus; Blade and Grip were out patrolling the perimeter with their bodyguards.

"Have you found anything?" We sat inside Desmun's tent, drinking tea and going over information the Captains managed to gather from the troops. The General wanted to know everything, no matter how insignificant it might seem.

"Three Red Hand troops went to meet with the High Commander, at least that's what they said they were going to do when they left right after moonrise, last night," Cordus grumped. Red Hand had camped ahead of the Farus army, just a little way up the mountain. They had to pass the outskirts of the Farus army to get back to Windle.

"Horsed or not?" The General asked.

"Horsed," Cordus answered. "But the night watch on the north side said they came back through after three marks, long before the late watch guards came on duty."

"How many does the High Commander have in Windle to guard him?" I asked.

"Seven, I believe," Solis replied. "What does that have to do with anything?"

"How hard would it be for two or three of them to ride double coming back with the others, drop off in that stand of trees between here and Windle and then attack several marks later when the watch changed, just to divert suspicion from the three that came through earlier?" Yeah, I hadn't liked what I'd smelled when the four had come to eat at our inn. There was a taint about them and that had raised my hackles.

Solis drew in a ragged breath. He was seeing this, too.

"Then we need to be questioning those in town instead of those here, perhaps," the General said.

"And we need to be quiet about it," Desmun grumped. "I don't want the High Commander to find out we suspect his guards unless we have solid proof." Solis, Nord and Cordus all agreed.

"We'll start with the stable hands," the General said. "Tomorrow, after breakfast, when the High Commander is inspecting his troops." He went every day—we knew that much—but was back in plenty of time for a better meal in town later.

I wanted to be in on that questioning, to make sure no tales were carried back to the HC or any of his troops. I didn't get any information after that; the bodyguards were sent away so the Captains could have a private chat with the General.

If I'd been alone, I'd have turned to mist and gone right back in. That wasn't an option with Warn, Maks and Ander with me. We ended up walking down to the stand of trees to see if we could find anything. The other three missed the hoof prints because of darkness, but I didn't. I also sniffed out the trees where they'd stopped to relieve themselves while they waited three or four marks to do their murderous misdeeds.

Three Red Hand troops had come—their scents were clear to me. They were likely well trained in hand-to-hand

# Chapter 5

combat, too. No wonder they'd beaten the two guards so badly. We walked back to the camp afterward, waiting at a table in the officers' mess tent while the Captains and General finished their meeting.

"Ready to go?" The General seemed to be in better spirits when he came out with Solis and the others. I stood with the others and we all walked toward Windle. Halfway there, the breeze carried a scent to me, which worried me greatly.

"Something's burning," I said, starting to trot and then to run. Solis was beside me in seconds, with Warn and the General coming behind at a slower pace. I was cursing when we raced into town—our inn was aflame.

"Someone's cut the well rope!" A man shouted. Things were chaotic as precious minutes slipped by.

"Get another rope," Solis yelled. "Find buckets now!"

Some brave souls had gone inside the inn and pulled the bodies of the innkeeper, his wife and daughter out. All dead. My group was the only one staying at the inn, and we'd been away when the fire started.

The great room inside the inn was mostly what was burning, but the wing with the guestrooms was beginning to catch.

"What do you need out of there?" I shouted at the General and Solis over the din while we passed buckets of water along. Those buckets were too little and much too late—I realized that quickly, but an attempt had to be made.

"Almost everything," the General shouted. I nodded. "I'll go," I said, and stepped out of the line. That night the entire town watched me shimmy up a tree that stood near the guest quarters of the inn, and then swing on a branch to kick out a window before climbing inside the burning building.

# Blood War

Smoke choked me immediately so I went to mist, gathered all our belongings quickly and then stayed mist as long as I could to account for the proper passage of time. Rematerializing, then, I began throwing things onto the ground below the window. We'd been on the second floor at the General's insistence—the better rooms were there.

Warn and Solis were beneath the window quickly, gathering our things and taking them out of harm's way. I was coughing hard when I got the last of it out, while soot and sparks flew around me.

The smoke was too thick, almost, to see through and I had to climb over the windowsill, leaping for the tree limb I'd jumped from to begin with. My hands barely caught hold of it while I coughed and gagged. I dangled there, still coughing my lungs out and hanging on in desperation.

The smoke had nearly gotten me and it took a while for me to stop coughing long enough to realize that Solis was shouting for me to drop down—the entire building was burning and the tree had caught as well. I let go of the limb and Solis and Warn caught me.

Our night was spent in the stable where we gratefully cleaned ourselves up in buckets of water after the fire was doused. The inn was a complete loss, however. The fire was extinguished merely to keep other buildings nearby from suffering the same fate.

Horse blankets laid on hay served as beds for us and we all slept. I was almost too tired to put up a shield around the stable, but I made sure it was done before I dropped off in complete exhaustion.

"Liss, wake up, girl," Solis tugged on my elbow. I'd been dreaming that I was in bed at home, my head on Roff's

# Chapter 5

shoulder. Light filtering through the stable window was blindingly bright as I blinked my eyes open.

"I'm awake," I muttered, sitting up on my horse blanket and rubbing my eyes with the heels of my hands. Dust motes and tiny bits of hay were suspended in the early morning light inside the stable. I smelled all of it, along with the remnants of a smoky haze left over from the burning of the inn.

"The General wants to see the bodies of the innkeeper and his family before they're buried," Solis said. I stopped rubbing my eyes and looked up at him.

"I want to see them, too." I stood quickly and went to find my boots. I'd slept in my clothes, so I pulled my boots on as fast as I could and clattered down the ladder right behind Solis. The General and Warn were waiting below for us, and we headed toward the healer's house quickly.

The bodies were in a shed behind the healer's home—all three victims were lined up on rough, makeshift tables inside it. They were all burned, but less so than the ones who'd murdered them hoped.

All three throats had been cut and they'd likely been dead already, bleeding out while the fire was set. The General saw the knife wounds right away and growled. Solis sighed.

The fire had destroyed any scent of the attackers—none of it remained with the bodies, but I figured I had a good guess as to who'd done this. The same ones who'd beaten two others who lay in comas yards away inside the healer's home.

When we went looking for other lodging after examining the bodies, we learned that the HC's messengers had arrived. They hadn't spoken to anyone upon arrival and were now closeted inside the HC's rooms at the other inn. Would we find out what their messages contained? My money was on the negative.

# Blood War

* * *



*Le-Ath Veronis*

"This one tried to kill himself after he was caught." Lisster had the man by the collar, shoving him into a chair beside Lissa's desk inside her study. Aryn sat behind the Queen's desk, his fingertips pressed together while he examined the intruder. He was young, like all the others, and Lisster and Rush had captured him as he scaled the wall to get away from Lissia.

"How?" Aryn wasn't looking at Lisster—he was still examining the young male, who swallowed uncomfortably.

"Poison—Lindis seeds."

"I see. Did the ones who hired you supply these?" Aryn's voice held strong compulsion. Grant sat nearby, recording notes on his handheld computer.

"Yes," the young man bobbed his head.

"Who hired you?"

"Said his name was Ibbett. Offered me a lot of money if I could get maps for him. Maps of this place plus some of the other cities."

"Did he say what the maps were for?"

"Said he wanted to sell them."

"Where did you meet Ibbett?"

"Hraede."

"I have a suggestion," Tony folded in with Gavin. Kiarra had given them the ability when they agreed to be alternate Spawn Hunters. They'd already gone to help with two batches of Ra'Ak spawn during Lissa's absence.

"What is the suggestion?" Aurelius and Garde walked through the door—they'd come quickly when Lisster called for them.

# Chapter 5

"Let's place compulsion on our boyo, here, and follow him back to Hraede." Tony grinned. He'd only gotten better over the years at espionage.

"Sounds like a good idea to me," Lisster shrugged and grinned.

"How quickly can we get counterfeit maps drawn up?" Gavin asked.

"Not long at all," Lisster said. "Lynx, one of Conner's mates, was an artist before he became Saa Thalarr. He still paints and draws. I'll ask him." Lynx showed up moments later and was given information on the maps required. "Let's see your drawing skills, young man," he laid an artist's tablet and pencils in front of the spy. The young man, shivering and blinking in astonishment at all the people who were simply appearing inside the room from thin air, lifted a pencil and began to draw.

* * *

*Vionn*

*Lissa*

"We're moving out tomorrow morning?" I asked, unsure whether I understood this turn of events. The HC held the ceremony with his seven bodyguards the night before—they'd bought four bottles of the best wine to be had in Windle for it. We hadn't been invited.

"We're moving out tomorrow morning," Solis confirmed. "Everything needs to be packed up; we'll leave here before dawn just to make sure the army is ready to head out at the right time."

"All right," I sighed and turned back to my tea. We'd rented a house—the widow who lived there had gone to visit her sister for two days while we needed a place in town.

* * *

# Blood War

Morning arrived, mist-covered and muffled as I stuffed the last of my belongings into my duffle and slung it over a shoulder. I hadn't missed riding, either, although Brownie was happy to get out of the stable.

The General rode before me, with Solis beside him and Warn next to me. It didn't take long to get to camp, where everything had been taken down, loaded up and made ready to go.

Red Hand was mounting up already when we arrived; the HC and his henchguards had gotten there shortly before we did. The two injured men had been left behind in Windle and honestly, the physician didn't expect them to live much longer. I blew out a sigh at the thought.

The army moved as quickly as they could but the ground began to rise into the mountains and it was harder going for the wagons.

"We'll be through the pass in another week," the General sighed as we stopped at midday to water the animals at a stream. "It'll be better after that, with a downward trail until we get to the first of the valleys. If we're lucky, they'll be there, waiting for us. If we're not lucky, they'll retreat to the farthest valley, which means at least another week."

I nodded at the General's assessment. Wherever we met up with Green Birth, I'd have to make a decision as to what to do. I still hadn't come up with a good solution to this dilemma and it worried me. It rained as the day wound down, too—enough to make everyone wet and miserable in the gradually cooling temperatures. It was going to be a cold night.

The General called a halt at a likely camping spot—at least it was mostly level ground, though we were flanked by thick stands of trees on both sides. The HC got his troops stopped only a little farther ahead of us on the trail.

# Chapter 5

He, with his seven bodyguards, came to eat in the officer's tent. While he was there, he never said a word to anyone other than his sycophants. He did glance our way several times while he was eating; his gaze wasn't friendly by any stretch. It made me wonder what the jerk was up to. The General breathed a relieved sigh when the HC and his mini-horde left.

The following day was steeper, higher and colder. I had my leather jacket on; nearly everybody was breathing misty breaths during the early morning. We rode into a thick fog around mid-afternoon, making it difficult to navigate. The fog was almost a light rain at times, which made all of us soggy and out of sorts.

Four fights broke out after we camped because everybody's temper was so short. At one point, Solis left Warn with the General and took me with him to see if we could sort out one of the fights.

"He cut me off!" One Regular, who had a black eye and split lip, was accusing the one he'd fought with, who was nearly as bad off. He also sported a black eye and a bruised cheek.

"In this fog, that wouldn't be difficult," Solis barked, causing both to take a step back. Two Sergeants were there already, the female Sergeant being one of them. She didn't look happy with the men.

"Do we have to put you in chains, or will this stop?" Solis went on.

"I'm done," the first one muttered. The other merely nodded, hanging his head.

"Put them on guard duty, on opposite sides of camp," Solis ordered. The female Sergeant nodded, issuing the command as Solis stalked off with me following at his heels.

He cursed softly as we walked toward the General's tent in thickening fog.

Dinner was a sad affair, with the fog penetrating the cooking tents. Campfires were impossible and everybody was grumbling. Even I was finding it difficult to deal with the situation, but placed my usual shields around the officers' tents before going to bed. A hit against the shield on the southern edge had me awake and shivering three hours before dawn. I misted outward, to find what had triggered the alert.

The fog was even thicker, now, and I hadn't thought that possible. Fortunately, my mist could see right through it, and my scenting ability hadn't gone away, either. Three Red Hand spies, who'd used the cover the fog provided, carefully made their way through camp and right toward the General's tent. Armed with knives, they cautiously placed their feet, intent on making little noise. Of course, the fog helped with that particular strategy, as far as the humanoids were concerned. I heard them just fine.

As mist I followed along behind, just to make sure of their intent, and when they pulled knives and started cutting into the back of the General's tent, that's when I grabbed them.

* * *

Cordus, Solis and Desmun glared at our three prisoners, who were quaking as the General paced before them. So far, no information had come, but that was about to change. I stood in the far corner of the General's portion of the tent, watching and listening as the men were questioned. No useful information had been offered.

Pulling out my knife—the one Glinda had lent me, I walked toward the man in the center—he was the tallest at nearly six feet. I carefully placed the sharp tip of the knife beneath his chin. "You will tell the General exactly what he wants to know," I said, placing more compulsion. I laid it on his two companions, as well. They talked, but didn't know much.

"We were sent to kill the General," the one on the left whined. "We weren't told why. We follow orders." He had dark hair going gray and looked like one of the HC's mercenaries. More than likely an assassin, brought along to eliminate unwanted allies and adversaries alike. I was standing in my spot in the corner again while the General and the Captains did the questioning.

"Why did the High Commander send messengers to the Pelipu?" Solis demanded.

"We were not informed," the man in the center answered.

"The Red Ritual for the god was performed in Windle," the one on the right offered. That had Solis and Desmun both growling. I had to *Look* to see what that meant, and it almost made me growl, too. They had a target in mind. Someone that they could accuse of heresy or worse. The ritual cleansed them from any responsibility for the torture and murder later. I wanted to hold my head—I felt a headache coming on. What new stupidity was this? Only it wasn't likely new stupidity. I figured it was an old, traditional stupidity. Amazing, isn't it, how some people will rationalize anything to get what they want?

"What shall we do with this scum?" Solis asked.

"I don't think the High Commander will come looking for them, do you?" the General looked at his Captains.

"No. He won't even ask about them," Desmun smiled grimly. The three men began to sweat, even in the cold, clammy air.

"Do it," the General jerked his head toward the tent's entrance. The spies were hauled away. I was thankful that I'd been left behind to guard the General. I wasn't fond of executions.

"Can I depend on you to let me know if anything else comes our way tonight?" The General asked me.

"Of course, sir," I nodded.

"You earned your pay tonight," the General said. "I'd like to go back to bed. You can turn in early tomorrow, if you want."

I nodded again and went toward my portion of the tent.

* * *

*Belen's Study*

Belen gazed upon the one who stood on the other side of his desk—the desk that Belen made to appear every time he chose corporeality. It had been several lifetimes—as humanoids measured time—since he'd had this one standing before him. "This is your choice, then? You have all the information?"

"Of course."

"I will be watching," Belen added.

"I understand completely."

Belen watched as the other disappeared.

* * *

*Vionn*

*Lissa*

The HC's eyes were on us whenever we weren't looking during breakfast the following morning. I'm sure he was wondering what had happened to his little band of assassins, but he would have to keep on wondering.

The fog was still thick and would cause problems as we made our way up the mountain toward the pass. I could find my way easily enough but was thankful that the General was

# Chapter 5

familiar with the territory and knew where he was going. The HC would have been hopelessly lost after five minutes.

The fog did cause problems; we didn't travel a third of the planned distance before the HC was forced to call a halt—the General had sent two messages during the day, both asking to halt and camp until the fog cleared. The tents were set up and the cooks had set about preparing an early meal when the messenger arrived at our tent.

"Message for the General. I was instructed to hand it to him personally," the boy said, holding the rolled-up paper back as I reached for it.

"What the hell for?" The General came through the slit in the canvas that separated his portion of the tent from mine. I didn't scent any taint about the boy, but I still watched him closely when the General came forward, his hand held out for the message.

"I was instructed to wait for a reply," the boy dipped his head respectfully to the General. The General looked briefly at the boy—he couldn't be more than seventeen—by his scent, anyway. He looked older, as if he'd been through too much already, and only expected more of the same from his life.

The seal on the rolled-up message was broken and the General opened it to read. He seemed a bit angry afterward, motioning the boy into his section of the tent to write a reply. He hadn't asked me to accompany him so I stayed where I was, listening carefully in case I needed to assist the General in any way. My help wasn't needed and the boy walked out a scant three minutes later, a freshly sealed message in his hand.

"We'll be entertaining guests after dinner," the General said, coming out again. His face looked worried, though. I nodded at his words.

# Chapter 6

*Wyyld*

*Office of the Minister for Defense*

Thurlow Burghin stood before the Minister for Defense, who was in charge of the Alliance armies, their spies, investigators, military tribunals and any other thing that might keep the Alliance safe and adhering to the law.

Thurlow wasn't particularly handsome, not as some measured it, anyway. He had thick, black hair, gray eyes, a slightly crooked nose and lips that were full and nearly sensuous. They were his best feature, according to the three female secretaries who'd passed him through office after office, from one ranking officer to the next, until he reached the Minister for Defense.

"Your record is impeccable," the Minister noted, setting the handheld computer on his desk. The Minister was in his sixties—still young for this day and time upon any number of Alliance worlds. "The Founder has personally approved your assignment to Le-Ath Veronis."

"Thank you, sir," Thurlow nodded respectfully.

"We need someone to act as Liaison with Le-Ath Veronis," the Minister sighed. "We are getting more and more arrests from there—people who have been hired by the remnants of Solar Red, all trying their best to gather information to send back to those murderous fanatics. I want someone on the ground, there, to hear those confessions firsthand. I want this stopped before it can start, do you understand? Our newest monarch on our newest Alliance world is being threatened, and I'm sure I don't have to tell you that Le-Ath Veronis is padding the Alliance coffers right now."

"I understand that, sir," Thurlow nodded slightly. "Why do we need someone there, though?"

The Minister rubbed the back of his neck uncomfortably. "Rumors have reached me, and those above me, even, that if the present Queen dies, all except the comesuli will be forced from the planet. You've read the information on Kifirin?"

"The planet or the demigod?" Thurlow asked.

"The god part," the Minister breathed a sigh. "He has been heard to say that if Queen Lissa dies, the others will be forced off the planet, except for the comesuli. That means the revenue that we are currently enjoying from Le-Ath Veronis will cease, and gambling will once more be done on non-Alliance worlds, more than likely. You understand, now, why we have an interest in all this? We very much wish to keep the Queen alive, by any means necessary. That is why we want to send one of our best. You are our eyes and ears. You will report directly to us, so we may see how urgent the matter is and take appropriate measures."

# Chapter 6

"Of course, sir. I understand." Thurlow didn't even twitch at the news. The Minister wanted to sigh again—his spies and undercover agents could all hide their expressions—quite well, in fact. They'd been trained in it, after all.

"You won't be undercover so much there; I've informed them that you are coming, in an effort to keep everyone apprised. We are obligated to keep all our Alliance leaders alive, after all."

Thurlow wanted to smile. Those leaders were kept alive as long as they agreed with the general consensus among the Grand Alliance Council. Assistance might come a little slower if the leader disagreed too loudly with the Founder and the twenty Charter Members that made up the Grand Alliance Council. "How quickly should I pack, sir?" Thurlow asked, a slight smile playing across his lips.

"Right away. I want you on a ship tonight. Passage is already booked. I'd provide an assistant, but I'm hoping that they'll do that for you. Ask when you arrive. Let me know if that request is denied."

"I will, sir." Thurlow dipped his head and turned to go.

* * *

*Le-Ath Veronis*

"Now is the time I wish Lissa were here, just to deal with this," Tony grumbled. The Alliance was sending a Liaison, while he and Gavin were scheduled to follow Paulin, their little artistic spy, off world to Hraede.

Paulin's employer, Ibbitt, might have connections to Solar Red, and Tony and Gavin were going after him. Lynx offered to come along, claiming a bit of boredom since he'd retired from the Saa Thalarr.

Gavin was doing his best to be pragmatic about the Alliance sending in one of their own to act as a Liaison between Le-Ath Veronis and the Alliance.

"It's only a bureaucrat," Gavin replied. "He'll follow others around and make a nuisance of himself, more than likely. Erland, Aurelius and Gardevik have already offered to keep him entertained and out of our hair while we tend to actual business. Flavio, too, has offered to help."

"But he's coming in right before we leave," Tony wasn't done, yet.

"Anthony, let us save this discussion for later," Gavin said.

* * *

"Child, we will be entertaining a guest this evening, at the palace," Flavio informed Roff. "Please dress appropriately."

Roff set his book down. He hadn't read much before, but now he found he had a fascination with it. Flavio's library was extensive and Roff's interests were wide and varied. He was currently reading a rather large book on the Ancient Greeks. Flavio smiled at Roff's choice and wondered if it might not hurt to have Roff point his inevitable questions in Wlodek's direction.

"I will wear my gray pinstripe," Roff smiled at his vampire sire.

"That will be fine," Flavio agreed. Flavio was worried, however. How were they going to explain to the Alliance representative that Lissa was missing? The media was already making their usual conjectures, since no interviews had been granted and there'd been no sightings.

The Council meetings, which had been televised at first for informational purposes on Le-Ath Veronis, were now fed to all Alliance worlds and there was quite a fan base. Many

# Chapter 6

across the Alliance tuned in to see if Lissa caught any criminals. Many hoped to see her fangs and wrote reams of fan mail to that effect. Since Aurelius and Gardevik had been handling the meetings, the usual rumors spread.

The thing that Flavio appreciated the most, however, was the renewed friendship with Aurelius and the increasing friendship with Gardevik, the High Demon Prime Minister. Flavio had come to respect him greatly.

Some of the Council's vampires might have gotten their way by applying pressure in the past, but that didn't work with Gardevik. In fact, all he had to do was sit there, staring them down and allowing a bit of smoke to curl from his nostrils. That generally restored order.

Aurelius, too, was used to that sort of thing, but employed a different tactic; pointing out any flaw a plan might have with gentle thoroughness. Few of them knew what a sleeping giant Aurelius truly was. Flavio was one of the few still alive who'd seen Aurelius fight.

* * *

"I thought perhaps the Queen might come and greet me," Thurlow smiled at Erland's discomfiture. Erland had been elected to go to the space station and meet the representative for the Alliance. Thurlow was well aware that the Queen seemed to be on yet another of her sabbaticals.

"I am sorry to disappoint," Erland sounded gracious, even if he truly wasn't. "Our Queen could not be here at the moment. Nevertheless, your welcome is most assured. Come, I will take you to the palace and show you to your suite. I'm sure you are weary of traveling. You are also invited to a formal dinner later, with members of the Council from Lissia."

Thurlow followed Erland while two vampires lifted his bags easily and came behind.

# Blood War

* * *

*Vionn*

*Lissa*

The mess tent was the meeting location of choice, and the sides of the tent had been lowered for privacy. I followed the General as he strode angrily toward the tent. The HC and his seven murderous minions were already there. All six of the General's Captains were also there, sitting apart from the HC and his guards.

I'd been sent to deliver messages to this one or that, and to gather messages while the General and the Captains had one of their usual, secret meetings after the HC's message had come. When I got back, it was already over. I had no desire to hear any of it, to be honest. I should have been more curious.

"Sit here, Liss," the General sighed, pointing to a seat, front and center. That shocked me. The HC grinned at my surprise. Well, *Looking* sounded like a good thing to do right about then, and what I found had me pissed.

In the past, I might have been frightened, or a little shaky, at least. Not this time. If these things masquerading as religious representatives thought they might have the advantage in this situation, then they needed to think again.

"We are here to levy charges," the HC intoned as he unrolled a heavy, parchment scroll. "We charge that Liss, bodyguard for General Hardin Wolf, is in actuality a demon in disguise. We intend to prove this over the course of the evening, with tried and true methods developed by our most holy brothers in Ialus."

Well, that sounded like torture to me. "What say you to the charges, demon?" The HC folded the scroll up and gave me a hard stare.

"I'm not a demon," I shrugged.

116

# Chapter 6

"We intend to prove it," he snapped coldly.

"You can try to prove it for the rest of your life, but it'll still be untrue," I said. "I'm not a demon, and anyone who has actually seen a demon would agree."

Solis was trying to get my attention by making minute gestures with his hand, but he could save the effort. I was done with these guys.

"Are you saying that you have seen demons?" The HC was nearly chortling. I was falling right into his trap.

"Oh, yeah," I nodded. "I can think of one in particular who'd have your head twisted right off your body if he were here. Would you like for me to invite him in?"

"You cannot summon a demon," the HC scoffed.

"Well, you can't have it both ways, then. Either I'm a demon and can summon other demons, or I'm not a demon at all. Which is it?" I had arms crossed over my chest, now, glaring right back at my would-be torturers.

"You are a demon; our holy writ proclaims that any creature with hair of flame, moving faster than the eye can see is a demon."

"Are you kidding me? My hair is more a strawberry-blonde. Not really a true red." I lifted a stray lock and studied it briefly.

"But none of us saw your movement when you removed Mardis' head." The HC was getting grumpy, now.

"Still not a demon," I denied his allegation.

"Then go ahead. Summon another demon for us. We wish to see this." The HC thought he was calling my bluff.

*Connegar, honey,* I sent, *can you bring Garde if he isn't busy?*

Connegar didn't bother to reply, he, Reemagar and Garde were there in about a blink. You should have seen the scattering of people when two blue giants and an apparent humanoid appeared inside the tent. It wasn't tall enough for Connegar to stand up straight, so he raised it with Power. Swords came out when that happened.

"The blue ones aren't the demons," I said. Even Solis was backed up against the canvas of the tent, staring. The HC's voice was wobbly when he asked his next question.

"Where is the demon, then?"

"Lissa, why didn't you call me sooner?" Garde came to stand next to me.

"I didn't need a demon until now," I answered dryly. "I'm fine, by the way, but that schmuck over there is trying to tell everybody here that I'm a demon. I tried to tell him I'm not. He wants to level charges and then torture a confession out of me. I called you because he may need to see a real demon."

"He wishes to torture my mate?" Garde's eyes went hard and he jerked his head around to stare at the HC. Smoke was coming from his nostrils by that time.

"Then what are you, if you are not demon?" The HC kept pushing his agenda, when he should have kept his mouth shut. He'd ignored Garde completely, too, and that wasn't a wise thing to do. There's an old saying on Kifirin—Never ignore the demon in the room. The HC was ignoring the demon—and two really tall Larentii because he wanted to torture a confession from the only female in the tent. How typical.

"I'm a vampire," I turned my attention to the HC. "Well, that's not completely true—they call some of my kind the Nameless Ones, but I don't exercise that option very often." Garde was still blowing smoke and staring angrily at the HC. I figured that guy was toast if he didn't shut up soon.

"A vampire?" It was a new word for Solis.

# Chapter 6

"You don't have anything to worry about," I tried to reassure him. "But I am sick of being here. What say we get this over with, right here and now?"

"Lissa, what do you have in mind, love?" Reemagar was on my other side, with Connegar next to him.

"I think we'll take the ones inside the tent, here, and go have a little parlay with Green Birth. I'm really tired of slogging through the fog and the rain they keep sending in our direction. I think I know what I want to do, anyway."

"Would you like for us to make the move?" Connegar offered.

"No, honey, I can do it," I said, giving him a smile. I went to energy, gathered power and moved the entire tent to the central valley where Green Birth had gathered. Then I caused the sides of the tent to roll up by themselves. If the HC and the others hadn't been scared witless and too frightened to move, they might have taken off running at that point. Instead, they had hands on swords or knives, staring at me wide-eyed.

"If anybody pulls a weapon here, they'll die," I said amiably.

The General, who'd been standing and gaping ever since the Larentii showed up with Garde, sat down heavily on a campstool. Garde still wanted a piece of the HC, I think, and was growling, blowing clouds of smoke and watching him like a hawk.

"I have sent out mindspeech for the leaders of Green Birth to come," Connegar informed me. I looked down at my feet where new, green shoots of grass were coming through rich soil with tiny white flowers, here and there. In only a few minutes, four of the Green Fae came walking out of the fog toward us.

# Blood War

"We would not have come if we had not received mindspeech from the Larentii," one of them said, pulling his hood back to reveal blue-green hair. Another, with sun-gold hair pulled his hood back. The other two, both with hair the brown of oak leaves in the fall, lightly tinged with green, also lowered their hoods.

"I think you would have come, if I'd told you," I snapped. They looked at me in confusion. "Now," I said, "I'm here to take care of this mess. General, I know why your King sent you—he has need of funds and looks to the lands belonging to Green Birth to provide those funds for him, in addition to handing out parcels of land and favors to his aristocracy. Does that sound about right?"

"It does," the General replied reluctantly.

"We have paid our taxes to the crown faithfully," the gold-haired Fae remarked.

"No doubt, but the King inherited a lot of debt with the throne," I said. "So he's looking for a quick fix. You were the target. Now," I turned to the HC, "what's the Pelipu's stake in this? Is it because he wants to control the lands or because he can't seem to control these people? Is that it? That he can't say hop and have them ask how high?"

"They are heretics," the HC declared.

"Heretic is such a convenient word," I said. "Nobody does anything like this unless there's something in it for them," I pointed a finger at the HC. "What is it? Control of the masses? Or maybe loss of the control of the masses? That there might be a sect in opposition of the Pelipu's religion—one that doesn't condone torture or scare tactics, or who doesn't believe that you can donate to the church and buy your way into the afterlife? Is that what he's afraid of? That he might not get his cocoa at bedtime?" Garde snickered.

# Chapter 6

I looked around at the faces in the tent—they were all frightened and trying to determine how we'd managed to travel the distance to Green Birth's lands in a blink, when it would have taken nearly two weeks under ideal conditions to get there on horseback.

"Well, this is what I'm going to do," I said. "I am sealing off these valleys from any other humanoids on this planet. They will be hidden. There will be a buffer zone in between, where trade can occur if Green Birth so desires. Otherwise, the lands will not be reached by others. Your king," I turned to the General, "will have to find another way to fill his coffers. I suggest fishing and sea trade. He has a fleet, tell him to use it. And the lands to his south can be farmed, if he can get those nobles of his off their asses to clear it." The General nodded, still showing signs of confusion.

"Now, you," I pointed at the HC. "I'm going to send you right back where you came from. And if you or any of your religion step foot on the soil of Farus with anything other than peaceful purposes on your mind, you'll die. How's that?" I went to energy again, gathered power and sent him, his seven cronies and all of his army right back to Ialus. I figured the Pelipu was having a hissy fit, even as I watched them disappear.

"You, go home," I pointed at the others, once I was back to myself. They were all staring at me now, their mouths open in surprise. "Solis, I think you and the General can stay here, if you want. That way, you two can actually be together instead of hiding all the time." Yeah, they'd been together for a long time, they just did their best to hide it from everybody.

"You can take them with you, Lissa. We could use extra security on Le-Ath Veronis," Reemagar suggested. I shrugged.

"If they want," I agreed.

"Now, you," I turned to the four Fae.

"We are satisfied with these arrangements," the gold-haired one said. "I am Tiearan Briar."

"Aren't you forgetting something?" I asked as sweetly as I could.

"What?" The blue-haired one asked.

"The reason I came," I said.

"Why did you come? We were expecting a Karathian warlock. Perhaps the King himself," Tiearan Briar said.

"You don't have his child," I said. "You have mine. I am Lissa, Queen of Le-Ath Veronis. The child you stole was a comesula, not the King's grandson. If you don't mind, I'd like him back now, please. Otherwise I will take this planet apart myself, and never allow two bits of it to join together again."

"I will take the Farus officers back to their camp," Reemagar whispered next to my ear. I nodded while I watched four Fae shoot troubled glances at each other.

"Go," Tiearan told one of the brown-haired Fae, who nodded and took off running.

"The child will arrive soon," Tiearan said softly, holding a hand out to keep me at a distance. He was all Fae, I could tell by his scent, as was the other, brown-haired one. The one with blue-green hair, though—he was half. Nearly twenty minutes passed before the brown-haired Fae returned with two more Fae, one of whom had Toff in her arms.

"You have to understand that we didn't know it had happened until six days after we'd taken the child," Tiearan sighed.

"What?" I said absently, reaching out toward Toff as the two female Fae stepped beneath the roof of the tent. Toff hid his face against the female's shoulder. That wasn't like him.

Normally, he squealed with laughter and reached out for me, no matter what.

"Toff, honey, come to your auntie Lissa," I said, reaching out for him. He gave an unhappy little sound and burrowed closer against the female Fae. That scared me, and I lifted my eyes to hers. She was young, as far as Fae go, perhaps two hundred years of age, with hair the color of red that maple leaves turned in the fall. And she looked frightened, too.

"Redbird desired to keep the child," Tiearan's words came from a distance. "She performed the mind-bond with the child, so he would stay with her. We did not intend for this to happen and we deeply regret it." I snapped right back to the present; I think my eyes and fangs were now showing exactly what I was.

"Explain to me exactly what a mind-bond is and what it will do to Toff when I take him away from here," I snarled.

If I hadn't had my Larentii with me, holding me back, I think I might have killed just about everybody inside the tent. Even Garde was holding me back, and he was almost as angry as I was.

Tiearan explained that a mind-bond was something the Fae could do if they adopted a child. The child would see the one performing the bond as a parent—and only them as a parent. The child would be their own person once they matured, but by that time, they normally considered the adoptive Fae their parent and no other. I was so angry when he stopped talking that I could have taken Vionn apart anyway.

"I am sorry," Redbird apologized, even while she held my Toff tightly against her. I wasn't buying that apology and she knew it.

"If there is any way to make this up to you," Tiearan said, "we will do our best to oblige."

"And just how would you propose to do that?" I hissed. "If someone stole your child and forced you to come and haul their ass out of a bind, and then ended up taking your child anyway, tell me how that would make you feel?" I was so angry my eyes were likely blood red and my fangs pricked my lower lip. That was nothing compared to the headache I now had.

"We would not like it," Tiearan refused to look at me. "We thought we would have to contend with the Karathian King over this," he muttered. "We expected to die for Redbird's mistake."

"And I want to kill you," I said. "And if my Larentii had not given me mindspeech, telling me that it will harm Toff if Redbird dies, well, you might already be dead," I growled. "Didn't you have enough sense to hand him to somebody who would keep him safe, instead of fucking with his head?" Connegar had also told me that the mind-bond was irreversible in a child as young as Toff—if we tried, he would likely die or be simple from the damage.

"I thought my daughter would keep him safe," Tiearan glanced at Redbird, who was playing with Toff and pointedly ignoring her father and me.

"So I get fucked over, for coming to save your sorry asses."

"There is nothing I can say or do, which will eliminate your pain or anger," Tiearan said quietly.

"So, I'm to go home, without my child. That's what you're telling me. Are you going to do this again? You get in a bind; you kidnap a child to get what you want?"

"We have never done anything of this nature before," Tiearan winced. "And it was to save our half-children that we

# Chapter 6

did it. We understand the threat of loss, but not the loss. We cannot repay this debt. We have no way to do so."

"We will send him to you when he reaches his maturity, so he may decide which world he would rather live in," the other female offered. Her name was Rain, I knew; they'd introduced both of the females after a while.

"Sure, after you've raised him and indoctrinated him," I muttered angrily. "He'll resent the fact that he has to live with relatives he doesn't remember."

"He will not have the talent and capability that we have, and that will separate him from us," Tiearan sighed.

"So, my child gets tortured, no matter what," I muttered, now close to tears. I knew what growing up without belonging felt like, and these Fae had condemned Toff to that existence.

"He will love Redbird, and she will love him," Tiearan tried to calm me.

"Forced to love her," I shot back, wiping away the tear that fell. "Tell me what good that does me?"

"We cannot replace a child," Tiearan replied. "I am sorry."

"I will go back with her," the blue-green haired one offered.

"Corent, no!" Rain was standing, now. His offer also had Redbird off her seat, holding a hand out to him. They were lovers; I knew it in that instant.

"It is only fair," Corent turned his gaze on Redbird. "You keep her child until he comes to adulthood. Nothing can relieve that pain for her. Therefore, it is only fair that you suffer, since you did not confer with us over this matter. You chose this yourself."

"Corent," Redbird whined. Well, somebody was used to getting her way.

"Fine." I stood up. "Don't ever come to me or any of my kind for help. Ever. And if this child is raised in anything other than a loving environment, I will still come and take this world apart and I won't waste time doing it."

"We will see that he is loved and cared for and I regret that this has harmed you," Tiearan stood with me. "I understand that you would not truly harm us, I felt the insincerity in your words. You are allowing your pain to speak for you. If there were any way to take that away from you, I would do it. If there were any way for me to take back my daughter's folly, I would do it. I only beg you to take care of Corent; he has never been anywhere except through these valleys, and only knows a peaceful existence."

"I'll put him with the comesuli, near the light half of the planet," I was crying again; I couldn't seem to stop. Garde had his hand at the small of my back, trying to comfort me without being obvious about it. "The farms and orchards are there," I lost it, then, and the Larentii had to haul us all home.

* * *

"Daughter, you almost destroyed us all," Tiearan looked at Redbird, as she bounced Toff on her lap. "And call that child by his given name," Tiearan went on. "That is only fair, and we will not be otherwise." Tiearan stalked away, leaving Rain to stare at Redbird. "You cost me my child," she said sadly, and rose to follow Tiearan.

* * *

*Le-Ath Veronis*
*Lissa*
Reemagar did all the talking for me when we took Corent to his new home. He nodded as we introduced him to Riff, the orchard overseer. I felt Corent might be more comfortable with trees around him.

# Chapter 6

Riff promised to find housing for the displaced Fae; Garde offered to bring clothing. I hoped Corent would be happy in his self-imposed exile; I wanted to lock myself away and scream and cry. I was doing my best to hold off on that.

In all my dreams, I had no idea that this would turn out the way it did. I folded myself back to the palace with Garde and the Larentii hot on my heels. I went straight to my bedroom, threw myself on the bed and started crying.

Connegar had the presence of mind to *Pull* back the duffle and blades I'd taken to Vionn—I'd left them behind in the tents. He also folded in Solis and General Hardin Wolf.

I learned all this when Connegar whispered what he'd done when he returned. I was still crying my eyes out, so Connegar told me he would turn Solis and Hardin over to Drake and Drew while Reemagar rubbed my back soothingly and Garde lay down beside me, trying to gather me against him.

I wasn't just crying for myself. I was crying for Giff and Roff, too. What would they do, when they found out? Roff didn't have the memory of his child, but what if he remembered one day? The news that his child was stolen and turned against him was going to be as painful as it could possibly be.

* * *

"The Green Fae did this?" Dragon shook his head in confusion. The Green Fae were always peaceful and nonviolent. To kidnap a child was unheard of, but to amplify the mistake by performing the mind-bond on a child who didn't belong to them, well, that was unconscionable. They sometimes did it with orphans or runaways, but this was nothing of the kind. Lissa had protected them, on top of all that. It was a senseless, selfish act.

"We can't get Lissa to eat," Drake and Drew sat down heavily on either side of their father. Dragon put an arm around each of his youngest.

"It'll take time," Dragon sighed. "I don't know what to do in the meantime. Of all the people for this to happen to."

"Problem?" Thurlow came in to sit at the kitchen island. He'd been given the run of the palace; he just wasn't allowed to barge into private suites or offices. The amenities were his to use if he so desired. He was quite surprised at the openness of all of it.

"A private matter," Dragon's scowl was back in place. "May we offer you something to eat or drink?"

"A sandwich, perhaps," Thurlow nodded. The comesula servant went about making a sandwich for their guest. Dragon and his sons rose after a bit, wished Thurlow goodnight and left the kitchen. Thurlow blew out a sigh. He had a difficult task before him, it seemed. The Queen had returned, he knew that much. He also knew she was extremely upset, which meant all her mates were upset. Thurlow would have to wait to meet her.

* * *

*Lissa*
"Lissa, sweetheart, you have to stop crying." Aurelius was there, somehow, and he'd pulled me off the bed. Being wrapped in Aurelius' arms was like being hugged by a bear. A really gentle, careful bear.

Gavin and Tony had gone to follow a spy, so they were both away. Aurelius was filling in for them. Drake and Drew had sat with me for a while, but they couldn't get the tears to stop any better than Garde could, or the Larentii. I don't know why they didn't put me in a healing sleep and be done with it.

* * *

# Chapter 6



*Earth*

*Gryphon Manor*

"What the hell were they thinking?" Dragon had called a meeting and nearly all of Lissa's mates were there, as were many of the Saa Thalarr. Kiarra cursed while she paced inside her kitchen, where the meeting had been called.

Drake and Drew were both looking haggard and unhappy. Radomir was furious and Rolfe was even angrier. Giff hadn't been told yet and Roff was still oblivious—Flavio thought it best not to bring him. Davan and Grant had been brought instead, since they loved Toff. Davan was silent and obviously troubled; Grant was nearly in tears at the news.

Shadow couldn't understand any of it. Erland was relaying mindspeech as fast as he could to Wylend Arden. This was one of the worst possible outcomes for this entire sorry affair. Karzac felt like cursing—just when it appeared that Lissa might have a child, albeit an adopted one, it was taken away from her.

"What did she do?" Erland asked. He was almost afraid to learn the answer.

"She put up a curtain that the others can't cross, to keep the Green Fae safe," Kiarra muttered. "This was after they kidnapped Toff. She didn't know what else they'd done until afterward."

"A Karathian would have killed them all," Erland mumbled his response.

"It's better for them in that respect, and worse for Lissa, at the same time," Kiarra snorted. "Now she has someone who exchanged himself for Toff. What good is that supposed to do her?"

Adam sat silently at the island and wondered at the absence of Griffin. Lissa's father should be there, or with

Lissa, yet he wasn't in either place. Adam sent mindspeech to Merrill regarding that fact. One of Merrill's eyebrows lifted at the observation, but he didn't reply.

* * *

*Le-Ath Veronis*
*Lissa*

"Avilepha, I cannot bear this." Kifirin had come, so Aurelius stole quietly from the room. I sniffled again and wiped my face with a sleeve.

"Kifirin, did somebody decide somewhere that Lissa needed to be continuously kicked, for some reason? That her life wasn't complete without shit happening to her regularly?"

"Lissa, that does not happen. Not like that. Betrayals come. You have had more than your share." Kifirin looked a little gray, I think, and that was unusual for him. "The girl could not have children with her half-Fae lover. Therefore, she took what had been handed to her. Her father thought to be kind, handing the child over for her to care for and she took it for herself instead. If that had been Wyatt, the same thing would have happened and Wylend would have torn the planet apart."

"You're saying it was better that Lissa took the hit?" I wiped my face again.

"No, m'hala. Not at all. The girl was selfish and did not think past her own desires. Many will be watching over Toff, now, to make sure he is well cared for. Including the girl's father. He is quite angry with her now."

"I'm sure she'll get a big tap on the nose for it, too," I muttered.

"Their race is immortal, my love. He will wait for Toff to come to adulthood, and then punishment will be given. Also, the Green Fae owe you a debt. They do not like to owe anyone.

# Chapter 6

It will remain with them as a very great burden, unless they can find a way to discharge it, someday."

"Oh, sure, they owe me a debt. They owe me my child. Roff's child. Giff's brother."

"Avilepha, I will be with you when you give the news to Giff. I will help with this. Rolfe will be there for Giff as well, since she is bearing a child of her own."

"Kifirin, I have the worst headache right now."

"I know. This is none of your doing, my heart's love. Yet the pain is yours, as it will be for Giff. Your Larentii are coming. They will make sure your night is as restful as they can make it. Sleep well, my little mate." He kissed me on the forehead as Connegar and Reemagar landed in my suite. My last vision, as Connegar was placing fingers against my forehead, was of Kifirin folding away.

* * *

"She is sleeping and we will not wake her for trivialities." Drake, Drew and Winkler all glared at the Alliance representative. Thurlow sighed and nodded.

"Please inform me when she is prepared to speak with me." He walked toward his suite in the guest quarters.

Thurlow was called later, but it was to sit in at a meeting while another wall-climber was interviewed.

"I swear, it was only a prank to see if I could get in," the young man wailed. He had no idea how much trouble he would be in, for simply trying to see Lissia for himself.

"This one knows nothing," Aryn tossed up a hand.

"You will not be allowed to return to Le-Ath Veronis, and you will be escorted to the space station with all your belongings," Rolfe growled at him. The young man gulped. He'd wanted to see vampires. He was seeing them now, and in less than ideal circumstances.

"You signed the agreement when you purchased your ticket," Thurlow explained as he helped escort the young man to the space station. He'd joined Hart and Nima, the two female Falchani guards, to send the prisoner away.

They'd all ridden in the shuttle pod with him on the way up. Thurlow handed out the lecture as the young man was herded toward the gate at the space station, still whining about his punishment.

"I can't ever come back?" Disappointment saturated the young man's voice. He'd barely turned gambling age and had spent a great deal getting his tickets and lodging.

"Your name will be on a list, therefore you will not be allowed to return," Thurlow replied. They watched as he boarded the ship and waited for the door to be closed. The ship took off shortly afterward.

"Thrill-seekers," Hart muttered as they walked toward the pod station to return to the planet below.

# Chapter 7

L*issa*

"Giff, I don't have good news, honey." Rolfe was there, his arm tight around her as she blinked at me in confusion. Giff had trusted me—always. I felt responsible for Toff's abduction, even though I wasn't. I was still trying to puzzle all this out.

How had it happened in the first place? I was back, too, to the fact that bracelets had been switched. Maybe I needed to have a talk with my grandfather, to see if any of the hired babysitters could have done this as a prank. It just didn't add up or make any sense at all.

Regardless, Toff was gone from us. We wouldn't get to watch him grow up. It made me weep, just thinking about it.

"No, he's not dead," I held out a hand at the terrible pain in Giff's eyes. "The Green Fae took him, Rolfe told you that. He was handed to one of their females, who didn't have children of her own. She decided she wanted to keep Toff. Adult Fae have the ability to perform what they call a mind-bond. It makes the child think the bonded adult Fae is their parent. That's what she did. Toff is so young that if we try to remove it, it could kill him or damage his brain. He didn't even recognize me when I tried to take him. He was holding onto that girl as if she'd been the one to give birth to him."

I was crying again and Giff was weeping in Rolfe's arms. Kifirin sat beside me and his arm came around me. Karzac came in after a few minutes, placing Giff in a healing sleep.

"Giff's child will come in a few days," Karzac sighed as Rolfe carried her gently from my study.

* * *

I waited for Flavio to bring Roff. I wasn't sure how he might react to the news about Toff, but I wanted him to know. I'd convinced Flavio to bring him so I could explain things as best I could.

Flavio stepped inside my study, Roff following close behind, his wings folded tightly against his back. He knew there was a problem; he just didn't know what it might be.

"Please sit," I motioned them toward the two chairs before my desk. "I have news that concerns you, Roff. And your family."

"What can that be, Raona? I do not recall my family."

"Yeah. I get that," I sighed. He'd called me Raona, but there was no affection in his voice. Once, that word had been uttered in adoration. I might never hear it spoken that way again.

"We know you can't remember some things," I studied his handsome face. He'd let his dark hair grow out longer, and Flavio had seen to it that it was cut and shaped so it would not detract from his looks or get in the way. "We were hoping the memories would return when Radomir offered his blood. That wasn't the case. Before that, we hoped the memories might come back on their own."

"I realize this, Raona. It bothers me at times, but I don't dwell on it; father says that those memories will either come or they won't, and there's no need to fret over it."

"He's right, except for this. You have a right to know, since this would normally affect you more than anyone else. Before you were attacked and turned, you were comesula, as you know. You still have some of those memories."

"I do. I remember having a wine shop on Kifirin." He smiled at Kifirin, who sat behind me. Kifirin had named the High Demon planet after himself.

"What you don't remember is that you had two children. Giff is your first child, Roff. She weeps when she sees you at times, because you don't remember her." Roff's eyes widened in shock.

"Giff is my child?" Roff attempted to process that information.

"Yes. You didn't remember her, just as you didn't remember me. You lost your memories of the ones closest to you, honey. That's why you don't remember Toff, either. Toff was your youngest."

"Toff—mine as well?"

"Yes." I was trying not to cry again, although tears were choking my voice. "Flavio told you that someone took Toff." Roff nodded his head, worry clouding his eyes, now.

"They were supposed to give him back as soon as I went to take care of a few things for them. But one of the Fae who took him decided she wanted to keep him." I was crying by that time.

# Blood War

Kifirin had to explain to Roff about the mind-bond. He also explained that when Toff was an adult, he would be allowed to choose where he lived. I think Roff knew as well as I did, exactly what our chances were in all that.

Gone were my hopes of seeing Toff as a winged vampire someday. I sobbed. Roff, as soon as Kifirin finished telling him the whole of it, rose from his chair and stalked from the room.

* * *

*Solar Red Headquarters*

"What do you mean; she was within our grasp on Vionn?" Tetsurna Prylvis snarled at the High Priest who stood before him.

Few knew that Prylvis had opened the door for Ra'Ak to take membership in Solar Red. They came willingly; accepting positions as Priests and High Priests and often did Prylvis' bidding, in exchange for the lives offered and the blood that flowed.

Prylvis had heard the title Khos'Mirai whispered among his Ra'Ak members in the past. Somehow, that one had long ago convinced many Ra'Ak that hiding among Solar Red's Temples was a wise thing to do.

"That fool Pelipu had the information and did not share it in time. He declared her demon and sent some of his to torture a confession from her. Obviously, that was a mistake. Somehow, they let her slip away and the lands the Pelipu sought to take are now shielded against invasion by any humanoids. Farus' shores have been locked against any who have other than peaceful purposes for a visit."

"You are correct—the Pelipu is a fool," Prylvis frowned in anger. "Our target within his grasp and he allows her to slip away. What say you, my Seturna? What should be the Pelipu's punishment for this offense against me and Solar Red?"

136

# Chapter 7

"The reason our target came to Vionn is still on Vionn, with the Green Birth Fae," the Ra'Ak High Priest replied. "And as I said before, the Green Fae lands are shielded against any humanoid entering. Those shields cannot keep me or my kind away. I feel we should set one of ours up as Pelipu—the current Pelipu will make a good meal for the one who will wear his face afterward. Then we attack the Green Fae lands in numbers, take what the Queen searched for and draw her to us in that way. You will have what you desire, Tetsurna."

"I like this idea. Very much," Prylvis nodded. "Perhaps you would like to take the Pelipu's place?"

"I had hopes, but did not wish to presume," the Ra'Ak bowed insincerely to Prylvis.

"Of course you may take his seat, then we will have what we want. Shall I contact Black Mist? Some of his would be welcome as we destroy Green Fae. I hear they are quite tasty to your kind."

"Allies from Black Mist will be more than welcome. I hear that some of my brothers may be among Black Mist's arsenal of assassins."

"I hear that too, High Priest. Go. Make the arrangements. We will attack the Green Fae on Vionn very soon."

* * *

*Le-Ath Veronis*
*Lissa*

"What is this?" Yeah, I was depressed. Grant had handed a comp-vid to me, and I didn't want to read it.

"The agenda for the Five-Year Conclave. It's coming up, you know," Grant said. "We have to go over the items and you have to decide how you'll vote—you can't just show up without information or preparation. Besides, one of the items on the agenda is the approval of religions on Alliance worlds. The current law allows each world to give permission for a religion to establish itself on their planet. This proposal would give the Founder and the Grand Alliance Council the final decision."

"That can't hurt, can it? Surely, they'd be fair. And it might prevent some of those worlds from taking bribes to allow Solar Red or the Red Hand to walk right in and set up temples." I lifted the comp-vid and thumbed through agenda items.

* * *

*Vionn*

The Pelipu of Vionn watched the one who paced before his high seat. He called it a chair but it was a throne—he just didn't want to alert the King of Ialus to the fact that he had designs on the throne the king held.

He'd hoped that Farus would now be under his thumb, the Green Birth eliminated and their fertile lands his to do with as he pleased. He could launch an army against other civilized lands from Farus; they had a sizable fleet of ships—enough to carry Red Hand troops from one country to the next.

For now, he and his mercenaries had been shut out of Farus, whose King was busy setting up trade with the countries farther south, specializing in fish and fish oil for lamps. Why hadn't he thought of those? He shook his head in anger.

"You say you can't ever set foot on Farus, if your intentions are impure?" The man before him stopped pacing.

"That's right. We've tried and the ones we sent are now dead."

"And there's an impenetrable curtain surrounding the Green Birth lands, too?"

"Yes."

# Chapter 7

"Well, I may have someone who can get around that for us, but he will exact a price."

The Pelipu snorted. "Money I have," he said.

"This one doesn't take payment in money."

"Then what does he want?" The Pelipu couldn't fathom anyone not expecting money as payment.

"Sacrifices," the other replied. "Lives, given to him to play with."

"Hmmph," the Pelipu replied. "I have plenty of that, and it costs me nothing."

"Do you wish for me to call him in?" The other one smiled.

"If it will get me what I desire, then of course I want you to call him in."

"Very well. I will bring him to you in a few days. Prepare for his coming. Have prisoners brought in."

"May I watch?" The Pelipu smiled with anticipation.

"If you wish."

* * *

*Black Mist Headquarters*

"What is your will, Viregruz my brother?" Ringolar, eldest of Viregruz's six chosen Ra'Ak, stood before Black Mist's founder.

"Ringolar, I believe the days the Khos'Mirai predicted have arrived. We are on the front steps of taking the Alliance. Soon it will be ours, to do with as we please."

Viregruz sat upon the jeweled chair a clan of Wizards had designed for him. He hadn't been able to convince Grey House to work for him, but he'd found another clan nearly as good. The Belancour Wizards had done fine work for him.

"It is too bad the Khos'Mirai is gone from us—we received much good advice from him, did we not?" Ringolar gazed at Viregruz.

"He and his clones," Viregruz agreed. "I believe he tired of his life; that is why he allowed himself to be taken. I can only imagine that one of the Mighty may have destroyed him. It is now our lot to carry on his work and reap the promised rewards."

"What is your desire, then, brother?"

"Solar Red has approached and asked for help taking Vionn. Tetsurna Prylvis says a shield has been placed around the Green Fae lands and the key to his target lies behind that shield. This shield only holds back humanoids. Your kind may breach it easily. I wish for one of our brothers to assist the Tetsurna and his forces. If we combine his strength with that of Solar Red and The Red Hand, at least in appearance, how easy will it be to attain our long-term goals?"

"Very easy, my brother," Ringolar grinned. "As for the shield, it's as good as gone," he waved a hand in dismissal. "It will take much to keep even one of our brothers out."

"Good. I believe Prylvis will not object if you take Vionn as your feeding grounds afterward."

"As I had hoped, brother," Ringolar grinned.

* * *

*Le-Ath Veronis*

"Child, I had no idea that this would trouble you so much, since your memories were gone. I might have asked Lissa to hold off telling you," Flavio sighed.

"Like you asked her to hold off telling me that I had children?" Roff was angry with his vampire sire—for the first time.

# Chapter 7

"Child, our intentions were good; you were a new turn and fragile. The circumstances surrounding your turning were less than ideal and quite traumatic. I held that information back. Lissa had nothing to do with this; in fact, she was quite upset that we decided to withhold the information for a while."

"Because she cared for me. Giff, too. And Toff."

Flavio didn't want to tell Roff that all three of those mentioned had wept grievously because he didn't remember them. He held back, choosing to nod at Roff's assessment instead.

"So Lissa was going to adopt my child because she cared for him, and his own father didn't recognize him any longer. Is that the truth?"

"Yes, child."

"Father, I am extremely angry over this. I am going to work at my winery for a while. I do not wish to be disturbed." Roff stalked from Flavio's study; Flavio heard the front door slam after a bit and sighed again.

* * *

*Hraede*

Paulin dawdled, as if he were putting off going to see Ibbitt. Gavin was now glad that Lynx had come with them—he was capable of shielding all three of them, rendering them invisible as they silently tailed Paulin.

Paulin had his portfolio of drawings slung over a shoulder as he stopped at a fruit stand, one of many small shops lining the streets amid the poorer sections of Hraede's capital city.

The drawings of the palace, the wall surrounding Lissia, as well as other key locations that Paulin had drawn were all incorrect—Aryn, Lynx and Gavin had seen to that. Even if these drawings fell into the wrong hands, they wouldn't be getting anything close to accurate information.

Smells of cooking wafted past them as they followed Paulin when he continued down the cobblestone street, eating his fruit and glancing about. Gavin was becoming impatient, but Lynx placed a steadying hand on his shoulder. Gavin nodded and calmed himself.

A baby's cries disturbed the near-silence as they passed through an alleyway. Children raced past them on the street when they emerged, playing games with one another. Paulin stopped before a doorway half a block away, adjusted the portfolio hanging from his shoulder and knocked on the door. Lynx folded Gavin and Tony inside the home, shielding them from sight.

The tiny reception area was barely big enough to contain all of them, but Lynx found a way. "Do you have what I asked for?" A short, ancient man with a bald head and wrinkles covering every bit of exposed skin asked Paulin.

"I do, Master Ibbett," Paulin slipped the portfolio from his shoulder and handed it to Ibbitt.

"Ah, let us see, then," Ibbitt led the way into the rear portion of the home, where the kitchen lay. He set the portfolio down on the tiny table and unbuckled the clasp.

"I knew I could trust your skills," Ibbitt crowed softly, holding up drawing after drawing. "I recognize this from the vid feeds." He held up a picture of the Council chamber. It was the only one Lynx hadn't altered. Everyone who lived on an Alliance world had seen that Council chamber. More than likely, others had as well. Things tended to get passed along on the black market, and that included information and images.

# Chapter 7

"Here," Ibbitt shuffled toward a small cabinet against a wall and pulled out a drawer. A pouch of coins was tossed to Paulin. "I appreciate your talent and the fact that you didn't get caught. They're locking people up everywhere, you know, over their paranoia," the old man said.

Paulin nodded and Ibbitt led him toward the door. Lynx, Gavin and Tony stayed behind with Ibbitt. They knew where Paulin lived and had arranged for him to be picked up when he got home. Their focus was now on Ibbitt and what he planned to do with the drawings.

* * *

*Karathia*

Wylend stared across the table at his son, who was focused on his breakfast. Erland had also come. "Brenten," Wylend said, causing Griffin to look up from cutting a slice of ham.

"Yes?" Griffin placed the ham in his mouth and chewed.

"What do you think Lissa will do when she finds out?"

"Be furious," Griffin stared at his plate.

"With whom?"

"Me, mostly."

"Child, you are wrong."

"Why do you say that?"

"She will be hurt and angry with all at this table. You know that, don't you?"

Griffin didn't answer for several seconds. "Yes," he nodded uncomfortably.

"And how angry do you think she will be, child, when she discovers that you were the one who removed Roff's memories?" Griffin looked up in shock at his Karathian warlock father.

* * *

# Blood War

*Campiaa*

"Do you see this?" Arvil San Gerxon and his chief of security stood behind the one-way glass in his office, staring down at the casino floor below. "And this is better than most of the others," he snorted in anger.

Few clients were gambling downstairs, and most of them worked on the wrong end of the law. That meant Arvil had to make sure they won regularly. His profits had gone down dramatically, all because of Le-Ath Veronis.

Several of his competitors on Campiaa had applied for and received approval to move their casinos to the vampire planet. While that might have made Arvil quite happy since he'd ended up with additional property, the ensuing reduction in visitors to Campiaa, added to the loss of payments from those former competitors, meant the money was only trickling in, now.

Arvil became furious every time he thought about it. His guests were abandoning Campiaa in droves, preferring to visit Le-Ath Veronis' casinos instead.

"I hear Black Mist has thrown in their lot with Solar Red, and they're all out to get the Queen bitch now," Arvil's chief of security noted. The man's face was scarred from too many fights throughout his lifetime, and his name was several generations past the one he'd been born with.

"What's that, Jos?" Arvil turned back to his chief.

"Black Mist and Solar Red are out to get the Queen Vampire," Jos paraphrased his prior statement.

"You're sure about this?"

"Absolutely. I wouldn't have brought it to you, otherwise."

"Do you have contacts? I might be willing to pay someone, just to hurry this up."

# Chapter 7

"I can put out an offer. If it is sufficient, I know Black Mist will be interested."

Arvil wanted to shiver at the mention of the Assassin's Guild. They weren't anyone to cheat or mess about with. Jos seemed sure of himself, however. "Fine, put the word out that fifty million will go to the one who can bring her down."

"That seems a reasonable sum," Jos grinned, his platinum caps gleaming in Arvil's artificial lamplight.

* * *

*Solar Red Headquarters*

"He's offering fifty million?" Prylvis lifted an eyebrow at Viregruz's words.

"Yes. And it's to accomplish something we are already planning," Viregruz chuckled.

"What do you say, brother," Ringolar began, "to offering this amount to any would-be assassin out there—and letting them know that Black Mist is making the offer?"

"Are you suggesting that we make it look as if we don't want to dirty our hands with this, and allow anyone with the desire to put fifty million credits in their pocket to provide a distraction for us?" Prylvis wanted to laugh.

"That's exactly what I'm suggesting," Ringolar agreed. "Let the bitch queen's guards weary themselves fending off attempts by amateurs, while we plan the real assassination."

"Is it decided, then?" Viregruz asked.

"Oh, yes," Prylvis agreed.

* * *

*Le-Ath Veronis*

*Lissa*

I hadn't seen or heard from Roff for six days. I wanted to ask Flavio about him, but dreaded what I might learn if I did. I didn't *Look*, either, for the same reasons. Aurelius and Garde were flanking me as we walked down the hall toward the first Council meeting I'd attended in six weeks. The media wanted to come calling, too, but I just wasn't in the mood. They'd have to settle for the feed from the Council meeting.

Kyler was in her usual corner; she gave me a nod as I walked in with my escorts. Giff was depressed and refused to see anyone, and that wasn't doing her any good at all.

I'd sent Rolfe to stay with her—I had other personal guards, after all, and Giff's child was coming; there was no way around that. Kyler announced our business for the day—increasing security around the perimeter of Casino City. We'd beefed ours up; they needed to do the same.

Adam and Merrill had come, with most of the casino owners following suit. Some of those owners had transferred from Campiaa. Erland, Adam and Merrill had advised me on which applications to approve.

Honestly, I hadn't been to Casino City since the first day it opened. I wanted to sigh as I looked over the crowd of vampires. Fifteen cities were now represented, and the members who'd died in the chaos earlier had already been replaced.

It was a well-known fact that solar-powered hovercraft provided transportation between the vampire cities and Lissia. Many Council members had drivers or assistants with them, now, posing as bodyguards.

I can't say I blamed them—there hadn't been any guards except mine when vampires had died inside these walls. I wondered if we'd need a football stadium before it was over, just to seat the members and their hired muscle.

Giff wasn't the only one depressed, either. I automatically searched for Toff every time I sat at the dinner table. One of my favorite memories had been of Roff trying to get him to eat with a fork, while Toff had been busily shoving spaghetti into his mouth with his hands.

That, however, was before Shala had tried to kill me; she'd staked Roff instead. It was also before Gabron showed his true colors. Briefly, I wondered where he was before putting him out of my mind.

"If we provide two-man hovercraft, we can patrol the walls faster and easier," a casino owner stood in the back to make a suggestion. We were allowing all of them to speak today, since their taxes would be used to pay for this.

"Is there a feasibility study available?" I asked.

"We arc putting one together," Adam said. I saw Crane and Dragon sitting next to Adam and Merrill—they'd folded in. They had a hefty interest in one of the casinos; they'd invested with Lynx, Russell and Will. Weldon, Martin, Daniel and David owned half of another one, with Radomir, Rush and Lisster. Yeah, members of the Saa Thalarr, including my new Crown Investigators, owned casinos.

"How quickly will we have the information?" I asked.

"In four days, I think," Adam replied

"Should we buy a couple of vehicles in the meantime, just to give it the practicality test?" I suggested.

"If you want," the casino owner who'd made the original suggestion was grinning.

"The crown will put up half the money," I said.

The next item on the agenda was how many wall climbers had been caught since the last meeting. That was a total of sixty-four. Too many.

"Are they doing it just so they can boast of it later?" someone asked.

"About half are," Lisster came in the room with a comp-vid that he handed off to Garde. Garde frowned at the message he was reading, and smoke curled from his nostrils. That wasn't upsetting or anything. I couldn't allow it to distract me, however, so we didn't interrupt the meeting.

* * *

"This is the message that was intercepted." Erland paced angrily inside my office. He referred to the message Lisster passed off to Garde during the Council meeting. Garde was there with Aurelius, Lisster, Radomir and Rush. In fact, all of my mates except Tony and Gavin had come.

Thurlow, the Alliance representative, was also there. I hadn't taken the time to meet with him before. He seemed a patient sort, thankfully, and he was poring over the message, just as the rest of us were.

The message indicated that some sect that called itself Black Mist now had a bounty on my head. They were a clan of assassins that would accept money to off anybody. Well, if they were offering, it meant that somebody else had offered them more and they were farming out the work.

Fuckers.

"I hear from reliable sources that Arvil San Gerxon may have put up part of the money," Erland said. I was beginning to learn that Erland worked as a spy for my grandfather. Oh, he kept that fact hidden very well; everybody thought Erland was wrapped up in Erland.

Except he wasn't. Not really. I think that's why he had a casino on Campiaa, originally. What better place to hear rumors one might not get elsewhere? The criminal element certainly flowed through Campiaa. It made me wonder whom Erland still had there, working for him.

"How much?" I asked. I thought I should know how much they were willing to pay to do away with me.

# Chapter 7

"Fifty million," Erland sighed. "This means that with all contributors combined, the Black brotherhood has been offered at least four times that much."

"So they're probably pooling their money." I sat back in my chair and rubbed my forehead. "Plus, the nutcases that come here and try to climb the wall may be trying to get to me so they can claim the biggest jackpot ever."

"Unfortunate, but true," Adam agreed. The objections I'd raised initially about making this a gambling planet and open to space travel had certainly come home to roost.

"Lissa, you are welcome to come to Kifirin," Garde said. "Jayd and Glinda have already offered."

"Lissa should not have to leave her world. I made this for her. Others are taking it over, now, although she raised her objections in the beginning." Kifirin wasn't happy with the current situation; I could see that right away.

*Lissa, I didn't know this would come*, Adam apologized mentally.

*None of us did*, I sent back to him. When I raised my objections, it had been because I didn't want the peace of Le-Ath Veronis interrupted.

"I will file this report with the Alliance," Thurlow had a handheld computer out and was tapping away on the screen. He copied my security team on the message, too. They were going to have a security pow-wow right after this impromptu meeting. That was fine; I had a couple of things I wanted to do myself.

* * *

"Corent, how are things working out for you?" I found him walking among the apple trees, putting his hands on this trunk or that. I envied him at that moment—walking through the orchards with no price on his head, no meetings to attend, no missing child, no puzzlement over how that child had been taken to begin with—he might miss Redbird, but he'd volunteered to come. I hadn't forced the issue. Today, his hair was a bright blue, reflecting the sky over our heads.

"Things are very well, here; the comesuli have a great respect for the land and the trees." I nodded at his assessment—Roff had it, too, when he'd been one of them. I wondered again where he was.

"Are you happy with your home?" He'd been given a small home for himself, and payment for his work—Kyler and Davan had taken care of it. He and the comesuli had access to computers and vid screens, too, and could either go to one of the cities to buy clothing and luxuries or order them on computer.

"I am happy with my home. I am learning new things as well, and that pleases me."

"We're about to build more schools on this side," I said. "With all the pregnant comesuli we have, we'll need them in a couple of years."

"The children are a joy," he actually smiled when he said it. "There were few births among my kind." I nodded, not mentioning the real reason we were standing there, having our conversation. "I did not expect to be visited by you, or treated as an honored guest," he went on. "And I wish to ask you where the Indis-Banuu came from."

"Indis-Banuu?" I asked, puzzled.

"The light-gathering crystal. Indis-Banuu means holder of the sun in my language. It is with sadness that I admit we drained most of what we had and destroyed some of it in the taking of your child. We could not get the sun to recharge nearly half of what we had on Vionn." Well, there it was. I wanted to weep at his admission. I worked to put it out of my mind.

"Oh. That stuff," I said as cheerfully as I could. "That came from Surnath. The crystal just litters the ground, there."

"There is such a world?" Corent drew in a sharp breath.

"Yeah," I shrugged. I had no idea why that excited him so much.

"Is there more here, that you are not using?" he asked. "I can use it to help trees and plants grow." Now I knew how they'd taken useless land and turned it into a garden. The crystal held sunlight and operated as a focus for their power. They'd used it to kidnap Toff, too.

"I don't know," I replied to his question. "If there's not, I'll get some for you if that's what you want." I didn't get any bad vibes from him—he wasn't planning to misuse the stuff.

"I do want some, if it's no trouble."

"I'll see you get it. Let me know if you need anything else. You're not in prison, you know. As long as you follow the laws here, you're as free as anyone else."

"I'll try to remember that. How should I address you, when I see you again?" he asked when I turned to leave.

"You can call me Lissa, unless you prefer something else. Bear in mind if you use profanity instead of my name, some of my mates may take exception."

"You would allow me to use your name?" He gave me a puzzled look.

"Why wouldn't I?"

"I would imagine I am not in good grace, at the moment." Corent hung his head.

"You didn't cause this mess on your own. If you hadn't volunteered to come, I would have left you where you were."

"I understand that. Now."

I nodded to him and folded away before I started crying again. Toff wasn't coming home to me. I had to get used to that.

* * *

"Child, are you well?" Tiearan waited for Lissa to disappear before making himself known to Corent. "Your mother worries."

"Father, did you hear what she said to me?"

"No, child. Was she abusive?"

"No, Father. The opposite, actually. She treats me kindly, as do the comesuli. They have not been informed why I am here. They treat me as one of them. The Queen has offered to bring me Indis-Banuu—which they use here to help supply power. I do not understand this at all."

"Do you have a place to stay?" Tiearan studied Corent's face.

"I do. Come, I will show you." Corent led Tiearan toward his home.

* * *

*Earth*
*Merrill Leopard's Manor*
"Brenten, while I understand that you were protecting Wyatt, I fail to understand why you did this to Lissa." Amara held her sleeping son in her arms while she watched Griffin.

He stood near a window in Merrill's old manor house in Kent, looking over the well-kept lawn surrounding the house. "Surely there was some other way. If she learns of this, you may as well forget you have a daughter."

"She has trouble recognizing me as her father anyway."

"Brenten, is this my husband talking, or someone who merely attempts to justify himself?"

# Chapter 7

"The switching of the bracelets is only a part of this," Griffin turned to face Amara. "I have rationalized my acts in the past. Often congratulated myself on making things come out in the best way possible, by sacrificing this one or that. I keep telling myself it is for the greater good. Yes, it causes me superficial pain, but that is all. I couldn't face this pain, Amara. I couldn't handle having my son taken away from us like that," he shook his head.

"And if I'd told Wylend, or anyone else, it would have turned out worse than it did. Wylend would have sent some of his and Vionn would have suffered, if not been destroyed outright. So I put this on my daughter, who has had enough pain as it is. I removed the memories from Roff because I knew, even then, that things would come to this."

"Lissa told him what happened. I heard that from Kyler. She says that Roff hasn't spoken to Flavio for days. She also said that Lissa will barely speak to anyone, locks herself in her room most nights, only does what she absolutely has to do and now has a fifty million-credit price tag on her head. I'm grateful I still have my son in my arms, Brenten, but what have you done to your daughter?"

"I won't have a daughter, Amara. Not when she discovers what I've done. And, I may not hold onto my Oracle status much longer—I feel that Belen may be considering what to do about this even now. I interfered, Amara. To save myself and to save my son. The one my daughter managed to give to us. Wyatt wouldn't have come to us any other way."

"Who else knows of this, Brenten?"

"Wylend and Erland know. When Lissa finds the truth, she'll be angry with them as well."

# Chapter 8

L e-Ath Veronis
Lissa

"Grant, why don't you take a break?" Thurlow Burghin, the Alliance rep, stood in my doorway, so I was giving Grant the opportunity to get away from this meeting if he wanted to. I would, too, if I could.

"Okay," Grant smiled and headed toward the kitchen to pick up a bottle of blood substitute.

"Mr. Burghin, come in and have a seat," I offered. So far, he'd been discreet and polite enough. I couldn't fault him on his manners. He wasn't bad looking and I couldn't help but think he'd probably like to be anywhere but here.

"Please, call me Thurlow," he smiled and sat in the offered chair.

"Would you like something to eat or drink?" I asked.

"Lady, no. If you and your staff feed me any better, I'll be too heavy to board ship again," he chuckled. He didn't look as if he had an ounce anywhere that wasn't hard muscle, but I didn't say that. It made me wonder what he'd done for the Alliance before coming on this little assignment.

"So, what can I do for you, Mr. Burghin—Thurlow?"

"What would you be doing now, if you weren't taking time to talk to me?" he asked. That made me sigh. Honestly, I wanted to crawl out of my skin and into a hole somewhere, until the pain that followed me everywhere I went had gone away. That wasn't something I'd tell anyone, however. Except for Gavin—or Kifirin, perhaps. I was feeling Gavin's absence the past few days, much more than I normally would.

"Please," Thurlow said when I didn't answer, allowing too many things to rush through my mind instead.

"Sitting on the roof," I said. He'd asked, I answered.

"On the roof? Why, lady?"

"Mr. Burghin, I'm not sure I can do this interview right now. My apologies." I stood up behind my desk.

"I've upset you."

"It wasn't you, or anything to do with you, I assure you," I muttered.

"Is it the price on your head?" He stood because I was standing.

"No, I'm sorry to say. I wish it were something as simple as that." I looked down at the immaculate surface of my desk— Grant, Heathe and Davan kept it that way for me.

"A price on your head is a simple matter?" His voice was almost gentle.

I wanted to tell him that if I desired, I could hunt the ones down who'd placed that price on my head. Moreover, I could make them very dead—all by myself. What I couldn't do was make a child mine again, when someone had stolen him away, body and mind.

"Walk with me," Thurlow said. I looked up at him. I truly wasn't in the mood to do anything except find a place to cry. Again. I don't know how we ended up walking out of my office together, or down the long hallway toward the front steps of my palace.

Long ago, I used to tuck my hand in the crook of Don's elbow and we'd walk that way. I felt the urge to lean on someone, but Thurlow Burghin was a stranger and he'd been sent by the Alliance, on top of that. Not someone I'd consider for an arm-in-arm walk.

"Where are we going?" he said after a while, when we passed the courtyard and wandered into the nearest vampire neighborhoods.

"Some of my friends live down these streets," I sighed. I hadn't seen Bryan lately. He was busy—I knew that. He coordinated all the news and edited the newsfeeds that went out to the Alliance daily. He probably needed help to do it, too.

* * *

Thurlow watched her face carefully, without appearing obvious about it. So many people thought that vampires were veiled killers, unfeeling and grim. He wondered what some of them might think if they were privileged enough to walk beside this one—weighed down with grief as she was. He wanted her to tell him what was wrong, although he knew already.

Long, strawberry-blonde hair was brushed away from her face with a graceful hand and then tucked behind an ear as she stared down a street; several grand houses stood there, surrounded by well-manicured lawns.

# Blood War

The grass that grew in the dim light on this half of Le-Ath Veronis was blue-green and looked nearly black when in shadow. The moon was out—if the planet had a normal orbit, it would be night, now. The Queen should be preparing for sleep instead of wandering the streets of the capital city.

"I know about the child," Thurlow surprised himself by saying.

* * *

*Lissa*

I stared at him stupidly for several seconds after those words came from his beautifully sculpted lips. I shouldn't have been surprised—the comesuli gossiped all the time. They probably knew all about it—what with Giff collapsing in on herself and everything. Why would I expect anything else from someone whom the Alliance had sent to spy and report back to them?

"I will not include that information in my reports," he said softly.

"Do you think I trust you?" I asked, walking away from him. He stepped up beside me.

"A missing child is not the reason I'm here," he replied.

"Then why are you here?" I turned away from him, afraid I might cry at any moment. I wanted to mist away from him and wondered if the Alliance had that information about me, too. Wondered what their dossier held regarding the Queen of Le-Ath Veronis.

"Many reasons. The Alliance wishes to keep you safe. I am their eyes and ears at the moment, charged with sending reports on just how safe you are. I'm not sure they're interested in personal drama, or the fate of one small child who was never legally adopted."

# Chapter 8

"There's the problem, I suppose. Legally. Isn't that what everybody bases everything on? The letter of the law?" I walked on and he followed. "Legally," I went on, "there shouldn't be a price on my head. Legally, I shouldn't be a vampire. Therefore, legally, we shouldn't even be having this conversation."

"I can't argue with your logic," Thurlow nodded. "If there was a way to make you feel better, I'd do it."

"I don't think there's a single thing that might make me feel better right now," I said. "Let's go back."

"If you want," he agreed. We parted once we were inside the palace and I headed toward my suite. It was empty when I arrived. Giff would always be there in the past, waiting on me so she could get me undressed and my clothing hung up.

She was huddled in depression somewhere with Rolfe, who was doing his best to make things better for her. I wasn't going to interfere with that. Once again, I wondered what Roff was doing, and if anyone was trying to comfort him. I lifted my silk tunic over my head, walked toward my closet and searched for an empty hanger.

* * *

*Hraede*

"Tell me why you wanted these maps!" Gavin's eyes were red and his fangs were pricking his lower lip. Ibbitt was frightened. He'd never seen vampires this close and angry, yet here were two of them, accompanied by another man. He wasn't sure what that one was.

"I-I had someone come to me, offering quite a bit f-for them," Ibbitt's voice quavered. "They didn't tell me why they wanted them."

"You will give me names and addresses, if you have them," Tony flopped a pad of paper in front of Ibbitt.

"He was supposed to go himself," Lynx said, after taking a brief moment to *Look*.

"I am too old," Ibbitt whined. And I have worked for these before."

"Then why don't you take us to them?" Gavin showed the entire length of his fangs.

"I have to set up a meeting," Ibbitt said. "Please, do not hurt me."

"Make the call." Lynx set Ibbitt's communicator on the table in front of him. Ibbitt nodded and lifted it with shaking hands.

* * *

*Le-Ath Veronis*
*Lissa*

"Lissa, why don't you spend a day or two at Grey House?" Shadow had my chin in his hand, forcing me to look up at him.

I'd dressed in pajamas and sat on the side of my bed, but that was as far as I'd gotten. I hadn't turned down the bed or anything; I just sat there, numbly staring at the floor until Shadow folded in. "Kyler and Cleo are both at Grey House at the moment."

"Shadow, I don't know that I'm in the mood for anyone right now, even though they're family." Yeah, I was figuring things out, finally. I was afraid to dig very far; the betrayal might be too big. What was I supposed to do? Say "thanks, Dad, for fucking up my life again?"

Other things were clicking into place, too—things like who else might have known, and when did they know? A lot rode on that, to be honest. If they'd known from the beginning, then my family would be whittled down to nothing and my mates would take a whittling as well.

# Chapter 8

"Come on, baby, come back with me. I don't get to sleep with you in my bed as often as I want." Shadow lifted me to my feet. "I'll open a bottle of wine and we can raid the kitchen."

"I'm not hungry."

"Baby, I got mindspeech from Drake and Drew, telling me you didn't come to dinner tonight. What do you think I'm supposed to do about that?" he leaned down to kiss me and folded me to Grey House at the same time.

"Raiding the fridge, son?" Raffian Grey walked into the dimly lit kitchen as Shadow was trying to tempt me with whatever was inside it. Raffian, Shadow's father, sat next to me on a long, stainless-steel island in the center of the kitchen. His legs nearly reached the floor; mine didn't.

"Want a glass of wine, Dad?" Shadow straightened from perusing the lower shelves, lifting the bottle of wine he'd uncorked for his father to see.

"Sure." Raffian *Pulled* a wineglass off a rack, and then *Pulled* the bottle toward him, using the power that seemed to come so easily to him and his family. "What's in there that looks good?" he asked while he poured wine. The bottle sailed toward Shadow, once Raffian's glass was full.

"There's ham, roast beef and turkey," Shadow grinned at his father. "And some roast chicken." He pulled a platter out that held most of a roasted chicken. "Come on, help me eat the chicken," he coaxed.

That's how all three of us ended up sitting at the island, eating leftover roast chicken, drinking wine and nibbling on banana cake afterward. I went to bed with Shadow after cleaning the kitchen.

Making love with Shadow is consuming. It's like fanning the flames of an out-of-control blaze. It leaves me completely exhausted when it's over. I slept in Shadow's arms and he didn't wake me, as he should have. He let me wake on my own. That was and wasn't a good thing.

* * *

"Geez," I mumbled, willing my eyes to open in what I thought was early morning. Shadow answered by kissing my forehead and then my eyelids. "Honey, I ought to go home," I lifted a hand to rub my eyes, but my Wizard grasped the hand and kissed my fingers.

"You can sleep a little longer, if you want," he murmured against my hair.

"What time is it?" I asked, still trying to get my eyes open.

"Baby, it's nearly noon."

If Shadow hadn't held onto me, I might have leapt off the bed. I had an early meeting on Le-Ath Veronis. "I thought you could bend time," Shadow was smiling as I frowned up at the face that looked down at mine. He stroked my hair back. "You can stay here all day with me—it's off-day. You can sleep or we can make love, or go for a swim or eat ourselves sick. Besides, I sent mindspeech and Garde is taking the meeting."

"Garde is taking too many meetings," I muttered ungratefully, sitting up in bed. I was naked—Shadow didn't like pajamas or any other thing that people might sleep in.

"He was happy to do it—in fact he told me to make you sleep as long as possible."

"Honey, I need to get up." I was trying to wiggle away from him.

"Come on, baby, stay just a little while longer," Shadow wheedled. Well, as wheedling went, it worked pretty well.

* * *

*Hraede*

# Chapter 8

Gavin and Tony had fangs and claws out as Ibbitt led them down narrow, stone steps, with hollows and grooves worn in places, they were so old. Gavin smelled moss, lichen and mildew; it was damp in this place and dark as pitch to anyone other than a vampire or someone who could change into a giant cat.

Lynx had the night vision of his avatar if he needed it, and he needed it now. Ibbitt was going strictly by feel—he had his right hand on the stone wall as he carefully made his way down, leading the three behind him. He'd placed a call, and someone, Gavin couldn't say who, had told him to come when he explained that he had the maps.

Gavin carried the satchel that held the drawings over his shoulder, while his, Tony's and Lynx's footsteps were all but silent as they followed the wrinkled, ancient Ibbitt. When they reached a door, Ibbitt pulled a key from beneath his shirt—it hung on a gold chain about his neck.

The key looked to be centuries old, but the lock clicked easily as if it were oiled and maintained regularly. Ibbitt swung the door wide and stepped inside an even blacker interior.

*I'll fold us out if there's danger*, Lynx sent mindspeech. Gavin barely nodded, as did Tony, and they followed Ibbitt into darkness. Ibbitt's footsteps crunched—it was an old trick; place nutshells or another, similar substance on the floor—it was meant to alert anyone inside to their presence.

Gavin could hover or lift himself, using the power afforded him as an older vampire. He lifted Tony and Lynx and sailed silently behind Ibbitt. Ibbitt found another door, and there was the dimmest light coming from the crack beneath it. He reached out for the handle and pulled the door back.

# Blood War

"Welcome, Ibbitt," a disembodied voice spoke. "Did you bring your guests with you?"

* * *

*Vionn*

"Honored guest," the Pelipu bowed slightly to the one who'd come, and then stared at Alvoritt. This is what you've brought me? was the question trembling on the Pelipu's lips, but he dared not voice it aloud. "Thank you, Alvoritt," he murmured instead. "I appreciate your efforts on my behalf."

The one Alvoritt had brought was of medium height, if that, and completely unremarkable. The Pelipu had been expecting a champion, at the very least—someone with a physique to match Alvoritt's description of a torturer, if nothing else. This one didn't appear strong enough to wield tongs, even.

"You have the prisoners?" Alvoritt asked.

"Of course. Would you prefer to go to the dungeons or have the prisoners brought here?" He hoped he didn't have to bring them here to his audience hall—he had expensive rugs on the floor and had no desire to toss them away if the blood flew.

"We'll go down," Alvoritt agreed amiably. He nodded deferentially to the one he'd brought in, who didn't even blink at the respectful gesture. Silently he followed as the Pelipu led them toward a doorway at the side of his audience hall. He waved off the guards, too, who prepared to come along.

"Stay here, I'll be perfectly fine," the Pelipu assured them; they were ready to ignore Alvoritt's unspoken command.

The dungeons were three flights of stone steps beneath the Pelipu's temple. The prisoners were kept in cages, nearly starved, and not allowed to bathe. The dungeon stank with old blood, excrement and death.

164

# Chapter 8

"I will not accept them if they are filthy and smell." Those were the first words the guest had spoken as they passed cage after cage.

"Then perhaps these," the Pelipu walked to the last cage. Inside it was a group of three men and one woman, all fairly clean—they'd been snatched from the market only that morning.

"Bring out two of the men," the guest ordered. The Pelipu snapped his fingers at the dungeon guard, who brought the keys. Another guard had to be brought forward to help pull two unwilling male prisoners from the cell.

"Oh, never fear, your turn will come to feed the god," Alvoritt crooned to the two remaining inside the cell as the guard locked the door behind him.

"Where would you like to do this?" The Pelipu's voice was tinged with the slightest bit of mockery—he imagined his guards might be forced to assist their guest.

"Here will be fine," the guest replied, immediately transforming into the largest serpent the Pelipu had ever thought to see.

At least forty feet of gleaming, coppery scales now stood before the Pelipu, with a head crowned with spikes and a multitude of sharp, needle-like teeth inside the gaping mouth. The two prisoners disappeared down the serpent's wide throat in seconds. The Pelipu only had a moment or two to marvel at what he'd invited into his temple before he followed the two prisoners into the belly of the monster.

The monster transformed back to a humanoid appearance, only now he held the Pelipu's face and form. The dungeon guards, just before they died, wept and begged for their lives.

* * *

# Blood War

*Hraede*

"Please, come in. We were hoping someone would come."

"I recognize this one." There were six inside the rock-walled room. All six were vampire; Gavin knew by their scent. One of them recognized Lynx; Gavin hadn't expected that.

"And I recognize you," Lynx nodded to the vampire, who stepped forward to study his three visitors—Ibbitt had been led aside and settled onto a chair against a wall. "It has been two thousand years or so, I believe?"

"That is so," the vampire nodded. "Are we in danger again, my friend?"

"Not from those—not here," Lynx replied. "Although there are rogues out there who may cause problems before this is over."

"Perhaps you should introduce us to your friends," the vampire said.

"Very well," Lynx grinned. "This is Gavin, and this is Anthony," he pointed out his companions. "These," he said, indicating the six vampires, "are the Rith Naeri—the Order of the Night Flower on Hraede."

* * *

"You are all former Kings of Hraede?" Tony stared at the one who'd known Lynx—his name was Rigovarnus, but Lynx called him Rigo.

"Yes. I was the first King to be made vampire. My heir was set to mismanage my kingdom. My sire had no desire to see Hraede suffer, so he turned me as I lay dying. I supervised my heir through his entire reign, and then the next six kings and queens as well, until Halimel came along. That is when I began the tradition of marking my subsequent vampire children with this." He tapped the side of his neck, where a tattoo of the Hraedan night flower lay.

# Chapter 8

The actual flower was such a deep purple as to appear black, and hung on a delicate stem, nearly upside down. Only the flower itself, with its petals fully open with tips curling upward, was depicted.

"We attempted the turn with two queens, but I'm sure I don't have to tell you how unsuccessful that was," Halimel added. "Then came Rondival, Alrenardo, Brinelodus and Yandiveri. Only we call each other Hal, Ron, Alren, Brin and Yan. It's a lot easier than those stupid proper names we were saddled with," Rigo almost smiled.

"But you arranged this?" Gavin was trying to sort out why they were there.

"We were hoping someone would come," Rigo agreed, nodding. "We worried for your Queen. We wished to learn how well she was protected, and if we might send a spy inside the Queen's city. We knew Ibbitt was much too old to go himself, so we watched the one he sent. Paulin is not particularly talented in espionage, but he managed to breach the walls. You have weakness there, my friends. Your Queen must be protected better than this. Those poisonous seeds Paulin held weren't really poison. He was led to believe they were, to impress upon him the potential danger of his mission. We wanted him to be caught and followed, to test the strength of the Queen's protection. No good vampire would allow a clumsy humanoid to get past them, if they truly wish to keep the Queen alive."

"What interest do you have in the Queen?" Gavin's eyes darkened.

"You'll have to forgive him, he's one of the Queen's mates," Lynx laid a calming hand on Gavin's shoulder. "As is the other one," Lynx jerked his head in Tony's direction.

"We wish to help guard her," Rigo said. "We have heard rumors and there is no denying the price that has been placed upon her head. Although we all wish to come, Rondival and Alrenardo have agreed to stay behind and keep up our long work."

"Why did you not apply for citizenship?" Gavin growled.

"Because none know we exist," Rigo sighed. "We are hidden. We control the crown, if it becomes necessary. We have done this for thousands of years. Hraede is stable, because of this. If there are those who seek to overthrow the current regime for their own gain, we mobilize and take down their armies. Other vampires are here who are registered and live beside Hraede's humanoid citizens. These vampires serve as our army, at times. For obvious reasons, we must remain as we are, hidden from all."

"These six helped me when I came here two thousand years ago to deal with the Ra'Ak," Lynx said. "Without their help, Hraede would have been overrun with spawn."

"So, no royal turns since then?" Tony was curious.

"None worthy," Rigo snorted. "Yan was turned three thousand years ago. We've had self-serving monarchs since then, except for three very good queens. We did not attempt the turn with them, for obvious reasons."

"And if we allow you to come to Le-Ath Veronis?" Gavin still wasn't sure.

"Bring us before your Queen and allow her to decide. We have watched her in her Council meetings—she seems adept at weeding out undesirables. We will submit to her scrutiny."

"I'll vouch for Rigo," Lynx said. "And I'll fold all of us to Le-Ath Veronis, if you want further proof."

* * *

*Le-Ath Veronis*

# Chapter 8

*Lissa*

*Lissa, where are you?* Mindspeech from Gavin was as scarce as grasshoppers with guitars, as my mother used to say.

*Honey, are you all right? I miss you. I'm in bed, right now.*

*I miss you, too. Will you meet us in your study in a few moments? We will be folding in with guests.*

*Okay.* I slid off the bed and went to get dressed again. At least Shadow had made sure I got plenty of sleep earlier.

* * *

"Lissa will be here in a moment." Gavin said, after Lynx folded all seven of them to Lissa's study at Gavin's direction. Four trunks were lined up against the wall, too—the four members of Rith Naeri had been prepared to travel at a moment's notice.

Rigo, as any proper vampire who was nearly eleven thousand years of age would, calmed his excitement. From the moment he'd seen the vids of the Vampire Queen, he'd wanted to meet her. And, if he were honest with himself, he wanted more than that. He knew that would likely never be, and steeled himself when he heard the quiet footsteps outside the door.

* * *

*Lissa*

Of the seven people inside my study, only one of them wasn't vampire. That one was Lynx, one of Conner's mates. He grinned at me as I turned a puzzled gaze to him. Surely, he'd been the one to fold everyone here from wherever they'd been. Saa Thalarr didn't fold anybody anywhere—unless they were completely trustworthy.

"Lissa, allow me to introduce four of the six members of Rith Naeri, the Order of the Night Flower from Hraede," Lynx's grin widened.

"Little Queen," the oldest of the four bowed slightly to me. The other three bowed a little deeper.

"Please don't bow, I don't expect it," I said.

"This is Rigo," Lynx introduced me to the oldest. "And Hal," Lynx said. Hal was the second oldest. I took their hands and they bent over mine and kissed it lightly, as if they'd been trained at court. Brin came next, followed by the youngest—Yan—who was three thousand. These were some old vampires.

"What can I do for you?" I asked.

"We wish to protect you," Rigo said. "We have become worried over the lack of protection and the price on our Queen's head."

"You are Queen to all vampires, whether they reside here or not," Hal said. His statement made my eyebrows lift in surprise.

"That's nice of you to say, but I think that would be a bit egotistical on my part," I said.

"We have a network of information; you would not believe the vampires who have chosen to stay upon their home worlds and still regard you as their Queen," Yan replied. "Some are very old and do not wish to start over elsewhere, especially as they are accepted on the Alliance worlds where they reside. Were it not so, they would have come long ago."

"Ah," I said. I could understand that.

"Why are we only now hearing that you're back?" Drake and Drew walked in, pounding Tony on the back. He grinned at the twins. They knew not to manhandle Gavin, though.

# Chapter 8

We introduced the four vampires to them. "They'll be on the payroll, looks like," I said. "Why don't you two show them to the guest quarters for tonight, and we'll see about something else tomorrow. Are you hungry?" I asked them. "We have blood substitute in the kitchen."

We ended up in the kitchen; the four new ones were quite pleased with the blood substitute. I watched them—Rigo especially. He had hair as black as Merrill's and his eyes were as black as Wlodek's. He looked weathered by time, though.

Hal was the handsomest of the lot, with dark-blond hair down to his shoulders and green eyes. Brin and Yan could have been brothers—both had brown hair and brown eyes, with square jaws and strong chins. Brin had a bit of a dimple in his chin, but some people might find that attractive. Rigo was the tallest, at six-two. Yan was the shortest at five-eleven, so not much difference in height.

Drake and Drew took them to the guest wing after they finished their bottle of blood substitute. Gavin came and nuzzled my neck. Tony sighed. He figured he'd get tomorrow night, I'm sure.

"Lissa, cara, are you all right?" Gavin pulled me against him as we made our way to my suite.

"Honey, things are kind of awful," I sighed. "There's just nothing we can do about it now."

* * *

Thurlow watched as Gavin lifted Lissa, got her legs wrapped around his waist and her arms around his neck. He was kissing her, even as he opened the door to her suite and went inside. Thurlow sighed softly before heading toward the front doors of the palace. A walk in the moonlight seemed appropriate.

* * *

*Karathia*

"I intend to see Lissa tomorrow," Erland yawned as he sat in a chair before Wylend's desk in his private study.

"How do you think that's going to turn out?" Wylend asked, watching Erland's face carefully.

"No idea," Erland admitted. "I hope, for both our sakes, that she doesn't blame us for the whole thing."

"This situation is a two-edged sword for me," Wylend muttered. "I can condemn Brenten for the treatment of his daughter, but he was doing this to save his son and my heir. What am I supposed to do about that?"

"No idea," Erland shook his head. "But that's my mate, either way. What would you do, if she were yours?"

"She is mine, only in a different way. I am still trying to figure this out."

* * *

*Le-Ath Veronis*
*Lissa*

I was sleeping, sprawled over Gavin, who had an arm held loosely about my shoulders, when I heard the call for the Spawn Hunters long before our sleep period was over. My palace was emptied of everyone that had anything to do with the Saa Thalarr, which meant Gavin, Tony, Drake, Drew, Winkler, Aurelius, Rolfe, Jeral, Radomir, Rush and Lisster mobilized quickly and disappeared. Even the healers were called out, including the ones who'd been teaching classes at the hospital in Casino City.

Kyler must have been with Flavio, because they folded in with Roff right after the others left. Gavin didn't even have time for a quick kiss before he folded away. I was hugging myself, standing in my study still dressed in pajamas when

# Chapter 8

Flavio, my niece and Roff appeared. Rigo rushed in, followed closely by Thurlow.

"My Queen, the Rith Naeri are now guarding the entrances to your palace." Rigo dipped his head respectfully.

"Thank you, Rigo." I shivered—it was early fall, now, and the air on this side of the planet was definitely chilly at times. Kyler *Pulled* in a robe for me and moved to put it over my shoulders, but Roff plucked it from her fingers and wrapped me in it. He pulled me against him, too, after I tied the belt. I looked up at his face. He still looked care-worn, but his face held grim determination. And why was he holding me? He still didn't have a clue who I was.

"Do we have enough to guard the palace tonight? What about the walls?" I asked as I trembled in Roff's embrace. He pulled me tighter against him.

"I have contacted your guard and mustered out extras," Thurlow surprised me. "Baxter and Dmitri are heading up the detail and fanning out extra guards. Lissia should be safe tonight, and we will make arrangements tomorrow, should it prove necessary." I thanked him softly for his words and his efforts on my behalf.

"Don't forget you have that trip to New Hesperia, this morning," Kyler reminded me. That made me sigh. A new vampire city had been settled and populated while I'd been on Vionn. It held around thirty thousand or so.

The applicants were under review just before I'd gone to Vionn, so I hadn't had final approval on all of them. Someone else had done it in my absence. They had a newly elected Council, but hadn't attended Council meetings yet.

That was one of the things I'd planned to discuss during my visit. I was counting on taking Drake, Drew, Gavin and

Tony with me, too. They were gone now, and I'd have to get up and be ready to go in another hour or so.

"I will come with you," Rigo offered. "When shall I be ready?"

"You need to be ready in an hour and a half," Kyler told him. "Meet here. Grant, Davan and Heathe will be going, to take notes in case anything needs tending to or provided for the new residents."

"I will go," Roff stated firmly, tightening his arm around me and almost daring Flavio to tell him no. Flavio flicked a glance at Roff but didn't say anything.

"I will go as well," Thurlow added.

"Thurlow, those are vampires we're going to visit," I told him, looking at his almost-handsome face. His sensuous mouth twisted into a grin.

"Lady, I am more than aware," he replied.

* * *

"Are we ready?" Grant was always excited to go on what he termed a road trip, even if it was only fifty miles away.

Davan was happy to get away from the palace; he offered me a smile as we walked through a side door and into the courtyard where a hoverbus waited. A vampire driver waited with the hoverbus, so Grant, Heathe and Davan loaded into the back, Thurlow and Rigo took the middle seat and Roff and I got the first row, behind the driver.

Roff had gone back to my suite with me earlier, never said a thing and lay down beside me while I stared at the ceiling. His hand crept toward mine eventually, until my fingers were clasped tightly in his. We'd stayed that way until we had to get off the bed, clean up and get dressed.

I worried about my Spawn Hunters, but had to put it out of my mind. I would be meeting the newly formed Council

# Chapter 8

from New Hesperia, and it made me wish for Garde or Aurelius to back me up.

I wasn't comfortable about this, and felt vulnerable without their presence. Aurelius was off killing spawn somewhere and didn't need to worry about an uneasy Vampire Queen. Garde had a meeting on Kifirin to attend in his official role as Prime Minister. Besides, I'd taken up enough of his time.

The vampire driver, who seemed happy to be driving the Queen around, opened our doors for us. I guess that gave him status or something. How was I to know?

The Council for New Hesperia was there to greet us formally, as we were ushered inside City Hall. Kifirin must have manufactured marble from thin air, I thought as we walked up grand steps and into the building.

New Hesperia's City Hall housed multiple offices, a meeting chamber, a kitchen area which held shelves of blood substitute and a bank of refrigerators quietly humming, keeping blood substitute cold in case you preferred it that way.

"We would like for more comesuli to visit us," the Head of New Hesperia's Council informed me as we were shown to their Council chamber. He was around five-ten or so and looked twenty-two, although his scent said close to a thousand. He also had blond hair, almost the color Gabron's had been.

I was trying to keep that from having any influence over my first impression of him, which wasn't very good, to be honest. I wasn't itchy, but felt on the verge of it, somehow.

He was demanding more comesuli, too. That was preposterous. We divided them among the existing cities as it was, according to population. The city councils were supposed to portion out the taking of fresh blood fairly among their constituents.

"You are getting as much as we can send," I said. "So many are pregnant right now, and we portion out the ones eligible for the bite fairly," I responded to his complaint.

"We thought we would be getting more fresh blood," the guy continued to whine.

"What is your name?" He hadn't given it, yet, only introducing himself as the Head of the Council.

"Geratt, Raona," he replied, pronouncing the G as a J.

"Geratt, were you promised anything before you came, other than a place to stay on Le-Ath Veronis?" I asked.

"But the rumors all said we'd get fresh blood."

"How much have you had since you arrived?" I asked.

"I have gotten to drink twice," he muttered, sounding angry.

"How much fresh blood did you get, where you lived before?"

"None, it was forbidden," he grumbled.

"Perhaps you'd like to go back there." I wasn't going to listen to much more of this. He'd gotten a taste for blood from the source, and looked to be on his way to becoming addicted. Apparently, Rigo thought the same; he was frowning at Geratt.

I made a mental note to check with the comesuli who'd come here, just to make sure they weren't abused when they offered blood. It looked like these might not have been trained to take blood properly, and I was out of patience with anybody who might mistreat the comesuli.

Roff, too, wasn't happy with this guy. Thurlow had as good a non-expression going as any I'd seen. I didn't have time to wonder about him for perhaps the fiftieth time.

# Chapter 8

"Come, let us walk through New Hesperia," Geratt offered, noticing, finally, that he was in a minority about getting additional fresh blood.

We walked out of City Hall with him, past the inevitable courtyard and down the center street leading up to City Hall. We passed a few grand manors, quite a few nicer homes and some that were more than adequate. The latter didn't seem to be occupied—the new residents had claimed all the nicer properties.

"My home is down this street," Geratt informed us as we walked along. I noted the street sign—the street was named after him.

How nice.

Of course, his mansion was at the end of the block and took up most of the cul-de-sac, wrapping around the circular area in a U-shape. Well, weren't we uptown? "I am looking forward to my first meeting at the palace tomorrow," Geratt smiled. Odds are he'd try to dominate it, too. We'd see how that turned out.

"Please, come and see what I've done with the house," Geratt went on. Heathe and Davan were already headed in that direction.

"Lady," Thurlow took my arm, just as my skin began to itch. I drew in a huge breath as wooden shafts were shot around us from nearly every angle. I turned everything around me to mist as swiftly as possible, mentally screaming out a distress call to anyone listening.

What I wasn't expecting was for Erland and Wylend to show up, nor what they did when they got there. Anything on that street that wasn't mist was burned to cinders in three blinks. Now I was seeing just what it was that Karathian warlocks could do.

# Chapter 9

*Lissa*

When I came back to corporeality, turning everything else within my mist as well, I learned what those wooden shafts had done. Davan was already dead and Heathe nearly so.

"No!" I shouted, struggling to get to Heathe before the last spark of life was gone. Cleo, healer that she was, got there ahead of me and nearly landed on top of Heathe, glowing like the sun. Davan was turning to ash as I knelt next to him and wept.

* * *

Sixteen piles of vampire ash—that's what we found behind houses—six behind Geratt's manor alone. Garde and Aryn had shown up quickly; I was staring at Geratt as he sat at a table at City Hall, looking guilty as hell.

# Blood War

Rigo held the other Council members off to the side—he'd placed a compulsion to end all compulsions, I think, and he was glaring at all of them. I pitied any one of them who might be involved in this.

Davan had been my uncle. *Had been.* We'd only known each other for a short time. He'd been so good—so grateful, even—for the job he'd been given, and the place he had at the palace.

I wanted to cry again over his loss, along with so many other things. Roff stood beside me, a hand stroking my jaw and neck carefully as he watched Garde question Geratt after Aryn placed compulsion.

"Tell me everything you know of this attack." Garde was blowing a lot of smoke. If his smaller Thifilathi came, we'd all have to leave and I figured Geratt would be dead quickly.

"They assured me it would be clean and swift," Geratt whined.

Where did you think you would hide afterward?" Aryn asked.

"I was promised transport back to Brisdan, if it appeared I might be implicated."

"How much?" Erland and Wylend were still there, and Erland now had Geratt's shirt gripped in his fist. "How much did they promise you for this? Because I can assure you, they meant for you to die here so they could keep the money for themselves. Only Lissa's quick thinking saved your sorry hide from those arrows, which killed her uncle, by the way."

Garde was still blowing smoke, but seemed content to have the warlock do some threatening. Thurlow was at the back of the room, watching everything and everybody.

We learned that three humanoids had hired Geratt and twenty vampires to kill me, for half the fifty million promised

# Chapter 9

by Black Mist. Three vampires had escaped and the humanoid masterminds were staying somewhere in Casino City, waiting to pay Geratt for my assassination.

Cleo had taken Heathe and Grant back to the palace; Heath had been really shaky but alive when she'd folded them away. I figured he'd be getting plenty of blood substitute the minute he got back. I looked up at Roff.

"Lissa, I am sorry," he leaned down and kissed me gently, wiping the stubborn tears away afterward.

"Me, too, honey," I put an arm around his waist and buried my head against his shoulder.

* * *

"I see them." Rigo spoke quietly to Aryn, Garde, Thurlow and Erland. Three men were gambling at a table nearby. Geratt had given names and descriptions. The names were assumed, but it was easy enough to fit the descriptions to the accents Geratt provided.

It was a simple matter afterward to track down where they were gambling. A vampire pit crew manned the craps table, and they knew not to say anything when Erland and Garde walked up.

"Please, come with us," Erland smiled pleasantly at the three. When one tried to bolt, Rigo had a hand on his shoulder and claws digging in. He came along quietly after that. A room was provided by casino management for questioning—the owner knew Erland well. He also knew better than to interfere.

"Now, you will tell us everything," Aryn placed compulsion. The three gulped and nodded.

* * *

*Lissa*

"Will you tell Griffin?" Wylend was saying good-bye, so I asked him to pass the news of Davan's death along—Davan was his brother, after all. Yes, I knew what Griffin had done. To me and to Roff.

I had no idea whether there was a way to restore Roff's memories completely or if their restoration would only cause further grief at this point. Roff had come to me somehow, whether he remembered or not. I was still trying to decide if I wished to speak to my natural father from now on. I did have one other request, however.

"Tell him I'd like Roff's ring back," I added. That caused Wylend's eyebrows to lift a little. "Don't pretend you don't know, Em-pah," I sighed. I was tired. I'd just lost another person I cared about and wondered if I had any male family members left who truly loved me.

I think Kyler and Cleo might be in my corner most of the time, but I didn't know where they stood on Griffin or if they even knew what he'd done to keep Wyatt away from the Green Fae.

"Granddaughter, I didn't know until it was over," Wylend said. "And I'd like to brush that tear away, but I don't think you'd let me touch you right now."

"I don't know that I'll let any male relative touch me again," I said and turned away.

* * *

*Karathia*

"You know about Davan." Wylend studied his son's face— Griffin had been waiting for him when he arrived on Karathia.

"Yes. This is going to hurt Jeral."

"It hurt your daughter. She knows, Brenten. She wants you to give Roff's ring back."

# Chapter 9

"I was afraid to *Look*," Griffin nodded, refusing to meet Wylend's gaze.

"Child, I hope you are done harming her emotionally," Wylend went on. "I would like to repair what little relationship I have with her."

"I thought I was done harming her," Griffin said. "Until Wyatt came along, causing things to shift."

"Do you love her at all?"

"She does not love me."

"That is not the question I asked. Has your son taken up all the love you might have for a child, now, and Lissa has become disposable?"

"Lissa shouldn't have been disposable," Griffin replied. "But her stepfather made her distrustful of any father figure. I had an uphill climb with her, every step of the way."

"And when you set her down in front of thousands of Ra'Ak and told her people would die if she didn't do something about it, that didn't improve things, did it? Especially since you'd admitted to her that she'd been the answer to the problems you were seeing and that you deliberately went looking for her mother, merely to produce the solution to those problems. That makes any child thankful for their life." Wylend didn't employ sarcasm often, but he used it now. "Child, look at me and tell me that you would still speak to me if I'd used you so grievously," Wylend tilted Griffin's face up with a finger.

"I wouldn't. I wouldn't forgive you, either."

"I know."

* * *

*Le-Ath Veronis*
*Lissa*

# Blood War

Kiarra had come with her three mates—Merrill, Adam and Pheligar stood with her. My two Larentii were there as well when I explained to Jeral, as best I could, what happened to Davan.

"At least I know you loved him," Jeral wiped his eyes. I was crying, too, and Roff was beside me, offering tissues.

"I did." I almost didn't get the words out; my voice broke. Cleo had to put Grant under and Heathe was sleeping, too. Davan had become such friends with both of them that I didn't know how they were going to deal with his death. "We can do a memorial in a day or two, if you want."

"I would like that," Jeral sighed. Davan was his brother, in addition to being his youngest vampire child.

"Jeral, come with us," Kiarra was urging him away; I was about to break down completely. Roff, Connegar, Reemagar and I left my study and Gavin, Tony, Drake and Drew were waiting outside. Karzac folded in as soon as we reached my suite.

"I will stay with Lissa," Roff announced as Karzac came toward me, fingers heading toward my forehead.

"Nice to see you, too, honey," I said before he touched me and I was out like a light.

* * *

"Get her undressed and put her to bed," Karzac ordered. Gavin was holding her up; she'd collapsed when Karzac placed the healing sleep.

"We will assist Roff; the others here need sleep, they are weary from killing spawn," Reemagar said. Connegar herded everyone else from the bedroom—they'd cleared quite a bit of spawn from a planet light-years away and were exhausted. The news of Davan's death hadn't helped, or the fact that Lissa had been attacked while they were away.

# Chapter 9

* * *

"I am required to notify the Alliance that we're holding them," Thurlow said, as the three men were locked inside the palace dungeons. They'd admitted under compulsion that they'd planned to take the Queen down, only they'd hired others to do it for them. Vampires seemed to be the logical choice, and they'd offered half of Black Mist's reward for evidence of the Queen's death.

They thought their plan couldn't fail. They'd hidden their tracks (or so they'd thought), and meant to collect the entire reward after their hired vampires killed the Queen. They'd counted on the Queen's guards tracking and killing the vampires involved afterward, never suspecting that a single vampire might live over it.

Geratt was in a cell separated from the others, so they couldn't reach or speak with one another. Geratt wore the cuffs to contain a vampire. Cell bars did well enough for the others.

"Do what you have to do, Thurlow, but remember these have conspired to kill the Queen. We won't be sending these back to the Alliance. This justice is ours," Garde snorted as he glared at the three humanoids.

"As the law allows," Thurlow agreed. A lesser crime would have sent the perpetrators home to their own world's justice. Murder or conspiracy to commit murder allowed the world on which the crime was committed to pass sentence.

"What are we going to do about the three vampires who are missing?" Rigo asked. They'd learned from Geratt that he'd hired nineteen vampires for the attack on Lissa. Only sixteen were accounted for.

"We'll send someone out," Garde said. "Trevor, perhaps, and a crew of handpicked vampires."

185

"Is Lissa still awake?" Garde asked. They'd left the dungeon behind and now walked through a side door leading into the palace, after Garde entered a security code on the keypad outside. Two vampire guards inside the door nodded them through—they were recognized.

"The Queen is sleeping," Dmitri heard the door open from the grand hall and went to double check, making sure the ones entering the palace were authorized to do so.

"Can you get a message to Trevor?" Garde asked. Trevor was a former assassin for the Council on Earth. Now he worked as Sheriff for Casino City.

"Of course. What should I say?"

"That we have three rogues loose. They were among the nineteen hired to attack Lissa today. Only sixteen were killed. We have the masterminds in the dungeon."

"Did any other Council members from New Hesperia know anything about this?" Dmitri asked.

"The Council members didn't. I intend to question the other citizens of New Hesperia to see if they knew anything or failed to come forward with information. I am quite angry over this." Garde proved it by blowing smoke. "I will check on Lissa before going home."

"I'll come with you," Erland said. Rigo and Thurlow refused to be left behind, and Aryn went, too, since the others were going. All walked swiftly and determinedly toward Lissa's suite.

"Roff, I only wish to check on Lissa," Garde opened the door halfway. Roff was in the Queen's bed, with Lissa tucked against him.

"Come ahead, her healer-mate placed her in a healing sleep. She will not wake." Roff turned on a bedside lamp.

# Chapter 9

"There's my girl," Erland breathed, sitting on the side of the bed and reaching out to touch Lissa's cheek.

"Did you find the ones in Casino City?" Roff asked quietly.

"We did. They're in the dungeons now," Garde replied. "But there are three other rogues who escaped. We have vampires hunting them now. I want to take Lissa to Kifirin with me, but I think I'd have a fight on my hands at the moment," he added. "The breaching of the walls and the attempts on her life worry me. Dmitri has an extra shift on guard duty. If you need me to take her out of here, get someone to send mindspeech."

"I can take her to Karathia just as easily," Erland murmured. He hadn't informed the others, but Wylend was sending out warlocks. There would be dead Solar Red, Black Mist and Red Hand by morning.

Rigo watched enviously as the little Queen, a bare shoulder peeking from beneath the sheet, slept against the winged vampire's chest. Thurlow watched Rigo, Roff, Erland and Garde, but held his face expressionless, as always.

Garde led them from Lissa's suite after a while, and Roff tilted his head to kiss the top of Lissa's head, mumbling words of love to her. Roff hadn't failed to notice that he'd been the first one Lissa had turned to mist earlier in the day, making sure he was safe from the arrows. The others had followed swiftly, but Heathe and Davan had walked too far ahead, preventing Lissa from getting to them sooner. Davan had paid for the trust he'd displayed with his life.

"I know you love me," Roff said softly, stroking a cheek. "And I know you loved my child. Both my children. I do not know of any other comesuli who can say as much." Roff leaned over and turned off the lamp. He hadn't needed the light to begin with—it was only a courtesy to their visitors.

* * *

*Kifirin*

"Gardevik, how is Lissa?" Glinda watched Garde's face as he sat at the kitchen island, a sandwich on a plate in front of him. He was tired and hungry—he hadn't eaten since early morning.

"Not that well—you know about her uncle who was killed." Garde bit into his sandwich. At least their cooks and kitchen help were very good, now.

"Yes. And I heard that Roff was with her when this happened. How is he?"

"Better than Lissa. She told him about Toff not long ago. He still has not gained his full memory, but he feels the betrayal anyway."

"Poor Toff. If someone did that to my girls," Glinda was as close to blowing smoke as Garde had ever seen her. She went Thifilatha when she turned—Glinda was the only female High Demon who'd ever done it. Female High Demons didn't turn as a rule. Garde wondered about her daughters, though, and if they might grow up with that ability.

"Anyone else would have killed over that," Garde agreed.

* * *

*Le-Ath Veronis*
*Lissa*

We held the memorial two days later and everyone in the palace went. They'd all liked Davan. He'd been shy and self-effacing, much of the time. Grant and Heath both spoke about what a good friend he'd been. Then it was my turn.

"I knew the moment I met him, that we were related," I said. "He bore the scent of my grandmother, whom I'd just met. Kifirin and I found him and the others—most turned as a convenience for the state of Beliphar. Most of you have no idea what I would give to have my uncle back again." I couldn't go past that—if I did, I'd break down.

Davan's ashes had been gathered and Jeral received them. He planned to take them to the light side of the planet, because Davan wanted to see the sun again. Since Jeral had been made Spawn Hunter, he could go wherever he pleased.

Griffin and Amara had come and they sat in the back, holding little Wyatt.

My little brother.

Well, he'd be kept away from me, more than likely. No justice in telling him what his continued existence with his natural parents had cost others. Of course, Griffin wouldn't be taking that chance. He and Amara folded away immediately after the service—they didn't even try to talk to me.

I went to find Kyler and Cleo afterward. "I want to take a little trip to the past," I told them. "I want to see my sister."

"I've been putting it off," Cleo nodded. "I'll feel better if you're both with me." She'd never met her mother, either. She'd been taken by Griffin while still a baby in the hospital on Cemdris, and moved to Earth. She'd grown up with adoptive parents there, while Griffin removed the memory from his daughter that she'd birthed twins. Did my father have the talent to fuck up lives or what?

"Then we'll go," Kyler said, pulling me away from my thoughts. She was the one to bend time and fold space.

It was a spring day on Cemdris and we found ourselves in a park. Children were running and playing here and there in the warm afternoon sun. A woman sat on a bench nearby, watching a dark-haired child playing on the swings.

She was tall, as Griffin was, and bore his brown hair and gold-flecked brown eyes. I stared at my sister Ardith, who'd been dead for centuries. She looked very much like my grandfather, the King of Karathia, and it made my heart weep—for myself and for Wylend. We'd never been allowed to know her.

"That's me on the swing," Kyler said softly. She stood between Cleo and me as we watched a seven-year-old Kyler playing. Griffin wouldn't be out and about—not during the day. He was vampire at the time.

"She was a physician and worked nights at the hospital, because that's when Em-pah could take care of me," Kyler sighed, gazing at her mother.

"You loved him then, didn't you?" I asked.

"Em-pah taught me so many things," Kyler said. "And he did love me. It's just that later, things went downhill."

"Yeah." I was in agreement with that.

Cleo had been staring at her mother instead of joining the conversation. She walked away from us, going toward Ardith. She sat next to her on the bench, too. Kyler and I followed.

"You're Ardith Endres, aren't you?" Cleo asked.

"Do I know you?" My sister turned to Cleo with a puzzled frown.

"No, I've heard about you from my sister, that's all," Cleo replied. "She said you worked at the hospital."

"Ah." Ardith thought she'd treated a family member or something. "How is your sister?" It was the proper question to ask.

"She's fine," Cleo said. "And this is my aunt Lissa." I nodded. Kyler had shielded herself, invisible to her mother.

"Very nice to meet you. What is it that you do?" she asked me.

"Oh, I'm a vampire," I said.

"Unlikely, since you're here in daylight," she smiled slightly.

"Well, that's how it started out," I agreed. "But not how it ended up."

"My father is vampire, that's in the records," my sister sighed.

"So was mine," I agreed. "We don't speak much, nowadays."

"Because he's vampire?"

"Because he doesn't tell me things," I said.

"Mine, too," Ardith agreed. "I think he keeps things from me, or uses the compulsion he has to make things come out the way he wants them to. I got tired of fighting it, after a while. I feel like a puppet and he's pulling the strings, making all the decisions. Sometimes I wonder how things might have been if he hadn't been turned."

"Same here," I said. "It gets a little old, using his kids to make things come out right."

"I loved him when I was little—he was up nights and he'd tell me stories at bedtime," Ardith had a faraway look in her eyes. "But when I grew up and got married, well, things changed."

"At least you had that love when you were little," I said. "I never knew my father growing up. I had a stepfather, who resented me because I wasn't his. I didn't meet my father until after I'd been made vampire. He sort of popped up, one day. Things haven't improved much since then."

"I understand. Look, it has been nice meeting you, but I have to get my daughter home and start dinner. Perhaps we'll meet again, someday." Ardith stood. "Kyler," she called. "Time to go home."

# Blood War

We watched as Kyler at seven jumped off the swing and trotted toward her mother. "Good-bye, Kyler," I said. "We'll see each other again, I promise." I smiled at her as she took her mother's hand and walked away.

"I remembered this day," the grown Kyler said, as we watched them disappear around a curve in the sidewalk. "I didn't know then why you'd be saying something like that to me."

"Now you know," I hugged her.

"Let's bend time again," Kyler said, and took us out of there. When we arrived at our next destination, it was night and we were standing in a street outside several small shops and eateries. Kyler, at the same age we'd seen her before, was sitting on a stool in a sweet shop, swinging her legs happily and eating ice cream. Griffin sat across a tiny round table from her.

"You've got ice cream on your chin, baby." That was Griffin's voice. He was passing a napkin to the young Kyler.

"Em-pah, what will I be when I grow up?" Kyler asked, as she swiped at her chin with the paper napkin. Griffin leaned over and got the spot she missed.

"Baby, you'll be amazing when you're older. Just wait and see. Promise you'll still love your Em-pah then?"

"I'll always love you, Em-pah," the seven-year-old Kyler declared, taking another bite of ice cream.

"I'll always love you, baby," he said. "I promise."

Well, that went for granddaughters. It didn't hold for daughters, apparently. I felt like crying again.

"Did you ask your daughter the same question, when she was seven?" I was there, standing beside the small table in a blink, asking my father a question when he didn't have any idea who I was. "Tell me why she's disillusioned, now."

# Chapter 9

Griffin looked at me, and I knew he had foresight, even then. "I did the best I could for Ardith," he replied. "Only some things—and some people—were more important."

"I can see that, now," I told him. "And the ones not so important you walk away from, isn't that right? Even though they might deserve a little better from you. You're no different from your mother, you know that?" I was crying when I folded away, leaving Cleo and Kyler behind.

* * *

"Lady," Thurlow was inside my private study when I folded in. Well, if he didn't know before, he did now. He didn't even blink, I'll give him that. I wanted privacy so I could break down and sob at my desk. Yet here he was, wanting something.

"Mr. Burghin," I wiped my cheeks with a hand that shook. "What can I do for you?"

"I didn't know what you'd be, all those years ago. I didn't even bother to go *Looking*," Thurlow sighed. "All I knew was that Griffin had flaunted what he had, yet again. Managed to father a child—when he was supposed to be sterile. Didn't even argue that much with me, when I pointed it out to him and levied the punishment. That should have been my clue. He didn't argue very much that time, and he always argued. Pointed things out to me that I should have gone to investigate for myself." He shook his head as I stared at him in shock.

"I was so full of myself back then," Thurlow went on as I wiped tears away and gaped. "Thinking how powerful I was and how things were going so well. I picked Kiarra, you know," he laughed humorlessly. "And then set her up as First when she took care of three Ra'Ak. Griffin had been First before that, did you know? I made him Fourth after that. He was very angry and that made me happy, I think. Something that

193 "

should have been beneath me, you know. I made other mistakes, too. Was sent back to the beginning for those mistakes. I've had to work my way back to the present, as you can see. I was sent to make things right between you and me, before I can move forward and take up my old work again. I'm beginning to think that's an impossibility, Lady. Do you know what the worst part of it is?"

I stared at Thurlow Burghin, my mouth now open in surprise, I'm sure. I wanted to sob. His name wasn't Thurlow. Close, but not. He offered a crooked smile with those sensuous lips. I had no idea if those were truly his or if he'd borrowed them or made them up from nothing.

Thorsten—of the Powers that Be stood before me. If he and Griffin had both been there, I might have let loose with the biggest scream of frustration ever. I might have attempted to slap them through a wall. That wouldn't solve anything, though. Not even a little.

"I no longer use that name," he said, as he watched emotions cross my face.

"Uh-huh," I muttered, looking down at my clean desk. I found myself wishing that Grant, Heathe and Davan weren't so efficient. And then I remembered that Davan was dead.

"I had nothing to do with that, and wasn't allowed to interfere with anything other than your life and the protection of it," he said.

"So. Not going by Thorsten, then. What the hell am I supposed to call you, now?" I lifted my gaze to stare at him.

"Thurlow is acceptable. All know me by that name, this time. I inserted records into the Alliance data banks so they'd recognize me and send me to you. I send the Alliance what they need, without giving them anything important," Thurlow said. "Solar Red and Black Mist moles are hidden in the Alliance too, you know."

"That's so wonderful to hear," I muttered. "And you still haven't explained what the worst thing was—what you said before."

"Yes, the worst part of all this," Thurlow smiled crookedly. "Love has a way of twisting your heart, did you know that? I didn't—not until now. Sometimes I wonder if this isn't part of my punishment—sending me to watch out for you, when they knew I'd love you. Knowing, more than likely, that once you learned who I was before, that loving me back would be the most impossible of things. I watch you with Gavin or Gardevik or any of the others, and I want to weep because for me that will never come. I cannot feel jealousy—that is impossible. Therefore, I have to hope. A hopeless hope."

"Well, if you think for even one minute that I have anything left in me right now, then you are very wrong," I said to him. "Where were you when I was little and needing that love?"

"I didn't bother to check on you," he lowered his eyes. "I thought you'd be unremarkable. I thought Griffin had found your mother because she might be the one capable, somehow, of having his child. I wasn't thinking."

"So. An unremarkable child. That's rich," I muttered. "Is any child unremarkable? Should they be?"

"I am learning," Thurlow looked at me again. "I beg you to be patient and not to close the door on me because of past mistakes. I also beg you not to reveal to the others who I am. Kiarra and Adam have no reason to treat me with anything other than contempt."

"Yeah." Thorsten had interfered, pretty much, with their daughter Anna Kay, while she was still in the womb. Placed a

M'Fiyah with an unborn child. He'd manipulated it, instead of allowing those involved to choose. That was forbidden and he'd done it anyway. That act had damaged Anna Kay and sent her off in a bad direction when she reached adulthood.

Dragon, too, might have a few words for Thorsten—Anna Kay had been intended for him. The whole thing had turned out very badly, and Anna Kay died before she turned fifty. Bad blood and bad history. My twins had explained that story to me months ago—how Anna Kay developed jealousy and tried to kill Grace. It was a sad story for everyone involved.

"As I said, I have had to work my way back to this time. There are other obstacles to overcome." He had that right—I was one of them. "This will be a challenge for me, I know," Thurlow went on. "But I beg you not to be cruel."

"Why would I do that?" I snapped. "If I treated you like shit, I'd be you." I misted away.

* * *

*Earth*

*Merrill Leopard's Manor*

"I have a memory now that I didn't have before." Griffin paced in front of Merrill's desk. They'd been as close as brothers for nearly two thousand years. Each of them had been on both sides of that desk many times.

"What memory? How?" Merrill wasn't sure he understood.

"Of Lissa. Only this was when I was still vampire and Kyler was seven years old on Cemdris," Griffin turned troubled eyes to Merrill. "Lissa, Cleo and Kyler had come, no doubt to see Ardith, my daughter. But they came looking for me, afterward."

"And Lissa said something."

"Yes."

# Chapter 9

"What did she say?" Merrill lifted the letter opener that Lissa had given him three centuries before—a replica of a Roman sword. He'd placed it in stasis; otherwise, it would have been worn thin from handling long ago.

"She told me I was no different from my mother."

"What did you say to that?"

"Nothing—I hadn't even seen her at that time. I thought she might have been slightly insane, but hitting upon a truth that I hadn't recognized before. I am my mother's son. When the child has outgrown their usefulness to me, I walk away in favor of the next one. Until they become useful again, as in Lissa's case. She was angry with me for bringing her into the world to serve my purposes—what I'd made her for. When she didn't show any signs of forgiveness quickly and Amara became pregnant, well, that was the time to dump my unforgiving daughter, wasn't it?"

"Brother," Merrill sighed, "it is one thing to choose sacrifice for yourself. It is something completely different to sacrifice others. I could not have sacrificed my children. If I'd treated Franklin or Jeffrey that way, I would have no hope of ever winning their trust again. I think Lissa will be watching you from now on, expecting the next betrayal."

"I know. I have been thinking a great deal about my mother in the past few hours. I expected the same from her, after a while. She drove every bit of love I had for her away with mistreatment and betrayal, culminating in what I thought to be the worst of all of it—when she drove me away from camp at age sixteen. That is nothing compared to what I've put Lissa through. She's right—I'm no different from Narissa."

# Blood War

"I believe you love your son." Merrill watched Griffin, who came to stand next to the window, staring over the moonlit lawn outside.

"I do." Griffin sighed. "I didn't see him. Never thought to *Look*. Lissa gave him to us, albeit unintentionally. My other children and grandchildren have been female. This is my son."

"So, you think you'll find it more difficult to mistreat your son than it has been to mistreat your daughters and granddaughters?" Merrill knew there was a sadness in Kyler that might never go away.

"I manipulated their births, so things would go as I planned. Wyatt wasn't planned."

"That's the difference? That's the excuse you use?" Merrill hadn't called Griffin out on this before, but he failed to understand things the way they were now.

"Lissa won't ever trust me. I've seen to that."

"That's an excuse to be cruel?"

"No, not an excuse, period."

"Well, your daughter and granddaughters went into to the past. I think it's time we did the same." Merrill rose from his chair behind the desk.

"Where are we going?"

"To see Lissa," Merrill said, and bent time and folded space.

"Oh, no." Griffin didn't want to see this, but it was where Merrill had taken him. A small figure lay in a hospital bed in intensive care, her head swathed in bandages and casts on both arms that lay upon the bed. A breathing tube had been inserted and the visible portion of the face was a mass of black and purple.

"Her mother's funeral is being held right now," Merrill sighed as he and Griffin stood at the end of the bed. "I thought about taking you to watch her stepfather do this to her, but even I can't stand by and watch that."

"Are you members of the family?" A nurse walked in, her voice curt as she asked the question.

"I am her father," Griffin's voice held pain.

"The one who did this to her?" The nurse was prepared to call for security.

"No, that one is in jail. He is only her stepfather. I'm her biological father." Griffin's words caused the nurse to snort.

"Where the hell were you, when this was going on?" she huffed.

"Missing in action," Merrill made the reply for Griffin. The nurse nodded; the handsome, black-haired man might convince her of anything.

"We'd like a moment, and you'll forget you ever saw us," Merrill laid compulsion. The nurse left the room without a word.

"This makes it real, doesn't it?" Merrill said softly to Griffin, who stood and stared as the machine forced air into Lissa's lungs. "And the worst part of it is we have to stand here and look at this, knowing there isn't a single thing we can do about it. Not one damn thing to ease the suffering. What do you think that was like for her, brother? To stand there and watch your mother get beaten to death, and then to take the beating yourself?" Merrill shook his head.

"I know you were tortured there at the end on Cemdris, but that was only a matter of weeks. Nineteen years it was, for your little girl. You took me to see Kiarra first, because you knew I'd focus my obsession on her and turn Lissa down later, sight unseen. You were the one to tell me I'd have a M'Fiyah with Lissa, after Wlodek asked me to teach her. You knew I'd ask you to remove the M'Fiyah without seeing her."

"Merrill, don't do this to me."

"You saw all of this, didn't you? Only you knew I'd fight you if Lissa was mine and you treated her this way."

"I don't want to lose what we have. We've been brothers all these years," Griffin begged.

"Griffin, how would you feel if that were Wyatt? Or Amara?" Merrill flung a hand toward the hospital bed. "Or do Lissa and your granddaughters mean so little to you?" Merrill went to the bed and lightly brushed fingers against one of Lissa's hands. "It's Daddy Merrill, sweetheart," he whispered. "Everything is going to be all right." Merrill turned back to Griffin. "If you had told me, brother, when it was time, it would have been easy enough for me to come and make the turn instead of that half-wit rogue, Sergio."

Griffin sat down heavily in the only chair inside the room and wiped his face with a hand. "Things wouldn't have turned out the same, would they, Griffin?" Belen appeared inside the room. "Our Lissa still had to be knocked around and Merrill, as her true sire and lover would never have allowed it. I'm not arguing with the outcome, only the methods," Belen held up a hand. "Don't you think it's time for a little support from her father?"

"She hates me," Griffin muttered. "I brought harm to her and to Roff."

"Yes—the innocent in all this," Belen nodded at the mention of Roff's name. "It is one thing to use your daughter and granddaughters, but another to deliberately bring harm to such as Roff, or his son. You took his memories, Griffin, and now his son is a stranger to him. What do you think your punishment should be?" Griffin lifted his face to the Nameless One.

# Chapter 9

"I don't know," Griffin turned away—he couldn't face the accusation in Belen's eyes.

"I am taking Wyatt's immortality," Belen said. "That is your punishment. If he gains it back, he will have to earn it."

"No," Griffin whispered as Belen disappeared.

# Chapter 10

*L*e-Ath Veronis
*Lissa*

Henri, Gervais, Robert and Albert stood before me. "Thank you for coming," I said. "We have three rogues out there somewhere, and I intend to track them down. I'd like your help doing it."

I'd sent for the misters and mindspeakers, who now worked for Flavio in the city guard. "If you agree to go," I told Henri and Gervais, "I now have the ability to pass on my misting talents—of turning to mist immediately. Would you like that?" It still took two minutes for them to go to mist, so it remained a weapon of stealth for them. I could change that, if I wanted.

"Lissa, that would be extraordinary and more than we deserve," Henri offered a polite bow.

# Blood War

"You know not to do that," I gave him the best smile I could, although it felt weak and watery. I was determined to get the last of Davan's killers, and doing something about it myself was probably better than sitting on top of my palace dome and crying my eyes out.

"I want Robert and Albert with me," I said. "But I want you two to go with me as mist. Take those bastards out as quickly as you can—you'll be able to form hands and claws only, if you want."

"I'm ready," Gervais agreed immediately. Henri had already decided. I put my hands on both of them; afterward they experimented, turning to mist in a blink and then coming back to corporeality.

"That worked," I patted their shoulders. "Let's go, before my palace guard and my army find out what we're doing." I folded them away.

When we found them, the three rogues had almost reached Casino City. They were bent on grabbing hostages and causing general mayhem as they attempted to get away from Le-Ath Veronis. They were about to get a surprise.

Lissia was the only city on Le-Ath Veronis surrounded by a wall; there was no wall around Casino City and our three rogues were about to reach the shops and eateries on the outskirts.

It was an easy place to grab hostages, I knew, and if they touched any of my comesuli, I'd kill them myself. I didn't have to, though; we were hovering over them as mist. I dropped Robert and Albert first, and as soon as they started fighting with the rogues, I released my misters, who performed above expectations. The rogues never expected to have their heads removed from behind while Robert and Albert distracted them by attacking in a frontal assault.

# Chapter 10

"Nice work," I commended my small vampire army, appearing beside them. Robert had a torn sleeve, but that was all. The dead vampires, now turning to ash, hadn't had much fighting experience, I could tell.

"Lissa, would you like to explain to us exactly what it is that you're doing?" Gavin demanded. Gavin, Tony, Winkler, Drake and Drew showed up after half a minute had passed.

While they were busy glaring at me, Garde, Karzac and Erland arrived. I think Connegar and Reemagar came in after that just to referee, if needed. Gavin looked angry enough to chew nails and spit tacks, so I was glad to have Larentii backup. I'd sneaked out of the palace without telling anyone so I could track the rogues. I didn't want multiple arguments with my mates, first.

"Robert and Albert took care of things initially, allowing Henri and Gervaise to take heads from behind," I said. "I was never involved." Gavin, arms crossed tightly over his chest, wasn't convinced.

"There's something else," Erland said. "You must come back to the palace with us immediately."

"What is it?" I turned to him. Erland looked worried.

"Lissy, your dad and stepmother are at the palace, and your stepmother is about to have a meltdown," Tony said. "That's the only reason we started looking for you, and we had to ask Reemagar to track you down since you went AWOL and we couldn't find you."

"Oh, lord, what's wrong?" I asked, beginning to get shivery and sick to my stomach.

"You must come, little mate," Connegar said. "It concerns your brother."

"Oh, no," I muttered, too terrified to *Look*.

"Kiarra, Adam, Merrill, Pheligar, Flavio and Kyler have also come, and Cleo is on her way with Rhett and Harvel, I think," Winkler added. Well, this was looking worse by the minute.

"Let's go," I said, trying to keep the quaver from my voice. "Robert, Albert, thank you. Same to you, Henri and Gervaise." I wanted them to know how much I appreciated their help.

I think the Larentii folded us back to the palace. I nearly breathed a sigh of relief when I saw Wyatt in Amara's arms, but that relief was a bit premature. Wylend folded in and he wasn't happy, I could tell that right away.

"What the blazes do you mean, his immortality has been removed?" Wylend thundered.

*Oh, dear God.*

"Belen handed out punishment for Griffin's premeditated mistreatment of Roff and Toff," Kiarra was at my side immediately.

"There is only one way out of this," Belen appeared in a flash of light. He had everybody's attention immediately. Thurlow had slipped in, and I hadn't seen him enter the room in a conventional way. Using a bit of his power, now, I suspected.

"And what is that?" Wylend forced himself to be respectful to Belen. Belen was the one who'd removed his heir's immortality, after all.

"Lissa has the power to restore Wyatt's immortality or allow the sentence to go forward," Belen said. "If the sentence is allowed to stand, Wyatt will either have to earn his immortality or die after a normal lifespan. If an accident does not take him first."

I was looking from my father to Amara to Belen. Griffin refused to meet my gaze; Amara's dark eyes were begging me silently for a reprieve. "Get Roff for me, please," I sighed. A few minutes passed while Winkler went to fetch Roff.

"Roff, honey," I said when he came to stand beside me, "I need your help. Belen here removed Wyatt's immortality, as Griffin's punishment for taking your memories and for setting Toff up to be kidnapped. Belen says I have the power to restore Wyatt's immortality, if I want. Otherwise, he'll either have to earn the immortality back or die as he normally would."

Roff was now staring at Griffin, his face set. He was learning that his memories had been deliberately removed, rather than having lost them after the attempts on his life. "You took away the memories of my children, and my love for Lissa," Roff rustled his wings. He was beautiful and angry at the same moment.

"I have no excuse," Griffin muttered. He wasn't able to look at Roff. Amara wept and Wyatt began to snuffle.

"My anger is directed at you, father of Lissa. You have not treated your child well at all. Have you?" Roff was coming into his own—I hadn't failed to see it these past few weeks. Amara sobbed.

"I have no anger for your mate, or your youngest child," Roff went on. "It appears that they stand to be harmed the most by this. If Lissa wishes, I will not stop her from reversing the judgment." Roff had gone to stand in front of Griffin, handing my father a hard stare.

"Whatever she decides, Griffin," Merrill spoke up, "our relationship as it was is at an end." I blinked at Merrill—he was handing out a judgment of his own, it appeared. His handsome face was set and he was angry. "I thought of you as a brother for so long. Thought you were providing assistance or favors because you cared for me in that way. I see now it was all a lie." Merrill disappeared in a blink.

# Blood War

The silence that came after Merrill's announcement was profound. Griffin hung his head—I knew he truly thought of Merrill as a brother and somehow, he'd managed to fuck that up, too.

"Well, then," I said. "Well." I glanced at Thurlow, who stood against a back wall. Rigo had come in quietly and now leaned against a wall nearby. Garde, Shadow and Kifirin had also come. "Before I give my decision, I want to talk about pain," I sighed, turning back to Griffin. "Pain we inflict on others or they inflict on us, intentionally or not. I think all of us here have had a little of that, from time to time. Some more than others."

I focused for a moment on my nieces, Cleo and Kyler. Kyler nodded slightly, as did Cleo. "I think I can speak for my nieces as well as myself, regarding this matter," I went on. "Whenever I've seen a child suffer, after suffering myself, well, I always wanted to take that suffering away. Speaking from experience, I know just how devastating it can be. When I was small and lying in my bed at night, in pain after being beaten by a jealous, sadistic man, I wished that someone would come and take me away from him. My mother was too weak and frightened to do it, so she and I both suffered. Griffin," I turned to my father. He looked up at me, finally.

"Do not make me regret doing this. Bear in mind that I'm doing this mostly for Wyatt and Amara. Least of all for you. Even though you've walked away from me, taken from me and mistreated those I love, you are still my father and I can't bear to see you suffer."

I dropped my corporeal body and gathered power around me, pulling it in until I was shining too brightly even for my overly large ballroom to contain. I loosed my power, then, giving Wyatt back what had been taken away. I could have

# Chapter 10

been vindictive and made Griffin suffer for his interference. I'd had enough of suffering, I think. I was learning, too. Griffin might not be able to blindside me again. Ever.

Amara was still crying, but these were tears of joy, now. Griffin had the oddest look on his face but no words, for either Roff or me. "Honey, let's get out of here," I took Roff's hand and folded away.

* * *

"Brother, your daughter is better than you," Jeral informed Griffin and folded away.

"My heir is immortal again?" Wylend wanted to make sure and attempted to lift Wyatt from Amara's arms. She allowed it. Wylend checked the baby over himself, grunting with satisfaction after a few moments.

Belen came to stand before Griffin. "I am still passing judgment upon you," he informed Griffin. "From this time forward, you will be unable to *Look* into Wyatt's future. You are blinded to his life path. I do this in retribution for your treatment of Lissa and Roff. As for Toff, you must find a way to compensate him. I will be watching and waiting to make sure this is accomplished. If you have not discovered it for yourself, yet, know now that your daughter will sacrifice herself before she will sacrifice any other. You should know that about her already, as any father should." Belen folded away.

* * *

"Lissa, where are we?" Roff hadn't ever been to the cemetery where Don's body was buried. He'd been close by— in Oklahoma City, but never here.

"This is where my first husband was buried," I said, leading him toward Don's grave. I was shocked to find not only that my name was listed on the other side of the double headstone, but a date of death as well; it corresponded to the day Griffin had taken me into the future.

I learned that Winkler, Weldon and Bill Jennings had done this. On my side, too, was an inscription—part of a quote from Theodore Roosevelt. It read, *Far better is it to dare mighty things.*

"My father was buried on Kifirin," Roff said, tucking his wings tightly against his body as we stared at the gravesite. After three hundred years, the stone was worn but the inscriptions could still be read.

"Would you like to go there?" I asked, turning to Roff. "Where is your father buried?"

"I took his ashes to Baetrah, when I was pregnant with Toff," Roff said softly. "He died shortly before my two-month came. I decided to visit the volcano then, leave his ashes there and ask Kifirin to take us to Le-Ath Veronis."

The two-month that Roff spoke of was the two months that every comesula was granted at the end of their pregnancy, so they wouldn't have to work before their child came. They were subsidized by the crown on Kifirin, if necessary—one of the few benefits they actually received.

"Well, let's go, then, but first let's get some flowers." We found a flower shop on Kifirin and I *Pulled* in a few gold coins to pay for the bouquet Roff selected. I then folded Roff to Baetrah an Hafei, the city below the volcano on Kifirin. We were joined by Kifirin as we began the long walk up the volcano's side.

"Here to ask the god for a favor?" He was smiling at me.

"Hi, honey. We're here to leave these flowers for Roff's father," I said.

"Then I will come with you," he said. We walked up a well-worn path that switched back often to make the climb easier. "Roff, did you make this climb while you were pregnant?" The path was quite steep in places.

"I did. Many pregnant comesuli came, to ask Kifirin for favors of this kind or that," Roff smiled. "Mine was granted."

"Lissa had much more to do with that than I," Kifirin said. We reached the top after a while. Baetrah was mostly dormant at the moment, with only a bit of steam and smoke coming from the center of the large caldera.

"Where would you like to drop these, Roff?" I asked, pointing to the flowers in his arms.

"In the center, there, if possible," he said.

"Of course it's possible," I told him, and turned us both to mist. We allowed the flowers to drop away beneath us once we were over the right spot, and watched as a tiny tongue of flame consumed them when they fell. Roff and I misted back to Kifirin's side after that.

"Do you have a wish, Avilepha?" Kifirin folded his arms around me.

"Nothing that can be granted," I sighed.

* * *

*Le-Ath Veronis*

"You're telling me that one of those three scum is related to the royal family on Twylec?" Garde was angry and let everybody know it. Aurelius wasn't pleased; neither was Flavio, Gavin or the others.

One of the three humanoids they'd captured at the casino—the ones behind the attack at New Hesperia—was a cousin to the Queen of Twylec and she demanded that he be returned to her.

After being given diplomatic immunity, of course.

"We have a confession, and she's still asking for this?" Tony fumed. Gavin was stone-faced and angry. Drake and

Drew were having a furious mental conversation with their father. Winkler sat at the opposite end of the conference table from Gardevik—if the High Demon went Thifilathi, Winkler didn't want to be anywhere near it. He was all for providing some sort of accident in the dungeon, but as a member of the Saa Thalarr, he couldn't be involved.

"What is the Alliance's stance on this?" Aryn had come and was now asking Thurlow for a ruling.

"It is never a good idea to damage relationships between worlds," Thurlow's words were ambiguous. "The Five-Year Conclave is approaching and we have not had the opportunity to gather allies. As the newest member of the Alliance, Le-Ath Veronis is in the minority and vulnerable."

"Fuck the Conclave," Garde growled.

"The Conclave is next month. Perhaps other arrangements may be made." Rigo had been patiently standing in a corner, listening to the debate.

"What other arrangements?" Gavin had been keeping his eye on Rigo. The vampire took his word seriously.

"It will involve some trust on your part. We will make arrangements to ship him to Twylec, with the royal blessing. And then," Rigo paused for a moment, "nature will take its course."

Garde stared at the vampire. Lissa had told him that Rigo, once Rigovarnus I, was eleven thousand years old and a King on Hraede before the turn. Now, he and five other vampires watched over the crown on Hraede, providing careful guidance and subtle interference when necessary. Hraede was stable and prosperous as a result—notoriously so.

"I am inclined to offer that trust," Gavin nodded to Rigo. Garde almost stopped in his tracks—Gavin would never trust lightly. Ever.

# Chapter 10

"Then I will go with Gavin's judgment and trust," Garde nodded.

"We trust this will not go straight to the Alliance?" Drake and Drew folded to either side of Thurlow, pointing their question at him. He was obligated, after all, to send regular reports to the Defense Minister.

"I hope I can earn your trust as well," he said. "My allegiance is with the Queen."

"Very good," Drake said. "Do not betray that trust, or place Lissa in danger."

"No fear, young Falchani," Thurlow replied with a nod.

"Do you need help?" Erland sidled up to Rigo.

"Perhaps, Warlock," Rigo smiled slightly at Erland. "I haven't failed to notice from the vid feeds that some of the enemy either disappeared recently or were found dead by an unseen hand."

"Maybe three hundred or so," Erland offered one of his best, heart-stopping smiles.

"Impressive," Rigo nodded respectfully to Erland. "And many from the highest echelons. Such a shame. Shall we pay a visit to Satris of Twylec, who languishes in his dungeon cell?"

"I will come as well," Aryn walked over. He'd heard the exchange between Rigo and Erland. He had no qualms about getting involved with this.

"We'll let you place compulsion," Erland grinned and folded them to the dungeon.

* * *

"What are you doing?" Satris of Twylec stood quickly. Three had appeared inside his cell as if by magic.

"Just wanted to offer a pat on the back for convincing your cousin, Queen Tamaritha, that your sorry skin is worth saving," Erland smiled. "Rigo." Erland turned to the ancient vampire.

"This won't hurt—but it may sting a little," Rigo tapped Satris' neck with the small needle he held.

"What in the name of the light was that?" Satris barely felt the prick but he rubbed the side of his neck anyway.

"Your death," Rigo's voice was even and practical. "And from now on, you'll believe you never saw us and that a spider bit you on the journey homeward."

Satris blinked in confusion as all three men disappeared as quickly as they'd appeared in the beginning.

* * *

*Lissa*

"So, not only do I have to go to the Conclave, we have to let Satris go because he's related to the Queen of Twylec?" My head hurt. Gavin, Tony, Drake and Drew had come to give me unwelcome news.

"That pretty much sums it up," Tony agreed. "But that's only one of them. You still have the other two, plus Geratt." I was aware of that—the trials were scheduled for the following day.

"When are we shipping him off?" I asked.

"Today. He should be at the spaceport now."

"I trust he's been cautioned not to cause additional trouble until he gets to Twylec?"

"Oh, no worries," Tony replied. I looked at Gavin, who merely shrugged.

"We have interviews this afternoon, for assassins," Tony reminded me. That was something I didn't particularly want to be reminded of. I'd been an idealistic fool—thinking there would never be a reason to execute anyone on Le-Ath Veronis. Trevor had come to take heads from the ones who'd sided with

214

# Chapter 10

the rogues inside my Council chambers, but he only did it as a favor to me. He preferred what he was doing now—working as Sheriff of Casino City.

Jeral came in and sat with Flavio, Kifirin, Aurelius, Garde, Aryn and me as we brought in the applicants for the two assassin/executioner positions. Of those we interviewed, one was from Beliphar, Jeral's homeworld, and I liked him very much. My goal was to find two like Gavin and Trevor. Trevor was tired of taking heads. I could understand that. Gavin wouldn't even consider it unless I asked—he was done with that part of his life.

Aryn was a King Vampire. I wondered if he even knew it. His compulsions were nearly as effective as anything Merrill could do and he employed that talent during the interviews.

We had two assassins before the afternoon was over, too. Garde and Aurelius asked most of the questions, with Flavio and Aryn chiming in from time to time. We wanted to make sure the vampires didn't want to kill merely for the sake of killing—that they would be swift and merciful when the heads were taken.

Kifirin gave final approval on both, and they were in accord with my choices. Learand from Beliphar and Dawes from Tulgalan were selected. They were assigned rooms at the palace—suites above the dungeons, actually—and a salary was established for both, plus other benefits and privileges. "Learand was a very good choice," Jeral told me later over a cup of tea in the kitchen.

"I think so, too, Uncle," I said, giving him a smile. It hadn't been long since Davan died, and it was difficult working with Grant and Heathe—all three of us moped around my study at times.

"I think that is the first time you've called me that," he smiled back at me.

"I'm only saying it because I mean it," I told him.

"I never thought to have a niece, or any family member," he replied. "And the opportunity to have tea with my niece is even more gratifying."

"I was hoping I'd find you together," Conner appeared beside us. I hadn't seen Conner for a while. I saw Russell, Will, Martin and Lynx often, but not Conner, even though Connegar was her son.

She was tastefully dressed, as always, and her long blonde hair was pulled back and clipped. Conner always looked as if she belonged on the pages of a magazine, she was so careful about her appearance. Russell, Will and Martin doted on her. Lynx was very protective and Graegar, well, he and Barrigar loved her more than anything.

"Lady," Jeral dipped his head to the Guardian. Conner gave me a hug.

"I have a message for Jeral, Grant, Heathe and you," she informed me. Conner escorted souls to the other side at times, and she was asked to deliver messages by those souls, now and then. I never thought to be on the receiving end of one, however.

"Grant and Heathe are in my study," I said. Conner's appearance meant Davan had left a message for us. I wanted to cry.

"We'll go to your study, then," Conner agreed. We walked—I wasn't in a hurry to hear this—it was tears waiting to come. Jeral placed an arm about my shoulders as we walked. I looked up at my uncle—he resembled his mother, Narissa, and my nieces, with darker hair and gold-flecked eyes. I didn't see much of Griffin in his face, but then Wylend Arden hadn't been his father.

"Grant, Heathe, this is Conner," I introduced her when we walked into my study. My two remaining assistants were going through stacks of mail. Today was the day for that, this week.

Conner was good—I'll give her that. She got us seated and comfortable before explaining to Grant and Heathe what she was and what she could do. They were shocked, I think, and shocking vampires is pretty tough to do, most of the time.

The message presented was a three-dimensional image, almost, much like a video or a live presentation, as Conner played the memory back to us when she'd taken Davan to the gate.

He was there, looking happy. I didn't expect that—he was happy. "I want you to take a message to my friends," he said. I wanted to weep at the sound of his voice. Jeral grasped my hand in his. "I want you to tell them what I see," Davan said. "I see a beautiful meadow in bright sunlight, with flowers everywhere. People are here, waiting for me. I know them. All of them, somehow, even though we haven't met. I feel happy and I can't explain it. Tell my brother Jeral that I don't regret what he did for me. Tell Heathe and Grant that I never thought to find such good friends. Tell them I love them. Tell Lissa that she shines like the sun, even in my memory of her. Nothing is forever, except the soul and love. Tell Lissa that for me." He turned away, then, fading into something we couldn't see.

I sobbed in Jeral's arms; he was brushing away tears, too.

"Lissa, I hate to interrupt," Thurlow appeared inside my study. Well, there wasn't any other way he could have just shown up as he did—the study door was closed and locked. He'd folded in. Conner didn't even blink.

# Blood War

"What is it, Thurlow?" My voice wasn't steady.

"The Ra'Ak have brought an army of spawn and are attacking your shield on Vionn. They intend to kill the Green Fae and the others inside the curtain."

There's nothing like fear and desperation to toss you right out of a grief session. Jeral was up and ready, too, the moment he heard the word spawn. Either he or Conner sent out the message; I had an army of my own at my back when I set out for Vionn.

Toff was there. Maybe they'd planned this—knew I'd come to protect that baby, if nothing else. Thurlow was coming with us, I noticed, and Kifirin folded in, bringing Aryn and Rigo. I sure hoped it was night there, otherwise Rigo might fry and I sure didn't want that to happen. "Let's go," I said, and folded all of us away.

Spawn had just broken through the shield when I arrived with my hastily formed military might. Eight Ra'Ak were there, driving spawn through the hole in my shield. They'd been the ones to destroy the barrier, and had used considerable power to do it. A ninth Ra'Ak, still in humanoid form, stood nearby, watching.

Saa Thalarr and Spawn Hunters went to work, challenging Ra'Ak and taking out what looked to be twenty thousand spawn pouring through a hole in my shield. All of them were heading toward the Green Fae's first valley as quickly as they could get there.

Dragon had come, as had Crane. Dragon went to his avatar immediately, preparing to wage war. Crane's giant Wyroc screamed a battle cry and engaged the first Ra'Ak he found. Drake and Drew, my twins, were also in Dragon form and fighting Ra'Ak. Radomir arrived and hit the ground as a giant Black Tiger, taking on one of two remaining Ra'Ak. My

# Chapter 10

focus was on the one still in humanoid shape. I decided to have a parlay with him. First, he wouldn't expect it, and second, I figured all my mates, Kifirin included, were going to be mighty pissed if I told them before I did it.

"Perhaps I should have just gone to kill the Pelipu, rather than letting one of your cousins have him for dinner," I said amiably, misting right in front of the humanoid Ra'Ak.

He hid his surprise well; I'll give him that. "But you failed to do so," he said. "I hear he was quite tasty—just the right amount of fat, as you might imagine. You are a bit thin but still quite tender, I'd wager." He grinned. I was about to be dinner, too, if this creep had anything to say about it.

"I'll fight the whole way down," I warned him. Yeah, I was watching to make sure he didn't turn scaly and coppery. Ra'Ak can eat somebody for lunch pretty quick.

"We haven't had a Saa Thalarr as a meal in a very long time," he went on. He was watching my every move, just as I was watching his.

"And you still won't get one," I said. "Not if I have anything to say about it."

"But I intend to have you as a meal," he went on, trying to mesmerize me with his eyes and voice, somehow. Too bad he didn't know that wouldn't work. I heard sounds of fighting and shouting behind me, but I ignored it for the moment.

"And you still won't get a Saa Thalarr, even if you manage to make a meal out of me," I said. "I'm not one of them."

"Then what are you?" He was stepping up the mesmerizing—it vibrated about him, much like the feeling you get while standing next to giant speakers. Still, whatever he was doing wasn't working, although he expected it to. I smelled the confusion around him because of it.

"Justice," I answered his question. "Have you heard of me?"

"No. Should I?"

"Let me guess—you were one of those flunkies hiding in the void, weren't you?" I asked.

"Not a flunky—they answered to me," he replied. He wasn't that remarkable, in looks, anyway. Brown hair, brown eyes, medium looks, medium height, medium build. That whole boom-box compulsion thing, though, that was something. It sounded as though he were used to being obeyed.

"You gonna have a tantrum if you don't get your way?" I queried.

"I will take this world apart, if things go badly for my servants." He jerked his head toward the battle going on behind me.

"Well, that's too bad," I said. I wasn't about to waste any more time talking him; not if he planned to use his Ra'Ak power to blast the planet. I disappeared in front of him, which didn't cause much of a stir, actually. He should have paid more attention to his history and pondered why a whole bunch of Ra'Ak had died on Kifirin not long ago. His head exploded, just as anybody else's might, when I misted inside it and blew myself outward.

Dragon and Crane had taken down their targets, Radomir had gotten his and Drake and Drew, in Dragon form, were chasing after the last Ra'Ak, after dispatching two others. This one was snapping and snarling at them as they chased him across a wide field. I'd never seen my twins' Dragons before; they were impressive—Drew's was silver, Drake's black.

*Want me to take care of that?* I sent.

# Chapter 10

*And spoil all our fun?* Drake sent back.

*Don't have too much fun; I don't want to watch Karzac put you in a healing sleep because you were dumb enough to get scale poison or something,* I grumped.

*Message received,* Drew replied and went on the offensive. The Ra'Ak was beheaded by massive jaws in less than a blink and everybody ducked for the inevitable dusting of Ra'Ak chunks. Now, it was down to the spawn; what remained of them, anyway. They were still running toward the valley where the Green Fae lived as fast as they could get there.

Spawn hunters were chasing after them; wolves, vampires—all were taking out spawn as quickly as they could catch them. Even one escaped spawn could destroy life on Vionn with a simple bite, and Toff was out there. Well, there was a solution to this and I was about to exercise my options.

*Sorry,* I sent to the Green Fae, *but the Ra'Ak know you're here, now, and they likely know you have my child. That means you can't stay.* I misted toward them swiftly, had all three thousand of them, including their half-Fae children and the Vionn who'd chosen to live alongside them, gathered and transported to Le-Ath Veronis in only a few seconds.

* * *

"I know these aren't your mountains and valleys," I said to Tiearan as he, the Green Fae and humanoid and half-humanoid alike blinked in shock at their new surroundings. "But it's the best I can do on short notice."

I'd set them down in an area just east of the last comesuli settlements and farms. The land there consisted of gently rolling hills, a river and a few streams and ponds. Plenty of ground, if you wanted to farm or raise animals.

The Green Fae didn't consume meat, but their humanoid neighbors did. They liked their milk, cheese and eggs, too, so they had cows, chickens and goats. I'd brought their animals with them; I just couldn't uproot trees or plants. They'd have to start over with those, but the comesuli could provide seeds, cuttings and the like.

"We were prepared; one of ours saw this," Tiearan admitted, refusing to look at me. "We have seeds and such with us."

Well, weren't we efficient? I looked up and saw Green Fae, their half-Fae children and the humanoids, all with pouches, bags and bundles. Crates, barrels and other things littered the ground.

"Doesn't sound like you're all that upset over it," I muttered.

"We have moved many times. Our seer predicts that the only reason we will leave this world is if we wish to. That is a blessing to us."

"Uh-huh." I was busy searching through the gathered people, trying to get a glimpse of Redbird and little Toff.

"She does not like being summoned, but she is bringing him," Tiearan murmured. "The child will still not come to you."

"Well, thanks for rubbing it in," I grumped.

"I did not mean it to harm or upset," Tiearan sighed. I wanted to ask him what he did mean, but held off. Redbird showed up, coming to stand next to her father. She didn't meet my eyes, but Toff was in her arms. At least he looked healthy and well-fed.

"We are again in your debt," Tiearan didn't sound happy. "And I find myself in need of asking you another favor."

"And what would that be?" I asked. "If it's to kidnap and mindmeld more comesuli children, I'll have your asses off this planet so fast your head will spin."

# Chapter 10

"We have already passed new laws to add to the old ones, so this will not happen again." Well, it was too bad they hadn't thought about that before they turned to kidnapping in the first place.

"I understand your thoughts on this, and it is unfortunate," Tiearan observed.

"You know, I think I'll send some of the older Larentii to you, and you can all sit down and talk logic while leaving the emotional side out of everything," I grumped. "What do you want, Tiearan?"

"Indis-Banuu," he reverently whispered the word.

"That stuff?" Surnath had given permission for me to take as much as I wanted. The crystal covered farmland everywhere and they were happy to get rid of it. "I'll be right back," I said, and folded to Surnath.

I was back in less than ten minutes with a thousand pounds of crystal, which I dumped right in front of Tiearan. "That enough?" I asked. "I can get more if you want. Also, just as a warning, it stays daylight here twenty-four out of the twenty-eight hours every day. I'll have someone come to put up homes and anything else you need. If you're done taunting me with my own child," I said, "I'll go now." I folded away, afraid that I'd become more angry and upset if I stayed.

* * *

"Your daughter has made a grievous mistake." The Green Fae seer came to stand next to Tiearan.

"You have already informed me, seer," Tiearan replied gruffly.

"It bears restating, as you cannot seem to control her," the seer replied.

<h1 style="text-align:center">Chapter 11</h1>

*Le-Ath Veronis*
*Lissa*

"What happened?" I asked, immediately concerned. Jeral was getting attention from Shane and Franklin, and that meant he was wounded. I'd folded back to the palace kitchen to get something to drink. Everybody else seemed to be there, too.

"Do not fear, child, it was a scratch and these two are taking good care of it," Jeral said, lifting my fingers with an uninjured hand and kissing them. I'd reached out to touch his shoulder—I wasn't ready to lose my other uncle. Jeral was reassuring me—he could see the worry in my eyes.

"Frank, you doin' all right?" I asked, shaking off my fear and doing my best to focus on Jeral's healing. Franklin and Shane were patching up a gash on Jeral's arm.

225

"I'm good. I hear that Oklahoma accent in your voice, little girl," Franklin replied. He looked so much like Merrill, with his black hair ruffled a bit and his piercing blue eyes focused on Jeral's wound. It made my heart hurt to look at him.

"The accent can't be helped sometimes," I muttered.

"I have never been to Earth," Jeral smiled. "It is a nice accent."

"I'll take you, sometime, and we'll get a chicken-fried steak," I said.

"I'll come," Winkler was ready to go right then. "Can we go back to that place you took me, all those years ago?"

"If you want to," I shrugged.

"I want to." Winkler came over to give me a hug. Yeah, I like my wolf.

"Thanks," I said. "Roff and I went by Don's grave. We saw what you, Weldon and Bill did."

"Lissa, I don't want to ever feel like that again," he hugged me tighter.

"Huh. I don't want to see your wolf inside a box, no matter how fancy it is," I grumped right back.

"I hear we need to put up some housing for Green Fae," Adam, Merrill and Pheligar folded in.

"Yeah." My voice was loaded with sarcasm.

"I'll come with you," Winkler offered. Therefore, it was only fair that my entire entourage went, including Rigo. I had to go *Looking* to determine that Thurlow had accomplished this somehow—Rigo could now walk in daylight if he wanted. I made a mental note to have a little talk with Thurlow—just not now. He came along, too.

"I do not wish to be left behind." Roff had come in and he was a little miffed, I think, that he couldn't go fight spawn with the rest of them. I wondered how his fighting lessons were coming along—Gavin and Tony were teaching him those skills. Rigo had come back from Vionn without a scratch—he was some kind of fighter, I guess.

"I won't leave you behind, honey." I smiled at my winged vampire. He smiled at me over Joey's head; Joey was tending to a slight scale poison on Radomir's arm.

* * *

"How many homes do you need, and what sort of amenities?" Adam asked Tiearan. He had a makeshift table with a rolled-out sheet of paper, complete with plans for a village on it.

We ended up with the humanoids on the eastern edge, the half-humanoid in the middle and the Fae on the western side. All had room to grow. Pheligar laid the pipelines for the water supply and each house was hooked up with solar power—all of it run with more crystal—what the Green Fae called Indis-Banuu. Well, they had plenty, now.

"You're welcome to trade with the comesuli, if you want," I informed Tiearan. He was quite surprised that we were willing to put up their village for them. They thought they'd have to start from scratch. Instead, they watched in amazement as buildings went up in very little time, courtesy of the power wielded by the Larentii and Saa Thalarr. Pheligar and Adam put up barns and fences for the animals, too.

Tiearan stopped me before we left them to settle in. "We do not like being indebted," he said.

"Do you know what a true gift is?" I asked him, looking into his leaf-green eyes. I figured he was thousands of years old, but I didn't have a gauge yet on Green Fae scents.

"What is this of which you speak?" He was curious, now.

"A true gift," I said. "A lot of gifts are given because the giver is obligated, somehow, or they expect something in return. A true gift is one freely given, with no expectations or conditions. That is what this is," I flung out a hand toward the newly erected village. "You are free to do with it as you will. This is yours, now. I know you will respect the land—I saw what you did on Vionn." I'd seen Redbird in the distance, leading Toff around—he was trotting happily behind her, his chubby fists filled with wildflowers. Roff still didn't recognize his child and I wasn't going to open that wound right then.

Tiearan was staring at Roff, who was helping Green Fae herd cattle into a fenced enclosure. "That one has wings," he said, surprised.

"That one is Toff's father," I looked Tiearan in the eye. "And if you hadn't stolen Toff, he would be the same—a rare, winged vampire one day. Only your daughter managed to fuck that up, didn't she?"

"She will treat the child well."

"Honey," I poked Tiearan in the chest, and he backed up a little, "I would treat that child well. Did treat that child well, as did many others who loved him. Your daughter took what wasn't hers to take. I saw her—scented her—when she brought Toff in after doing what she did to him. She's a spoiled little bitch, Tiearan. Is that your fault, or somebody else's?"

"I did not wish to instigate a confrontation." He held up both hands.

"Then learn some fucking manners," I muttered.

"Tiearan, perhaps someone else should interact with the Queen." A new Green Fae stood next to Tiearan, now.

"You are?" I had arms crossed over my chest, trying hard not to let my anger take control.

# Chapter 11

"Zervias, lady," he nodded to me. "I am the seer for this tribe. I attempted to tell them not to take the child, but they were desperate and ignored me."

"Do you hand out bad advice?" I asked him.

"Not as a rule, lady."

"Then why weren't they listening to you?"

"Some are headstrong, and want what they shouldn't."

"I can see that." I was still glaring at Tiearan.

"It was my idea—the kidnapping," the female called Rain came forward. "So now I am without my child, when it was Corent I was trying to keep by my side."

"He's only fifty miles away," I said. "He can live here if he wants. I have no argument with him. You just got added to my shit list, though."

"What would you have in exchange, or as punishment?" Rain asked.

"What is wrong with you people?" I asked, tossing up a hand. "You can't go around trading things for babies. Is that what you think? Look at yourself." I was glaring at Rain. "You were desperate to keep your child. Put yourself in my shoes for a minute. Imagine what it would be like if that child no longer recognized you as his mother. How would you feel about that?" I was pissed, and she was just now getting that idea. She backed up and stood behind Tiearan, now.

"I will say this, though," I went on. "If your daughter breathes a word to Toff, trying to say bad things about his father or anyone else on this planet, as soon as that child is grown, I will take her so far away from the rest of you and leave her on a deserted world somewhere, she'll never be able to get back to you. That world will be shielded, too, so she can't skip or flash or whatever it is that you do, to get off it. Do I make myself clear?"

"You can do this?" Zervias asked.

"I have a whole planet full of former Ra'Ak and Elemaiya, who would be more than happy to tell you just what I can do," I snapped.

"You know who I am?" Kifirin was at my side, suddenly, blowing smoke.

"Dark Lord," Tiearan went to one knee and bowed his head.

"This is my mate," Kifirin put his arm around my shoulders. "She is what I am, and has spent too much effort in your direction already. When the child comes of age, I will pass judgment upon you myself, for all your errors."

"I told you," Zervias hissed at Tiearan.

"You will be confined to this world," Kifirin went on. "I expect you to treat all as fairly as you can, and if the child suffers in any way, you will answer to me."

"Leave Corent and Zervias out of it," I said, looking up at Kifirin. He was the god, now, and nothing else.

"I will do as you say," he inclined his head to me. Zervias was weeping as we folded away.

* * *

"And we thought it was going to be terrible to offend the Warlock King," another Green Fae came forward. "Instead, we have offended the Lord of the Dark Realm and taken his mate's child. How have we come to this?"

* * *

*Black Mist Headquarters*

"Brother, Mordain is dead, as are those Prylvis sent. Their spawn have been destroyed and the Green Fae have disappeared. Saa Thalarr came to Vionn."

"Our brother is dead?" Viregruz hissed. "That is preposterous. Did the Saa Thalarr take him down as well?"

# Chapter 11

"I have interrogated Red Hand troops who were nearby. They say not—a red-haired woman stood before our brother, then disappeared shortly before his death. We believe it was the Queen of Le-Ath Veronis. Our plan has been interrupted, brother." Ringolar was angry and very close to shifting. He had no desire to shift before Viregruz, however. His brother abhorred such loss of control.

"You believe she killed Mordain?" Viregruz lifted a dark eyebrow.

"Yes. No one else was near."

"She will die for killing our brother, then. Double the price on her head. That will keep her busy fending off amateurs while we make our plans. The Five-Year Conclave is approaching, is it not? How difficult do you think it might be to attack her there? She is obligated to attend."

"That might be accomplished, brother. And it may be easier than you think. All we need is a bit of cooperation from our Solar Red allies."

* * *

*Le-Ath Veronis*
*Lissa*

"Lissa, you have to stop torturing yourself with this." Winkler stood with me outside the Green Fae village. Rain fell around us as I kept watch, hoping to get a glimpse of Toff. The Fae had used their talent to bring rain to newly planted crops, and everyone was staying inside if they could.

"I know. That stupid Conclave is coming up, too, and I've barely looked at the agenda. What if Toff doesn't come back to us?" I looked up at my handsome werewolf's face. Winkler was using some of the Power granted by the Saa Thalarr to keep rain off us as we talked. Reaching up, I smoothed a lock of black hair away from his forehead.

"I used to dream about us. About you putting your hands on me," Winkler's smile was gentle. "Come back to the palace with me. We'll make the bed bounce and then you can read all that boring crap."

"Rubbing it in because you don't have to read boring crap anymore?" I asked.

"Absolutely. All I have to do is bite heads off spawn. You have no idea how nasty those things taste."

"You poor thing. Should I order room service so you can eat before we bounce? Just to get the spawn taste out of your mouth?"

"I think I can stave off hunger until the bed has been bounced from one end of your suite to the other."

"You know my palace is filled with vampires. Their hearing is very good. All of them will know exactly what's going on."

"Is Gavin at the palace?"

"Probably. In the office he shares with Tony."

"Good." Winkler gave me his best, wolfish grin.

"That's just mean," I slapped his arm.

"Nope. Just getting back at the stuffy vamp, that's all." Winkler folded us to my suite.

* * *

*Twylec*

"We will fill your coffers if you allow us to establish our temples on your world."

"But your religion has been outlawed by the Alliance." Tamaritha, Queen of Twylec sat upon her jeweled throne, watching the one who stood before her. He claimed to be a simple priest of Solar Red. She had her doubts—she wasn't a fool. Nevertheless, her world was in financial ruin—the crown had demanded from and taxed the population to excess. She'd occupied the throne for four years, and those four years had been fraught with disasters and loans come due from other worlds.

She'd borrowed from others, just to pay the old debts. Now the new ones were asking for payment and she had nothing to give. Crops had been bad, newer technology could be acquired elsewhere and disease had killed off herds and a large portion of the population, as well. Twylec was not on anyone's list to visit, nowadays.

Except for Solar Red priests.

Her cousin, Satris, had already made a deal with those devils. He'd been held in the dungeons of Le-Ath Veronis for plotting to murder their Queen. Only Tamaritha's protests and requests for diplomatic immunity had gotten him away from there and returned to her in one piece.

The two friends he'd conspired with had been left behind—they weren't related to the crown. Satris had railed at length that he'd lost two friends and cursed the Queen of Le-Ath Veronis while he did it. He'd also cursed the vampire who'd agreed to kill the Queen for a portion of the reward money. Cursed him for not dying, as the others had.

Tamaritha had grown tired of his irrationality and hushed him after a while. She should have left him on Le-Ath Veronis, she decided, and asked her healer to be sent in for the headache she'd gotten. Satris was being kept away from the throne room and Council meetings, too—he'd developed a terrible cough her physicians couldn't cure. Nowadays, listening to her cousin's coughing and whining annoyed her greatly.

"How much will you pay to establish your temples here under a different name?" Tamaritha asked, coming back to the priest before her.

# Blood War

"Ah, now we begin to see reason," the priest gloated.

* * *

*Le-Ath Veronis*

*Lissa*

"Here is the agenda for the Conclave," Grant laid the handheld computer before me.

"Lovely," I muttered. I was supposed to go through and review all the petitions, et cetera, so I could cast a vote.

The Alliance had five hundred eighty-six members, so we were going to meet in one big meeting hall, I suppose. Everybody would have bodyguards and personal assistants with them, so you could multiply that number by at least six. There were three hundred sixteen items on the agenda.

"We're supposed to get through all this in a week?" I asked in disbelief. The General Alliance Council, comprised of the twenty Charter Members of the Alliance, reviewed petitions to join and things of that nature, but the laws governing all the Alliance had to be debated and voted on by the monarchs, presidents, despots, autocrats or whoever seemed to be in charge at the moment. That meant I had to go.

"At least half of it is electronic vote, with no debate. Those are laws that are already in place and only need approval to remain in place," Grant pointed out.

"Oh. Well, I guess I better read through this, huh?"

"Yeah. Get crackin', Queenie pants," Grant grinned.

"Did you call me Queenie pants?" I lifted an eyebrow at Grant in surprise. Some of his shyness had gone away. Truthfully, I was happy to see it go.

"It's more respectful than itty-bitty pants," he pointed out. Well, somebody had overheard my twins, then.

# Chapter 11

"Can I go?" Grant changed the subject. "To the Conclave, I mean?"

"I was planning on taking you and Heathe." I didn't add that Davan would have gone, too—if he were still with us. I was allowed to take up to nine people with me. I'd have to take Grant or Heathe—possibly both; I needed them to keep up with appointments and take notes.

That presented a problem. We'd informed the Alliance (through Thurlow), that meetings during the day wouldn't be a problem. Let them make of that what they would. Grant and Heathe needed to have that ability, too. Grant was in my study; Heathe had gone to run an errand. Just as well, I could only do one at a time.

"Grant, when did you eat last?" I asked, turning the small computer in my hands.

"This morning. Why?"

"Can you bite, without, well, you know."

"Without what?" Grant wasn't getting this.

"She means without giving the climax." Thurlow folded in. "I can do this for you, lady."

"I'd prefer to do it," I muttered. "I know you did Rigo."

"I did. You need to take him with you," Thurlow informed me. Grant was now staring at both of us, not sure what was going on.

"Grant, if I give you blood, you'll be able to walk in daylight like some of the others," I told him. Grant had a light in his eyes and he was smiling, now.

"Can we do it now?" He was practically bouncing with joy.

"I have to give formal permission, first," I said.

"And you must be gentle," Thurlow added. Grant frowned at him.

"As if I wouldn't," he huffed.

"Come here," I motioned for him to stand beside my desk as I stood up. "Now. My blood is a gift to you, Grant," I said. "You will take no harm from it. There are no bindings or conditions, it is freely given." I pulled my collar aside, so he'd have a clear space to deliver the bite.

"I will be gentle," Grant said, grasping my neck in his hands and pulling me against him. He pressed his lips to my neck, delivering a careful kiss, and then I felt his fangs pierce my skin. I must have drawn in a breath, because Thurlow was there beside me.

"Lara'Kayan, it will be over soon," he was stroking hair away from my temple while Grant drank. He also told Grant when he'd had enough and Grant pulled away, licking stray drops of blood off my neck. He was nearly asleep when he looked into my eyes and smiled. Thurlow folded all of us to Grant's suite of rooms, and got him onto his bed. Grant was asleep already when that happened.

"Now, you," Thurlow said, lifting me in his arms before I could protest and folding me to my bed.

"I have work to do," I complained, but light was forming around his fingers, lulling me to sleep as they gently stroked my face.

"Sleep, my lady," he breathed, and just like that, I was out.

* * *

"She is sleeping," Thurlow allowed Rigo to step inside Lissa's suite. Rigo walked silently over the thick rugs scattered across Lissa's marble floors.

"I only want to touch her," Rigo whispered. Thurlow nodded.

# Chapter 11

Rigo settled on the side of the bed and lifted one of Lissa's hands, kissing each of her fingers. Before Thurlow could protest, he had her pulled against him, her cheek settled against his chest. "I have dreamed of this," Rigo whispered.

* * *

*Lissa*

I was awake four hours later, eating a meal that Karzac set in front of me. He'd angrily crossed arms over his chest and waited for me to eat while I zipped through tons of information on my handheld computer.

All sorts of laws were being put forward, including what to do with surplus recyclable materials. That bothered me—one of the proposals was to dump it on an uninhabited planet. Well, maybe not inhabited by humanoids—I was going to check that out myself.

Another proposal suggested that each member planet be allowed to decide which religions to approve. That raised my hackles and made my skin itch furiously. Approval of that item would open the door for those Solar Red fuckers—I just knew it.

I wanted the Founder and the Grand Alliance Council to have final approval, and the matter would be debated during the Conclave. If it were left to individual worlds, then Solar Red and Red Hand could waltz right in under an assumed name to murder and plunder, all in the name of their state protected religions.

Yeah, I was all for religious freedom, as long as it supported the population instead of killing and sacrificing. I'd seen firsthand what they could do. I didn't want to see any more of it.

"Karzac, please sit, you're making me tired by standing there." I scooted out the barstool next to me and patted the cushion. Karzac came to sit next to me. "Honey," I said, "look at this." I passed the small computer over to him and let him read the proposal. He looked at me as soon as he finished skimming the resolution.

"As long as Solar Red changed their name, they could be approved across the Alliance," he muttered, his green-gold eyes troubled at the thought.

"Anybody could do this," I muttered, "including Red Hand and Black Mist; all they have to do is set themselves up as a religion," I snorted.

"And by the time the Alliance figures out exactly what they are, they may not have enough support among the Alliance worlds to get rid of them again. They may be plotting a takeover," Karzac snorted.

"Oh, good lord," I muttered.

* * *

There was no sleep for me that night, which upset my twins quite a bit. I was busy, reading information on every ruler on every Alliance world. I knew, just by pulling up their records, which ones had been invaded already by Solar Red or Red Hand, under a different name. I figured a lot of them had taken money under the table, too, to allow the torturing assholes in.

Erland doesn't appreciate being wakened out of his beauty sleep—I learned that, but he and I had a long conference inside my study that night. I also had a promise from him and a promise from my grandfather, by the time it was finished. No way was I going to approach my father—he hadn't even bothered to say thanks when I'd restored Wyatt's immortality.

Maybe he'd been too insulted when I'd told him he wasn't any different from his mother. It was time, too, to have a talk with Kiarra. I waited until she was awake; I had to *Look* to get that information.

"Hey, Adam," I folded into the kitchen at Gryphon Hall while Adam was having a cup of tea and reading stock reports on his handheld computer.

"Lissa, sit down and have a cup of tea with me." He was smiling. Adam isn't hard to look at, by any stretch of the imagination. He reminded me of an English actor that had been popular when I'd been snatched away by Griffin. Long dead, now, but Adam bore a slight resemblance.

"I'll get my own tea," I motioned for him to sit down again. I'd interrupted him, not the other way around. He didn't seem to mind, either, that I'd just shown up, without any notice.

"I'm used to it," he smiled and went back to his computer. I made myself a cup of tea and was sipping it when Kiarra and Merrill came in for breakfast.

"Lissa, what brings you here?" Merrill asked, coming to give me a peck on the cheek.

"I just wanted to talk to Kiarra about the Ra'Ak that I killed on Vionn." Kiarra had gone to pull something for breakfast from the fridge, but she turned to look at me when I spoke.

"What about him?" she asked. "Dragon said you had a few words with one of them before you killed him, but he didn't know what was said."

"We had a few words, all right, but he was stalling for time, trying to work his mojo. He wanted a Saa Thalarr under his thumb," I said.

"As if that's possible," Merrill snorted.

"Maybe not for you, Merrill, because of what you were before—a King Vampire that wasn't susceptible to compulsion. Or to me, because of what I am. He thought I was Saa Thalarr. And let me tell you, the compulsion, or whatever it was that he had, might have taken one of the others down. Some of the Spawn Hunters, for sure, and maybe others. He was full Dark Elemaiya before he became Ra'Ak. Have you heard of that, before?"

"That isn't good." Belen folded in, shining brightly before gathering his light and forming a corporeal body.

"Yeah. That's not good," I agreed. "And if there's more of those schmucks out there, well, who knows what will happen? If somebody challenges them, can they just place compulsion to win the battle or send somebody back to destroy things from within?"

I was thinking about my twins, Gavin, Tony and Jeral. It made me feel sick, to be honest.

"Conner's inviting us over for breakfast, so I don't have to cook," Kiarra had gotten silent mindspeech, her beautiful face set in a frown as she received the message. All of us were folded to Connor's, I didn't know by whom, and Franklin was sitting down beside me in a blink, telling me I was exhausted and needed to eat and then sleep. He'd gotten his hands on me, first thing, using his healer's skill to fix what he could.

"Honey, I appreciate the concern, but this is scary," I muttered. Franklin sat down and ate breakfast beside me—Shane and Thomas had fixed enough to feed a real crowd. It was a good thing, too—a crowd showed up. I listened while Kiarra, Belen, Conner and just about every other Saa Thalarr came in and talked the whole situation over.

Dragon and Crane were there, of course, with Grace and Devin. Fox folded in with Wlodek, Weldon and the rest of her mates. Gilfraith came to give me a hug. I patted him on the back and smiled. Cleo arrived with her mates; Glinda even

# Chapter 11

folded in, Jayd and Garde right behind her, with both tiny girls asleep in carriers. The babies were growing, though, and that was nice to see.

"Are you stirring up trouble again?" Russell came in and patted me on the back.

"You haven't seen trouble, yet," I teased him halfheartedly.

"We can't seem to get a handle on this, to tell if there are any more out there," Kiarra sighed after conferring with Conner, Dragon and Grace.

"There are plenty of other voids—Lissa only sealed up the biggest one," Joey was helping himself to the breakfast buffet.

"So, there could be Ra'Ak everywhere, and a lot more full-blood Elemaiyan Ra'Ak," Dragon sounded worried. "Who would know about the Elemaiya—enough that we might figure this out?"

Well, Griffin must have been listening in, because he folded in shortly afterward, his mother—my grandmother—gripped by the collar. She looked as if she'd been freshly washed and dressed, and I hoped Narissa hadn't given Amara too much of a fight while she did it. "I think maybe Lissa can get answers out of her. I wasn't able to, before, and I only started thinking about that recently," Griffin muttered.

He didn't meet my eyes as I stared at him. He was right, though—when he'd taken Cleo, Kyler and me to meet Narissa, she'd told him then that it was a good thing I'd placed compulsion.

Of course she'd tried to cover it up, muttering some nonsense about Wylend and a spell he'd cast. I hadn't thought anything about it either, at the time, thinking that Wylend Arden, as King of Karathia and perhaps the strongest warlock on that world, had managed to achieve that particular result.

He hadn't. He'd only been able to keep Narissa from telling others whose child she'd had. Compulsion had nothing to do with it. Her talent, combined with Friesianna's, had likely accomplished that feat.

"So, grandmother," I began, "tell me about the Elemaiya and compulsion."

"Many might have some form of compulsion," she snorted. "But that's not what this is. We use another word for this," she snapped. She didn't want to be there, no doubt about that. I put a plate of food together and handed it to her. She ate as if she hadn't had a meal in days. Most likely that was true.

"Then what word do you use and what, specifically, is this?" I asked when she'd slowed down on her eating.

"We use le'meruh," she muttered.

"Extreme coercion," Griffin explained.

"Only a few are born with the talent," Narissa went on, scraping up the last of her eggs with a fork and a wedge of toast. "Bright and Dark. It is coercion so strong, few can withstand it—even those among the powerful. The ones born with this gift have to be handled carefully, so they don't turn on the others. Friesianna was born with it. Became Queen, as soon as she was old enough. Some say she forced the old Queen to step aside."

"Is the old Queen still alive?" I asked.

"Don't know. She was forced from camp and we never saw her again."

"The new Queen is the one who made the deal with the Dark ones and the Ra'Ak?" Griffin was getting in on this. I didn't care, as long as we got to the bottom of it.

# Chapter 11

"Yes. But she has done many things in the past that should not have been." Was it me, or was my grandmother starting to sound more reasonable?

"So, not everybody agreed with her? That sounds like she forced some people to do her will, then."

"Yes. Many were afraid to say anything against the Queen's decisions, because of it." I wasn't sure whether I wanted to ask my grandmother if she'd been for or against the Queen on that one.

"Rabis tried to warn her, but she ignored him as she usually did. He also tried to warn her against the alliance with the Dark ones and the Ra'Ak, but when she refused him that time, he disappeared and did not return."

"Rabis was their Seer," Griffin said softly, when I raised an eyebrow. "He knew I had the gift."

"She still plays Queen, though she doesn't have a drop of power to her name—even the le'meruh is gone, now. She holds court and her pretty males are still lined up to do whatever she asks. They've killed for her, as often as not. She'll kill to get a handful of berries away from the ones who've gone out to pick them, rather than lift a finger for herself." There was contempt in my grandmother's voice. Well, she'd just described what I thought she'd become.

"Mother, don't sit there and tell me you didn't follow along right behind her, all those years when life was good."

"I did." She didn't look at Griffin when he spoke to her. "I should have gone to Rabis and asked him about it, long ago. He'd learned to keep his mouth shut, though. He wasn't volunteering anything, unless he thought there wasn't any other way. She would have gotten rid of him, too."

"So, you're saying that Rabis wasn't there on Kifirin with the rest of you?"

"No. There were a few others, too, that have disappeared over the years, one or two at a time. Rabis was the last to leave, before we met up with my granddaughter there. I wish Rabis had told me about her." Narissa nodded in my direction; she seemed particularly miffed that she hadn't been informed of my existence.

"My fault," Griffin said. "I knew somebody would come looking for her, so I brought her forward in time. I thought she'd died in the future, too, just as most of the others did."

"That's why he didn't see her. She skipped over some years." Narissa snorted.

"Around three hundred," I muttered. "Grandmother, I have to say you sound a lot more reasonable now than the last time I saw you."

"My great-granddaughter," she mumbled.

"I did it." Cleo came in and looked down at Narissa. "When I made my pronouncement, it broke any remaining compulsion that Friesianna had on her. I didn't realize it until later. That doesn't mean she's undeserving of what she got," Cleo held up a hand. "She still had some will left in the matter. She just chose not to exercise it."

"Until now," Narissa looked at Cleo. "It brought home to me just how mortal we are. Friesianna is killing, whereas she didn't do that so much before. The Ra'Ak influence, I think, in addition to her alliance with Baltis."

"Let's get back to the le'meruh thing," I sighed. I might have to go back to Evensun and sort out a few murderers. Later.

"I don't know that there were any with the talent left on the Dark side," Narissa went on. "The Ra'Ak, though; they're full of stories about how some of their own will come for them and make them Ra'Ak again."

# Chapter 11

"Is she saying that the Ra'Ak took or were handed the Dark Elemaiya with le'meruh, and they were made Ra'Ak?" Kiarra had been silent, listening carefully up to that point. Now she was thinking the same thing I was thinking.

"All I know is that they disappeared. It makes sense, though, and Rabis may have known about it, but I do not know where he is, either." Narissa was looking hopefully at the table. Cleo went to get another plate of food. A glass of milk and some coffee were provided, too.

"Thank you, I haven't had coffee in a long time," Narissa sipped it, first.

"Sounds like we need to find Rabis," Kiarra muttered. I was in complete agreement. We talked for a little while longer, but my grandmother didn't know anything else of value.

"They'll kill me when I get back," Narissa whined when Griffin moved to take her.

"I know what to do with her," I sighed. The Green Birth Fae owed me, so I set up fifty acres near the Green Birth settlement for my grandmother. I think everybody who'd been at Conner's came along, just to see what I intended to do.

Adam put up the house and I placed a shield around it. Narissa couldn't get past a certain point, and nobody could come in past a certain point. Food and other things might be left on the perimeter for an exchange, but that was all. Narissa was in a prison of sorts, albeit a comfortable one.

"I expect you to hand over regular reports," I informed Tiearan, who now stood among us. "Make sure she has food and clothing. If she needs anything else, let me know and I'll make a decision."

"We will do this to discharge part of our debt," he agreed.

"Let me know if she mistreats anyone," I added. Tiearan nodded.

# Blood War

* * *

"Where should we start looking for Rabis?" Kiarra blew out a sigh. We were in my private meeting room, which we seldom used. At least it held all of us, although not everybody got a seat at the table.

Even the Spawn Hunters were there this time, and Drake, Drew, Gavin and Tony were giving me looks, letting me know that they'd been left out. Well, I'd grovel in a little while. When this started, I didn't know that it was going to be anything except a conversation with Kiarra and possibly her mates. Now it was something quite different.

"Can the Saa Thalarr still use the gates?" Tony asked.

"Yeah—they were only closed to the Elemaiya and the Ra'Ak," I said. "Who else uses them besides that?"

"Just us and some of the Wizard clans," Griffin replied. "I know Glendes uses them at times—it's easier than folding to some places."

"Well, we probably need to scatter to find Rabis, then," I sighed. "There are a bazillion gates and he may be near one of them, hoping it will become useful again, someday."

"That makes sense," Griffin agreed.

*You don't have time to search through all the gates*, filtered into my mind. Well, there he was again, and this time he was sending mindspeech. And then the vision came, so clear I felt I could reach out and touch the leaves of the trees he was showing me.

"I have to go," I said and disappeared amid shouts from those around me.

# Chapter 12

*B*lack Mist Headquarters
"Le-Ath Veronis is closed against us." Ringolar watched his four remaining Ra'Ak brothers closely. "We can't set foot on the planet, but it is common knowledge that the Reth Alliance Conclave will be held in less than a month. Viregruz agrees that we should go there, my brothers, and avenge ourselves."

"We can kill many birds with a single strike at that affair," Dalstone agreed. "Shall we go disguised?"

"That would be perfect," Ringolar chuckled. "They think to take us—we will show them otherwise."

"But we did not see how our brother died," Farthis argued. "We only saw the darkness when he left us. The cameras attached to his optic nerves ceased to function, suddenly."

"He was distracted and attacked from behind. That is easy enough to determine," Ringolar scoffed. "You always worry, brother."

"There is a way to harm Le-Ath Veronis, without setting foot on the planet," Levecus said. Of the brothers, he was the quietest.

"How is that?" Ringolar turned to him.

"Imagine this," Levecus began, and as he outlined the plan, Ringolar smiled.

* * *

*Avendor*

I looked from one to the other. Rabis wasn't nearly as tall as the one who stood beside me. We'd come to a small clearing, surrounded by trees that bore knobs of fruit. At the time, I didn't bother to *Look* to see what kind of trees they were; I was focused on Rabis and what he might tell me. I also shoved aside what Rabis' scent told me—that could wait.

"I was hoping to meet you eventually," Rabis nodded respectfully. His hair was darker—a reddish-brown. His youthful appearance belied his age, too—he was older by far than my grandmother and looked younger. "Would you like to sit?" he asked. "The grass here is soft enough."

We sat. Rabis studied me for long moments, as if he were struggling to see past an invisible shield. The taller one sitting beside me turned away to hide a smile.

"You want to know about le'meruh," Rabis finally announced. He seemed satisfied with me somehow, as if I passed his scrutiny in some way.

"Mostly I want to know about Dark Elemaiya with the talent, who may now be turned Ra'Ak."

"Ah. The seven brothers," Rabis nodded. "And the seventh one, who is not Ra'Ak, may be the worst of the lot. He

# Chapter 12

is the seventh son of a seventh son, and among the Dark half of the race, that is not a good thing."

"That's comforting news," I muttered sarcastically. I wondered, too, what in the nine levels of hell, as Gavin was so fond of saying, might be worse than a Ra'Ak.

"They are plotting against you," Rabis added.

"Tell me something I don't know," I sighed.

"Le'meruh is a terrible weapon in the wrong hands," Rabis began. "It can only be removed by the one who placed it, or by the death of the one who placed it."

My skin began to itch immediately.

* * *

*Earth*

*Merrill Leopard's Manor*

"Will you give this to her?" Griffin held the small box out to Radomir. Radomir had to *Look* to see what it contained.

"Ah." Radomir wasn't sure he wanted to be the messenger in this instance, but was afraid it might not get to Lissa, otherwise. Radomir knew, too, that Merrill had been approached by Griffin for this errand, and Merrill had refused. A rift had occurred between Merrill and Griffin, and many among the Saa Thalarr worried that the long friendship had ended permanently.

"I'll see that Lissa gets this," Radomir said and folded away.

* * *

*Le-Ath Veronis*

*Lissa*

I was standing at the edge of the Green Fae village, again, watching them go about their daily business. Fall gardens were being tended, seedling trees planted, bread baked—I could smell it from where I stood.

# Blood War

No sign of Redbird, though—she was probably inside one of the homes, taking care of Toff. Roff had an arm about me, seeing and smelling what I did. Corent stepped around one of the small houses and walked toward us.

"The child is doing well," he came to stand beside me. I nodded; I didn't trust myself to speak. Right then I might have wept if I tried to say anything. So many terrible things were happening, and I felt it was all heading toward an awful end.

The worst part, too—was that I seemed to be at the center of it. I'd come to the Green Fae village, hoping to get a glimpse of Toff. Roff refused to be left behind—he wanted to see the child they'd stolen from him.

That's where Radomir found us—standing beneath the trees surrounding Corent's new home. As soon as Corent learned the Green Fae had come to Le-Ath Veronis, he'd joined them.

Radomir knew I was close to tears. He silently placed a small box in my hand. I should have known what was inside— I opened it anyway. Roff's ring lay nestled on a scrap of satin.

Amara must have packed it up; I couldn't see Griffin doing anything that considerate. "Honey, this was yours," I pulled the ring from the box and offered it to Roff. I was crying by that time.

"Do not weep, my love." Roff's wings unfurled and Radomir and Corent were shut out as he wrapped them about me. Only Roff and I existed inside the shelter of those wide, soft, leathery wings. The ring was lifted carefully from my palm as I tearfully held it out to him, and he accepted it, slipping it onto his left ring finger. It fit.

That could be attributed to Griffin, I think. He held the power to resize it to fit Roff's larger hand. It should never have been taken away. What had Griffin thought to accomplish by

# Chapter 12

taking it? Was that his final assurance that Roff would have no memory of his children—or of me?

"Lissa, come with me to the winery," Roff whispered, as he wiped away my tears.

"All right," I was trying to stop the tears from falling. Roff leaned down to kiss me, pulling his wings back.

Corent and Radomir were both gone, although there were a few Green Fae staring, not far away. I folded Roff to his winery. I'd never been there—too many things had happened surrounding its building and operation, most of which involved Roff's forgetting me.

We walked up wide, stone steps into the place; I was amazed at how automated most of it was, but then Merrill and Adam had a hand in building it. I shouldn't have been surprised at all.

Bottles were filled by one machine and corked by another. Two comesuli were there, supervising all the other comesuli employees. Roff led me to them.

"Roff, how are you?" The older of the two nodded to Roff. He had dark hair and his scent shocked me speechless. The one standing next to him only deepened the shock.

"Markoff, you may stop being polite, I have my memories back." Those were Roff's first real words with his brother, I'm sure, since Shala had staked him. I stood there like a fool, staring at Roff's brother and nephew.

I shouldn't have been surprised, however; I had vague memories of Roff telling me, when he and Giff had come to Merrill's from the future, that his brother and his brother's child had stayed behind on Kifirin to take care of his business. I was wondering why I'd never met them before.

"He did not wish to take advantage," Roff was doing a good job of reading my mind. And the fact that he'd remembered was also a huge surprise.

"Honey, when did you remember?" I asked.

"I already remembered some, but all came to me when I saw the ring," he twisted it on his finger. "Lissa, this is my brother, Markoff, and his child, Dariff."

"I am so sorry I haven't met you before," I held my hand out to Markoff. He took it, smiling shyly. Markoff was slightly younger than Roff—about fifty years if my nose was accurate. Dariff, his child, was Giff's age, which was close to ninety.

"Giff has been spending time with Markoff and Dariff, whenever Rolfe has been away," Roff explained. "Markoff has kept me updated, though I had no memories for the longest time. I wondered, at times, why he was telling me all these things. All is clear to me, now."

"I welcome you back, brother," Markoff's smile widened.

"Markoff, where are you living?" I couldn't believe this had slipped past me for so long.

"I have a very nice home near the light half; Roff made sure of it early on," Markoff replied. "Dariff and I live there and visit the capital twice a month. Roff arranged for our numbers to be the same." He tapped the bracelet that he wore, which indicated his two bite dates.

"Please come and have dinner with us, when you're in Lissia next time," I said. "Both of you. You're family." I was feeling terrible by this time, and the fact that Toff's situation was what it was made me feel worse.

"We would be honored to have dinner with the Raona," Markoff dipped his head. "I have heard that Toff is now on the planet, even if he has no memories of us." Well, the whole memory thing was getting to be an epidemic, looked like.

# Chapter 12

"Lissa, you had no hand in this, I did not mean to make you feel bad," Roff put his arm around me.

"I'll just need some time," I said.

"There are some things that I should check on here, and other things to discuss with my brother," Roff bent down to kiss me. Yeah, he probably had plenty to talk about with his brother.

"I'll see you at the palace," I said, preparing to fold there and lock myself inside my suite. I had a meeting in the afternoon, but that was three hours away. I could wallow in misery until then.

"Lissa, do not look so sad, I beg you," Roff had my chin cupped in a hand.

"I'll be fine," I said, and folded away from him.

* * *

"Lissa, there is another pile of stuff to go through," Grant was standing outside my suite, waiting to ambush me, I think. He had a smile on his face, at least, and he smelled like waffles. Grant was already getting into the solid food thing, I could tell. I didn't want to look at piles of stuff; I wanted to huddle in a corner, somewhere. I sighed and followed Grant instead, as he headed toward my study.

"Little Queen," Rigo met us halfway there. Thurlow joined us quickly.

"Lady, is there something I can do?" Thurlow asked. Well, he probably knew how I was feeling, even if the others didn't. I rubbed the space between my eyes—the headache was coming on. "You need to eat and relax," Thurlow said as we walked through the door of my private study. Heathe was there, waiting for us.

"Heathe, will you and Grant go to the kitchen and ask Cheedas to make something for the Raona?" Thurlow asked.

There was a Command in his voice that might have competed with the strongest of compulsion. Both my assistants trotted happily out the door and down the hall.

"Please sit, tiessa," Rigo murmured, taking my hand and leading me toward the chair behind my desk. Things slowed around me, as if time were different at that moment. Rigo settled me into my chair, kissed the hand he held, and then knelt next to me. Thurlow reached out with careful fingers and touched my forehead, taking the headache away while I blinked at him in confusion.

"I am keeping watch, my beautiful lady," Thurlow told me softly. "We will not be interrupted. Lissa," he sighed, "Rigo and I, well, our hearts are in these hands," he cupped both my hands in his and then knelt before me, right beside Rigo. He kissed my palms, then looked up at me, his sensuous mouth twisting into a sad smile. "I know that forgiveness for me may be long in coming. I was a fool, love. A terrible fool."

"I beg you not to turn me away," Rigo pleaded.

"Rigo," I reached out to touch his face—he was old as a vampire—older than Gabron, even, and I knew that he'd been the one to keep Hraede on an even track and stable for a very long time—he and the other kings he'd turned. Rigo kissed my palm and rested his forehead there afterward.

I stroked his face with my free hand and ran fingers through his hair. Rigo rose and lifted me, sitting in my chair and then pulling me onto his lap. I was wrapped in his arms and he was rocking me gently, telling me he was worried. About me.

"I have never attended a Conclave, because of my vampirism. I had to send our kings and queens with preliminary advice and remain in contact as much as I could. Now, with Thurlow's gift, I can go with you. Both of us must

# Chapter 12

go with you, in addition to any others you can take who might provide protection. I fear for your life, tiessa." Tiessa. It meant beloved, in Hraedan.

"I don't know what to do about both of you," I pulled away from Rigo.

"Lara'Kayan, you are not obligated to do anything, only please do not shut us out," Thurlow replied. "Get to know us. Talk with us. Sit with us. We will be happy with that, until you learn the depth of what we feel for you."

"Fine." My fingers shook as Rigo set me on my feet and rose—we all heard Grant and Heathe returning with a meal for me. Rigo leaned down and settled the gentlest kiss on my mouth before stepping away, just as my two assistants entered the study.

* * *

"Aunt Lissa, I have a suggestion." Kyler and Cleo had come to my study, where I'd been reading through three hundred sixteen agenda items for the Conclave. My eyes were crossing and I wasn't getting any real information anyway, so I welcomed the interruption.

"What's the suggestion?" I looked up at her. Kyler had settled on the edge of my desk and lazily swung a leg as she smiled at me. Cleo, also smiling, had sat in one of the chairs in front of my desk.

"Well, since great-granny Narissa is here, what would you say to bringing the others—the ones you took away from Kifirin because they didn't want to be involved in Friesianna and Baltis' war against you? You can set them up on the other side of Narissa's area, and she can talk to them through the shield."

"That's a good idea. Talking to Tiearan all day won't improve anybody's temper," I nodded after considering Kyler's suggestion.

"Kyler and I are afraid they may become a target," Cleo added quietly. Her comment had me jerking my head in her direction.

"You think so?" I stared at her.

"Yeah. Even though they have no power now, how hard would it be to snatch them up and make them something else—like Ra'Ak or something? Once they become immortal again, any talent or power they had will come rushing back."

"Like misting and mindspeech do with the vampires," I said, staring at my niece. Thoughts of Ra'Ak with le'meruh filtered through my brain. We didn't need more of that.

"Those things can manifest in quarter and eighth bloods, maybe even sixteenth bloods," Cleo agreed. "That's how a few vampires with only a little Elemaiyan blood can mist or mindspeak. You know Tony is only an eighth blood and he can mindspeak. Think what might happen with a full-blood Elemaiya."

"You just made me all goose-pimply," I shuddered. "We have to bring them here, now. I'll be scared to death for them—and us, if we don't. Are the ones on Mendenath the only ones?"

"No, Aunt Lissa. There are others, scattered here and there, that abandoned the Bright camp through the years. The Dark ones have already been picked up by the Ra'Ak. It's only a matter of time before they search these out."

"Kyler, how many others are out there?" If anyone would know, it would be the Larentii and Kyler was pretty much a Larentii, she just wasn't huge and blue.

# Chapter 12

"Aside from the sixteen on Mendenath, around seventy or so," Kyler said. She knew what I was thinking. "Do you want us to gather them up?"

"Yeah." I gave a heavy sigh—I felt exhausted. "Go ahead and bring them to the spot just east of the Green Fae settlement, we'll put them there."

Narissa would be in a buffer zone between the two—she was locked inside her own little prison. She'd be able to see all of them and talk, but none could cross the barrier I'd set up. That was my punishment to my paternal grandmother for offing her parents and doing other nasty things throughout her long life.

Kyler and Cleo nodded and disappeared.

* * *

"Where are we going?" Gavin demanded. I'd commandeered everyone at my breakfast table the following morning.

"To pay a visit to Le-Ath Veronis' newest arrivals," I replied cryptically. When we arrived at the designated spot, we found a village already there. Kyler and Cleo had not only brought the remaining Bright Elemaiya; they'd somehow convinced their Larentii mates to help.

With the Larentii there, everything had been set up quickly. I just shook my head at how efficient and powerful they were. I saw Callan, too—he was helping his Aunt Zela move a few belongings into a newly constructed house. Zela noticed we'd come and since she recognized me, immediately came over to talk.

"Thank you for bringing Callan to me and thank you for giving us this home. We are learning slowly to take care of ourselves." I nodded at her thanks. Most Elemaiya didn't bother thanking anybody.

# Blood War

"I'll see that some animals are brought in so you can raise your own meat, if you want. And you're welcome to trade with the others; bear in mind you'll abide by the laws here, or you'll be punished just like anyone else." I watched her—she seemed to be in charge.

"We expect nothing less," she agreed.

*I'll keep an eye on them*, Kyler sent the silent message. I nodded slightly. I needed to get back to my palace; I still had work to do before the Conclave.

* * *

*Solar Red Headquarters*

"Your dinner, Tetsurna Prylvis."

"Thank you, Zellar." Prylvis nodded as Zellar, Viregruz's hired Karathian warlock, made a plate appear before Prylvis. Prylvis was entertaining Viregruz and his brothers at his compound on Mazareal.

The evening's entertainment had already occurred—Prylvis had watched as Viregruz and his brothers consume several youths his Blood Captains had captured the day before. Once Viregruz was finished with his meal, steaks had been cut away and cooked for Prylvis' favorite dish.

"I don't understand why you bother to cook it," Viregruz watched as Prylvis raised the fork to his lips.

"It's tender this way, Lord Viregruz."

"Ah. I prefer it my way. Screaming and all."

"I enjoy the screaming as well. It's why I invited you to dinner."

"And it's only polite for your guests to bring something, is it not?" Viregruz drew a finger through a puddle of blood—his and Prylvis' dinner had died atop the table.

# Chapter 12

"This is quite good, Lord Viregruz," Prylvis chewed another chunk of humanoid steak. "Tell me of your plans to destroy the bitch Queen and her planet."

"It will be easy enough to get to her—we have plans to join Twylec's retinue. After that, it is a simple matter," Viregruz snapped his fingers.

"What if it's not so simple?" Prylvis stopped chewing for a moment.

"A contingency plan is in place. It involves a tremendous effort on the part of my brothers, but I believe it will come out well, should they be required to use it."

"What about her planet? We've taken money from San Gerxon, after all. Surely he will be made happy if Le-Ath Veronis is destroyed."

"Oh, he will be more than happy, I assure you. We all know what happens when vampires are exposed to sunlight, do we not?" Viregruz's smile was malicious and wide.

* * *

*Le-Ath Veronis*

"Giff?" Markoff led Roff inside his home. Roff had been there before, but not since he'd been turned. Dariff walked behind Roff, unsure how his cousin was going to react to her father, or to the return of his memories. Giff was now heavily pregnant and Rolfe had brought her to Markoff when he'd been called to hunt spawn on a faraway world.

"Uncle?" Giff wandered out of her bedroom, wearing a carry sac that held her baby pouch slung over the opposite shoulder. She'd just wakened, it appeared.

"Child, I am sorry you went through such misery on my account," Roff pulled his oldest child against him, and kissed the top of her head.

"Father, do you remember?" Giff wept as she turned her gaze on Roff's face.

"Yes, my little one. I remember."

* * *

"Lord Warlock." Rigo nodded to Erland, who appeared in Lissa's library. "How goes the assignment?"

"Good and bad—I found the information, but it wasn't good news when I found it. Nice work on Satris, by the way. My spies tell me the whelp now has a disease the physicians can't cure."

"Many years of research and working with poisons, venoms and such," Rigo shrugged off the compliment. "If they find the cause after his death, they will only believe he was bitten by a spider during his travels. It is uncommon but not unheard of."

"How long will it take?"

"Perhaps a few months, at the most. We will achieve our objective in the long term. At the end, he will wish for the quick death our Queen would have commanded."

"Tsk, tsk," Erland muttered, shaking his head in mock sympathy. "Perhaps Lissa should raise the topic of Diplomatic Immunity at the Conclave."

"That, my friend, would be inadvisable. She is new and many will be waiting, as vultures do when an ox is dying."

"I know. At times, I feel the need to cover myself in oil, just to slip through the tripe and garbage of Wylend's court. Lissa will have to contend with five hundred times that when she goes to Conclave."

"I fear that no amount of diplomatic oil will keep her from the shock that is coming. She will be snubbed and mistreated by many, I fear. Not only because she is a new monarch, but because there is a price on her head. Most will be placing as much distance between that and themselves as they can get. It is never wise to befriend one who is marked by the Assassin's Guild. That is usually a death waiting to happen. If one gets too close, one might be targeted as well."

"Sadly, it's true," Erland agreed. "But they don't know what Lissa is made of, or some of her mates."

"You know I wish to be included in your number," Rigo didn't meet Erland's gaze.

"We know. All of us do. We're just waiting to see if she offers a ring now or waits awhile." Erland cleared his throat.

"You have bets riding on this, don't you?" Rigo lifted an eyebrow.

"Yes, but it's embarrassing to admit it."

Rigo surprised Erland by laughing out loud.

* * *

*Lissa*

I had a private meeting with Erland to discuss his spying assignment, and Erland wasn't willing to let me get away afterward. Well, my desk got broken in, that night. Nobody can accuse Erland of being unimaginative—in bed or out.

I met up with Solis and Hardin, formerly Captain and General, as we walked out of my study. Solis and Hardin were now part of my palace guards. They were patrolling the halls as Erland and I made our way to the dining room after a quick cleanup.

"Solis, Hardin," I nodded to both of them.

"Liss, we seldom see you," Solis smiled.

"I hear that a lot," I said.

"Mostly from her mates," Erland gave a long-suffering sigh.

"Oh, you poor thing," I swatted at Erland, who managed to evade my hand. "Did they find a good home for you?" I asked, turning back to Solis.

"They did. We travel to the light side on off days and have sun bulbs installed in the bedroom for the days we stay on this half of the planet. Flavio told us not to invite any vampires inside."

"Well, not unless you want them to fry," I said. "Only a few of us can stand the light of day."

"I wasn't sure what you were talking about when you told us you were vampire on Vionn," Hardin told me. "I'd never heard of anything like that."

"There aren't any vampires on Vionn," I explained. "If there were, they'd likely have been hidden. Even on the worlds that recognize vampires as citizens, they don't mingle much with the general population. They're just too vulnerable during the day. No sense in inviting trouble, don't you think?"

"I understand that part of it," Solis said. He and Hardin were both armed with laser rifles and long, heavy steel blades strapped at their side.

"Have Drake and Drew offered to teach you to fight with two blades?" Just the thought of it made me smile.

"Yes, and we've started the training. We were also informed that they won't let us wear two swords until we're proficient." Hardin was smiling, now.

"Let me know if you need anything," I said, when Erland took my elbow to coax me away.

"We're fine," Solis called after us, and I was ushered into the dining room.

Adam, Merrill and Kiarra had come for dinner, which was served the minute Erland and I were seated. Gavin was seated on my right, so we would be going to bed as soon as he

# Chapter 12

could get me there. "Tomorrow is our anniversary," Adam said, putting his arm around Kiarra. "So I'd like to invite all of you to the Chessman tomorrow night for dinner. I have a private room reserved." Well, he ought to be able to reserve it, since he owned the thing and all. Looked as though we were going to get dressed up and go to Casino City. Honestly, I hadn't been there since the first day it had opened.

* * *

"You know who I am?" Connegar and Reemagar blinked at the one who'd come to them inside Lissa's library. Lissa and her mates, including a few extras, had gone to the Chessman Casino in Casino City to celebrate Adam and Kiarra's anniversary. Connegar and Reemagar had been invited, but they had no desire to sit in the midst of such a crowd so they'd stayed behind, choosing Lissa's library to relax and talk instead.

"Of course. Many Larentii would recognize the Mighty Hand," Connegar bowed deeply and respectfully to the tall man.

"I have an assignment for you," the man said. Although he was tall, he was still three feet shorter than Connegar, who was nearly ten feet tall.

"We are honored to accept," Connegar bowed again. "What is it that you wish, Bright One?"

The Mighty Hand outlined exactly what he wanted from the Larentii, who readily agreed. After all, it would protect Le-Ath Veronis and thwart those who sought to bring harm to Lissa. Under normal circumstances, Larentii wouldn't be allowed to interfere past the protection of their mate.

"It will be done swiftly," Reemagar spoke for the first time.

# Blood War

"Thank you," the tall man said, offering a crooked grin. Connegar and Reemagar couldn't help but smile back.

* * *

"We were married in Vegas," Adam said. He'd been asked to tell the story by members of the Saa Thalarr. I could tell it was a favorite and one I'd not heard before. "Kiarra wanted no part of it," Adam added, grinning. "I had to force her to marry me."

"You should have seen the look on her face when we made her march down the aisle," Lynx snickered. "She wouldn't buy a dress, either, so the rest of us picked it out. Tiger and Wolf had to dress her. She wouldn't put the thing on."

I'd only met Tiger and Wolf that evening. They were retired, but both were members of the seven Saa Thalarr when I'd helped Dragon on Refizan.

"She didn't have a ring for me, either," Adam laughed. "I ended up getting a piece of her unicorn horn." He held up his hand to show me the pale, gold band. It matched the ones worn by Merrill and Pheligar, too, I recalled. She'd given them a piece of herself. That was amazing, in my book.

* * *

"Heathe, if I give you my blood, then you'll be able to go with us," I told him. I'd waited until the following afternoon to make the offer, so we could wade through a pile of work first. He'd sleep afterward, that was a given, so I had to time it right.

Heathe was shocked out of his shoes, I could tell, when I offered him blood. Thurlow and Rigo had come immediately after I made the suggestion; I'm sure Thurlow had known this was about to happen.

"Will you allow one of us to hold you, while Heathe takes your blood?" Rigo wanted this, I could tell. Very much. After

264

# Chapter 12

thinking about it for a moment, I nodded to Rigo. He pulled me against him and gestured for Heathe to approach.

"No climax, Heathe," I whispered, before reciting permission.

"Shhh," Heathe said, and breathed on my neck. Rigo held the back of my head cupped in his hand, my body tight against his as Heathe leaned in for the bite. He was careful and it didn't hurt much.

As soon as Heathe licked off the last of the blood, Thurlow folded him to his suite. Rigo stayed behind. Grant cleared off the sofa in the corner and Rigo took me there to sit and recuperate for a while. Grant offered a bottle of blood substitute, but Rigo was already pulling his collar open.

"Come, tiessa, take from me," he offered.

"Honey, I don't know how to hold back the climax," I whispered.

"I am hoping that remains true," Rigo smiled. The corners of his eyes crinkled a little when he did that and I think I was lost, then and there. Well, I might have to talk with my mates. I sure didn't know what they were going to do if they had to add somebody else to the roster.

Grant stole quietly from the room. "Come, tiessa, do not feel embarrassed or afraid," Rigo leaned in to kiss me lightly. "You are not obligated; still, I just want this one small thing from you."

"All right," I leaned my forehead into the hollow of his shoulder, right against the tattoo of the night flower on his neck. He didn't hurry me so I sat there, breathing in the scent of him for a while.

If duty, loyalty and honor had a scent, I think it would smell like Rigo. I lifted my hand and slipped it around the back of his neck, placed a kiss of my own and bit. Rigo held me tightly against him as his body convulsed with the climax. Thurlow found us like that, still sitting together minutes later, neither of us willing to move for a while.

* * *

*Twylec*

"You will take us with you, or we will report to the Alliance that you have allowed Solar Red to build temples upon Twylec," Ringolar held his humanoid shape, as did his brothers. If Tamaritha knew what it was that stood before her, she would have dropped to the floor in a faint.

Ringolar thought about eating her and taking her place, but she had a lover on Jhirnain and he had no desire to get involved. Tamaritha had plans to share rooms with her lover.

Ringolar and the others could use the extra time to hunt meals while the Queen was occupied with sex. They had their own agenda and the pathetic mortals wouldn't survive anyway. Ringolar smiled at the thought.

Tamaritha frowned at the five that stood before her. "I can only take ten, and I need my bodyguards," she snapped. "Four guards are not enough, and I need my assistant at my side."

"Ringolar, take Farthis and Dalstone with you; Levecus and I will handle the other errand," Zethias smiled at Ringolar, nearly allowing the lengthy tongue to escape his mouth.

"Very well," Ringolar nodded in agreement with his brother. "That will leave you with six guards plus your assistant," Ringolar nodded toward Tamaritha. This was working out so well; the Vampire Queen would come to the Conclave, leaving Le-Ath Veronis vulnerable so his brothers could create havoc in her absence. Ringolar wanted to laugh at how simple it would be.

# Chapter 12

"We leave in three days' time; do not be late to board ship," Tamaritha whined.

<h1 align="center">Chapter 13</h1>

*Le-Ath Veronis*
*Lissa*

Erland sat on a corner of my bed as he directed two comesuli who were packing my clothing for Conclave. My warlock had a list of events, parties and meetings, so it looked as if half my wardrobe was going with me.

Giff's baby pouch was about to pop any day and she'd not been to work since her final two months had begun. I hoped Rolfe got in before the baby came, so he and Roff could both be there for Giff. Rolfe was off fighting spawn, as most other Spawn Hunters were.

Eight of us were going to Nemizan. In addition to Heathe and Grant, Thurlow, Rigo, Garde and Erland were going. Reemagar refused to be left behind, so he was going in disguise. He was identified as Larentii on the list I submitted to the Alliance Security Detail; he just wouldn't look like a Larentii to anyone else. We were obligated to give complete details on everyone we brought with us.

It was a first for Garde, too; this was the first time a High Demon had gone anywhere near the Alliance Conclave. Kifirin hadn't come to see me for several days and he wouldn't be interested in going to Conclave anyway.

My twins wanted to go, as did Gavin and Tony, but Kiarra was sending them out regularly to take care of spawn. They grumbled about being left behind, but it just wouldn't work if they had to disappear in the middle of something. Rigo's Rith Naeri were staying behind to guard the palace. I wondered if there was going to be a problem with security at Conclave due to the price on my head, but I really didn't have time to worry about that.

Reemagar planned to fold us to Nemizan—we didn't have to take normal transportation. Grant had let the Alliance know that we were going straight to the hotel where we'd be staying, once we arrived. They didn't ask questions regarding our travel arrangements and we all breathed a little easier.

What also interested me was that the Founding Member, Ildevar Wyyld, and the Grand Alliance Council seldom made personal appearances at Conclave. They sometimes attended meetings through live vid-feeds, but they didn't feel the need to be there in person.

I found myself wishing I could do that. Sadly, a personal appearance by the one in charge was mandatory. If the one in charge couldn't attend, a legal representative had to be approved weeks in advance by the Grand Alliance Council in order to vote on agenda items.

The whole thing was likely designed by the Conclave itself so that every five years, a different world received a windfall

# Chapter 13

from the visiting members and the ensuing tourism surrounding the event. It was like the Olympics times one thousand, complete with political gymnastics.

* * *

*Nemizan*

"I have all of us shielded," Reemagar said quietly when we landed inside the hotel lobby on Nemizan. If the desk clerk thought to give Grant the cold shoulder, he should have thought twice about treating a vampire badly. Grant only had to give slight compulsion and we had keys to our suite right away.

I learned immediately what being a new and unimportant member of the Alliance meant—we had the worst rooms in the place. I knew that because I misted through the other suites on our floor, just to check. Pointedly ignoring any personal or sexual activity, I focused on the amenities instead.

It was a good thing we didn't need the toilet, too, because ours didn't work. I laughed when Grant showed me that—he stood and flipped the switch over and over, trying to make it evacuate. Nothing happened. He and I high-fived over it, too— there wasn't any need to call maintenance and invite potential spies into our suite.

The royal family on Nemizan had been in charge of handing out the suite assignments, and it wouldn't do to snub any of their cronies. The other attendees all got better treatment and nicer suites. I, on the other hand, could be snubbed with impunity. Le-Ath Veronis had no allies, cronies, political bed-buddies or ass-kissers to look out for us.

Our suite was cramped, too, with three small bedrooms instead of the five larger ones requested. Well, we were lucky to have Reemagar with us—he fixed us right up, stretching out spaces and adding rooms with a blink of amazing power.

What did it matter that our suite now extended thirty feet into what was previously empty space? Reemagar shielded the addition from prying eyes and the hotel looked as it always did to anyone who might cast their gaze toward the seventeenth floor.

The other rooms had everything from fresh flowers to food or fruit waiting, and some even had servants and escorts. Well, they didn't have a Larentii with them. I could have wallowed in expensive chocolate and bathed in champagne if I wanted; all I had to do was tell Reemagar and it would have been provided.

As it was, I only requested shields and those had already been placed. Don would have smiled and called me a cheap date. I think Reemagar considered it, but Larentii seldom let their sense of humor show.

In addition to Reemagar's shields around us, I put up some of my own and Thurlow did as well; I felt his powerful shields vibrating against mine when I set them.

"I think we should disguise our Queen when we leave," Reemagar said as we prepared to go out to dinner. We had a meet and greet scheduled in the morning at nine, but nothing before then.

I figured the folks who already knew and liked each other would be getting together that first night, to eat, drink and carouse. I didn't know anybody and felt no need to schmooze. For my evening disguise, Reemagar gave me black hair and made me taller, causing me to blink at my new image in the mirror. It was more than strange—I'd never in my life colored my hair.

# Chapter 13

The hotel was huge—six hexagonal buildings set in a large complex. Each of the six rose in a tall, architectural statement constructed of steel, concrete and glass. The buildings were connected around a hexagonal courtyard and the complex resembled a honeycomb. I saw the lush courtyard and surrounding hotels as we rode a transparent elevator to the lobby.

Restaurants lined the lower floors inside each building, and we went through six before we found one willing to place us on a waiting list. While we waited for a table, I watched as numerous Conclave attendees waltzed in, with and without reservations, and were all led inside the restaurant quickly.

Someday, maybe the restaurant staff would learn not to snub vampires. Rigo stepped up to the host and in ten seconds, we were led to a table.

Lobbying was illegal with the Alliance, but that didn't keep people from trying—they just couldn't be obvious about it. They were present in droves, going from table to table and offering to buy meals, drinks or generally attempting to strike up conversations. A lot of them were successful, too.

Rigo had a word with our waiter, and that meant we didn't wait long for drinks or food. The meal was excellent and Reemagar checked it with power, first, just to make sure it was all right.

It didn't escape my notice, though, that not a single lobbyist approached our table. Rigo would have sent them on their way, but somehow, they weren't even trying. Shaking my head, I finished my fish and resolved to ignore it.

Reemagar didn't eat or even pretend to do so. He kept us shielded against harm as the rest of us ate and talked. When we got back to our suite, Reemagar folded away so he could feed on sunlight. I envied him, sometimes.

# Blood War

Heathe and Grant shared a room that had two smaller beds while Thurlow, Rigo, Erland and Reemagar all had their own rooms, thanks to Reemagar's talent for enlarging things so they'd fit. I had the largest bedroom and Garde slept with me the first night. Yeah, I like my High Demon just fine, thanks.

* * *

"Here is our registration," Grant handed information to the admissions clerks while we waited to gain entrance to the meeting hall. Heathe held the case that contained our palm-sized computers and everything else we needed during the day.

I'd dressed finely in a belted cream chiffon tunic and dark green, raw silk pants that flared and floated about my legs and ankles. A low-heeled, designer shoe in dark brown rounded out the outfit, except for the tasteful jewelry—all protection jewels designed by Shadow. I'd French-braided my hair, too, so it wouldn't be too much of a bother.

A committee of employees stood behind the registration desk as we checked in—all eight of us. Erland had a hand at my back, Rigo, Garde and Thurlow were scanning the crowd and I knew Reemagar, who looked enough like Garde to be his brother, had cast what he called Nexus Echo—if there were anyone close who voiced ill feelings toward me, my Larentii mate would know it.

Nexus Echo was a trick the Larentii had; the Saa Thalarr employed it at times, too—it picked up information if their name or a topic of interest came up. That's why they would often show up to add their two cents if somebody was talking about something that concerned them. I hadn't tried it myself—it felt too much like voyeurism.

# Chapter 13

The registration took too long and I worked to keep boredom and then anger away while our identification and information was checked and double-checked. Finally, we were sorted out with the welcoming committee, who all stared at me at one time or another while they went through their routine.

Eventually, we were handed ID clips that stuck right to our clothing. My group breathed a collective, deep sigh of relief as we were allowed through the door and led into a very large meeting room by Alliance security.

Our assigned table was off to the side and near the back. Grant and Heathe brought their own recording devices, but more were provided at our table. Everyone else had them, too. It didn't really matter; many in my party had perfect recall anyway, and some of us (Reemagar and Thurlow) could play back images in 3-D if they wanted.

While I sat at the table making small talk with Rigo, Thurlow and the others, I recalled going to meetings when I'd worked as a court clerk in Oklahoma City. We went to conferences on harassment, human resources, policy changes, all kinds of things. Nothing as momentous as this could turn out to be.

At least we all knew each other, pretty much, back at the courthouse. I didn't know a single soul, here. I will say this, though; the Governor of the Realm from Refizan, with his eight guards and assistants, stopped by my table. "You look very much like the one who saved Refizan, many years ago. I've watched those ancient vids many times." He smiled and held out his hand. I stood to take it.

"I enjoyed my visit to your world," I told him truthfully. I had—even though it had been three hundred years or more in the past and dangerous as all get out.

# Blood War

"Welcome to the Alliance," he said and moved away.

The next one to pass our table wasn't nearly as friendly—it was the Queen from Twylec and she had ten with her. She hissed out a rude name as she passed, but that wasn't what had me drawing in a breath and almost coming out of my seat—if Reemagar and Thurlow hadn't been sitting on either side, holding me down, I would have gotten out of my chair right then and there and things would have gotten ugly.

Queen Tamaritha of Twylec was being trailed by three Ra'Ak, all in humanoid form. I'd thought these meetings were going to be interesting before I came. Now they were going to be not only interesting but also dangerous—to the hundredth power.

The entire morning was completely boring; I heard a few snores throughout the crowd—a late night spent drinking and carousing, followed by three long and tedious speeches made by Nemizan's King and the President and Vice President of the Reth Alliance Conclave will do that to you every time.

* * *

Heathe, Grant, Rigo and I all had blood substitute for lunch, while everyone else except Reemagar had a meal served by the hotel. "You really drink that stuff?" That might have been the fiftieth time I'd heard a variation of that question during the mingling throughout the meal. I wondered if any of them were going to call me a fucking vampire.

I had a retort ready, but I think they knew better than to do that. Instead, I smiled and asked if they'd like to join me. I didn't get any takers. Wisps of smoke curled from Garde's nostrils from time to time, and I speculated as to whether any of those people knew that not only did they have an angry High Demon within striking distance, but I had their scents down and would never forget them.

# Chapter 13

Twylec's contingent managed to stay away from me, though, after their Queen's first insult. They should. I was watching them like a hawk and I think Rigo, Reemagar and Thurlow were, too. We discussed several agenda items that afternoon, but they didn't really amount to much and the votes were cast quickly.

The item I wanted to discuss most came on day four—that's when it would be decided whether each world could approve its own religions. I wanted my say and Grand Alliance Council oversight on that one.

Grand Alliance Council oversight meant that each petitioning religion would be carefully investigated by the Grand Alliance Council before they were allowed to set up temples and collect donations on any world. In Solar Red's case, they'd be investigated before they could set up temples and start maiming and killing.

Meanwhile, there was a lot of other political bull crap to get through, and if Queen Tamaritha's pet Ra'Ak didn't tip their hand before the meeting was over on the seventh day, I intended to find a way to follow them right back home, and they were going to get a quick send-off. I wondered if Tamaritha, cousin to Satris who'd helped kill Davan, knew what was following her around.

I learned later that more than half the Alliance members had been invited to a dinner and ball held that evening by the royal family on Nemizan. Of course, I wasn't invited. That was fine with me—we went back to the hotel and had a quiet dinner.

Afterward, Grant and Heathe put a list together of all the members who'd made a point of insulting us. More than two hundred had gone out of their way to be rude. Of that two hundred or so, twenty-seven had vampires on their planets. I found that interesting. Were their vampires being mistreated? I asked Grant and Heathe to check on that for me when we returned to Le-Ath Veronis.

We were watching the late local news before going to bed, and all stations had reporters positioned throughout the Nemizana Palace, talking to this world leader or that. It was truly boring, too, until my name was mentioned.

"It hasn't gone unnoticed," the reporter stated, "that Queen Lissa of Le-Ath Veronis has chosen not to attend. Some contend that it is due to the price on her head. Many leaders are concerned for their safety, as they are forced to be in such close proximity to Queen Lissa during the meetings." Then they cut to this member or that, most of whom had already made their feelings known about me already.

"I can't say that the Alliance is capable of protecting all of us, with that much money being offered for her death. It makes me wonder just why she has a price on her head to begin with." That was the president of Deveiphis speaking—she was a petite brunette who affected a delicate shiver at how much danger she might be in. It made me wonder how she'd gotten her job.

Overall, I was stunned at the media firestorm that now surrounded me. I hadn't been invited to the stupid ball to begin with and now they were accusing me of snubbing people or putting them in danger. Figures.

Twylec was putting them in a lot more danger, the way I saw it. I found myself wishing Le-Ath Veronis had never joined the Alliance. Erland rubbed my back and shoulders while I watched the entire debacle and then the reruns.

"Don't let them get to you—politics can be a backstabbing business," he murmured. "We'll get through this."

Well, I hadn't heard his name dragged through the muck like mine had been over this thing or that. Before, when Gabron had sold me out, that media feeding frenzy had been awful. I didn't find out until later that Kifirin removed all damaging information concerning Gabron from memories and records, just for me. The ones it had affected the most, though; we still remembered.

Reemagar had to place a healing sleep that night; I would have tossed and turned if he hadn't. The following morning brought more surprises, too, and none of them were good. World leaders and heads of state were demanding that their tables be moved as far from mine as possible.

That wasn't all I knew, either. Reemagar and Thurlow knew it too—Twylec's Ra'Ak had just made their intentions clear and it chilled me to the bone. I'd known since the first day that these were connected to the one I'd killed on Vionn. They had le'meruh as he did, and had just placed their deadly coercion on the members who attended the ball the night before. It terrified me—if they had plans to take over the Alliance, this was the way to do it.

I heard Tamaritha laughing over the moving of tables at one point. Not only was she clueless to what was going on around her, she didn't think I could hear from that distance. The Queen of Twylec should have studied up on her vampires. Honestly, if there'd been any vampires on Twylec, they would now have a standing invitation to relocate to Le-Ath Veronis, all expenses paid.

"I feel they are accomplishing their goals in this way, and will cause no physical harm at the Conclave itself," Thurlow whispered in my ear as we took seats at our table. Nobody else was within forty feet of us. It felt as if we clung to a small, round raft, adrift in a sea filled with manipulated hate, fear and disgust.

"What kind of harm do you think they've caused by casting coercion on the leaders of more than half the Alliance?" I hissed back. "If they get the green light to approve their own religions, and you can bet they'll vote that way in two days, what kind of harm do you think is coming?"

"Lady, do not upset yourself, I beg you," Thurlow said gently, taking my hand and kissing it.

"This is so fucked up," I sighed.

"Le-Ath Veronis may be an island in this storm, if the worst comes," Erland breathed next to me. I sat between him and Thurlow at the table. "Wylend has refused to join the Reth Alliance many times, and Karathia is heavily shielded as a result. We do not depend on Alliance troops to protect us. At least we know that Kifirin, Le-Ath Veronis and Karathia will stand, even if the others fall."

"Erland, that's not the answer I want," I turned to him and searched his beautiful, dark eyes. "I'm thinking of children, sacrificed to Ra'Ak and Solar Red's sadistic lusts. As soon as this Conclave is over, I'm hunting those bastards down and killing them. It's the only way I know to neutralize the coercion they've placed."

* * *

Erland turned on the vid screen the moment we arrived at our hotel, and we watched special news vids broadcast across the Alliance. This was what I'd asked Erland to do for me through his spying efforts—a reputable journalist stood before a temple on one of many worlds he'd investigated, which had ties to Solar Red or Red Hand.

He spoke of how those religions had posed as legitimate organizations or blatantly offered money to place their

# Chapter 13

temples on Reth Alliance worlds. Somehow, too, the journalist had smuggled spies inside two temples. We saw human sacrifices in living color, via hidden cameras.

A list of worlds was given, all belonging to the Alliance, which now had temples attributed to other religions but belonging to Solar Red. A spokesman for the Founder and twenty Charter Members of the Grand Alliance Council, who'd formed the Reth Alliance in the beginning, blamed the worlds themselves for not providing complete information on the religions before they were approved, and the worlds were blaming the Alliance, of course.

None of those worlds admitted that they'd taken money in any way, and Twylec wasn't on the list of exposed worlds. The Ra'Ak influence, I'm sure. It looked to be a good-sized battle shaping up over the whole thing. My honey Erland had come through for me, though, with flying colors. I think I told him I loved him at least half a dozen times.

"I would have done this before, if I'd known it would get this kind of response," he smiled down at me after getting a few kisses and a long hug.

The night was long, though, and every leader that had coercion placed by Twylec's Ra'Ak were calling the vids contrived or false and accusing the journalist and his backers of manufacturing lies in order to further a political agenda.

Yep, no matter where you are, politics and politicians are the same. Sadly, many Alliance citizens believed them, so we were at a stalemate and no better off than we were before.

"Lissa, I do not wish to alarm you, but the hotel is on fire," Reemagar interrupted my vid watching.

"Crap," I muttered. "And we haven't even had dinner, yet."

* * *

# Blood War

News crews were on the scene as we all trooped into the central courtyard at the hotel's insistence, while the fire stations responded to the fire in our building and the two on either side. Yeah, somebody was after me, and the journalists already had that information. They'd heard from several factions and individuals already, all claiming responsibility and all hoping that Black Mist would pay them the reward money in the event of my premature death.

Some people will do anything for money, and some people will pretend to do anything for money. Journalists were falling over themselves as they attempted to get interviews with me. They shouted stupid questions such as "Were you afraid for your life?" or, "Will this force you to leave the Conclave early?"

I wanted to give them the finger, but thought of Gavin and didn't. He would view that as conduct unbecoming any vampire and be embarrassed on my behalf. It was funny, actually, that Gavin was now my conscience.

The not so good news came later, and if there's worse news than somebody trying to burn down your hotel, it's that the hotel is now kicking you out because you're a security risk.

How could I blame them? It didn't do anything to improve my temper, though. I was ready to fold home and fold back in for the meetings each day. We were approached by Alliance security, however, and were assured that they had a safe facility available for our use and protection.

When I arrived at the facility (under heavy ASD guard), I figured they'd already prepared for what had just happened—there were accommodations for all my crew, including a stockpile of blood substitute shipped in from Le-Ath Veronis.

The facility was windowless, belowground and quite sterile—no paintings, comforts or extra supplies were provided. It reminded me of a bomb shelter, circa 1960s Earth. We set up our shields again.

The hotel staff might have been very surprised to learn that even had the rest of their hotel burned to the ground, our rooms wouldn't have been singed. That's where the shields had been placed and they would have held no matter what.

We had guards now, right outside our rooms and outside the facility, too. A lot of trouble to go to, I think, when we could have saved them the effort. I wanted to go home. Nobody wanted me on Nemizan—except the ones trying to kill me and collect the bounty.

At least on Le-Ath Veronis, some of the citizens were glad to see me. Thurlow, who'd been quiet until now, looked at me as if he were reading my mind. "We can sneak away with none the wiser, Lara'Kayan. You should go if that is what you want. We can be back in plenty of time."

"All right," I nodded. "Who wants to stay and who wants to go?"

Garde, Rigo, Grant and Heathe stayed to keep up appearances; the rest of us went to Le-Ath Veronis. We hadn't been there ten minutes before the attack came.

* * *

*Black Mist Headquarters*

"The mirrors are placed, brother," Zethias smiled. "They believe they are safe on the darkened half of their planet. They will learn differently in a matter of ticks." Viregruz watched the monitor—he wished to see a major portion of Le-Ath Veronis' vampires die. His brothers on Nemizan were working to bomb and then burn the Queen's hotel suite—all knew that vampires were vulnerable in a fire.

*We have failed with the explosion and fire,* Viregruz received mindspeech from Ringolar. *It is likely her Larentii mate placed shields and we cannot compromise those. The ASD has now placed the target in an underground bunker, where it will be more difficult to reach her. Send our brothers; we will implement the other plan.*

*Very well,* Viregruz returned. *They are coming now.* Viregruz turned back to his monitor after sending Zethias and Levecus to Nemizan.

* * *

*Le-Ath Veronis*
*Lissa*

Solar mirrors—many of them—carefully placed at just the right angle, directed the sun at Lissia, my capital city. Any vampire not hidden away in a darkened spot might have been fried, if it hadn't been for my Larentii's ingenious designs.

I wasn't sure how they'd known to place them ahead of time, but they'd done it. Light-gathering nets, invisible to the naked eye, were placed in just the right spots and bled the reflected sunlight away, shooting it outward into space.

My attackers thought they'd kill vampires—and lots of them. My vampires didn't even realize they were under attack. Thurlow and I destroyed the solar mirrors—he knew the Larentii trick of separating the atoms, and they floated harmlessly away. The nets were left in place, however, in case someone else got the same bright idea.

"Are there any news crews fresh on the planet?" I stalked through the hallways of my palace, guards, servants, mates and comesuli trailing in my wake. I wanted to know if anybody had been notified so they could circle like vultures and record images of vampires frying.

There were a few words I wanted to say to them if that was the case. Information was provided; Gavin, Tony, Drake and Drew supplied it with help from Trevor and his department, and we had six news crews in a meeting room at Adam's casino in no time flat.

"What did you know, and who told you?" I demanded, after Merrill had come to place compulsion for me. They'd all gotten information—after paying a hefty fee to a high-ranking advisor on Twylec. They didn't look comfortable, either, when I informed them that the show they'd come to see had been canceled.

"You knew something was going to happen and you failed to notify anyone." I was beginning to feel extremely angry. Turning to Gavin and Tony I hissed out, "Get Bryan." Bryan arrived quickly, with a handpicked news crew. He asked the questions, I stayed out of the picture. I was supposed to be on Nemizan, still, twiddling my fingers inside an underground bunker.

Connegar folded in and I gave him the biggest hug, after giving one to Reemagar, who was offering me the Larentii equivalent of a foolish grin. They'd protected Le-Ath Veronis.

I held both their hands as the news crews spilled their guts to Bryan, and they trilled softly when I found out how bloodthirsty the journalists really were. They wanted to see death and destruction and were ready to interview guests from Casino City after happily recording vampires screaming, dying and turning to ash.

With help from my oldest vampires, I now had half a dozen news crews in front of casinos in Casino City, all telling viewers via live feeds about the crisis that had been averted on Le-Ath Veronis.

"We have no specific information," I heard one reporter say as I stood with my mates and security team, my arms crossed angrily over my chest. "We only know from an unidentified source on Twylec that an attack was planned, and someone among the news crews passed information to the authorities so the attempt could be prevented."

Bryan had one of his vampire reporters there, and he was asking questions. We hadn't told the news crews to spill their guts to him so he was getting the runaround, but he knew it was coming. He asked the questions anyway, and anyone watching the newsfeeds would see evasive reporters.

The information that I'd wanted to be passed along was given out—that Twylec had somehow been behind all this. When the newsfeeds and interviews were over, we sent the news crews packing—Trevor and his department made sure they were loaded up and moved off world in as little time as possible.

* * *

*Black Mist Headquarters*
Viregruz cursed and then proceeded to destroy his private study. His brothers would have to destroy the bitch Queen, but their plans included destroying Nemizan with her. No matter—in the aftermath, the Reth Alliance would be scrambling, making it easy for him and Solar Red to take it over.

New leaders would come quickly and more le'meruh would be implemented. Viregruz calmed himself and sent for a Blood Captain. Prylvis would be notified and Solar Red would prepare to send out more Ra'Ak priests at a moment's notice. The Reth Alliance would be theirs—sooner than anticipated.

* * *

*Le-Ath Veronis*
*Lissa*

# Chapter 13

"Thank goodness that's done," I muttered as Gavin followed me to my suite. I was shocked to find Roff and his brother, Markoff, waiting outside the door.

"Lissa, Giff's child has come," Roff said. I stared at him. He should be with her, celebrating. He seemed sad and upset instead.

"What's wrong?" I said immediately. Markoff's face reflected the emotion displayed by Roff, so I knew something had happened.

"Rolfe is trying to convince her otherwise, but well," Roff stared at his shoes.

"What my brother is attempting to say," Markoff took up the conversation, "is that Giff fears for her child. She knows of your father's betrayal and interference, and of the price on your head. She refuses to allow you near the child. She worries that Toff will not be the only child taken. I know this is a blow, and I have her resignation," Markoff handed an envelope to me.

I stared in shock at the envelope now in my hand. It was addressed to me—in Giff's hand. "The baby is all right?" I looked up at Roff.

"Yoff is fine." His face looked gray. The baby was fine—I just couldn't see him. Giff wouldn't allow it. If a more crushing blow could be delivered at the end of that long and awful day, I didn't know what it might be.

"Rolfe is trying to convince her that this is foolish," Roff held out a hand.

"Tell him not to bother. I'm going back to Nemizan, now." I folded away before anyone could stop me.

I'd wondered why Giff hadn't come to see me after I'd told her about Toff. It was obvious that Griffin wasn't done harming me yet. He'd saved Wyatt at Toff's expense, and the expense of everyone around him. Since he'd broken the rules and interfered, there was no telling how many ripples that act had created, or how many lives might be affected before those ripples stopped somewhere. I intended to go to Nemizan, just as I'd said, but I took a detour, first.

The Guardian stood at the top of the Oklahoma State Capitol building three hundred years in the past. Night had fallen and a few stars twinkled overhead as I stared over the city. I remembered well the scents in the air around the city; it was early spring in Oklahoma.

In nearby Nichols Hills, Gavin and I walked the perimeter of Winkler's borrowed mansion. If I'd known at that time just what my life might come to, would I have stood in the sun in a wheat field instead of digging into the soil to preserve my life? I didn't have an answer for that.

* * *

*Earth*

*Merrill Leopard's Manor*

"Things have just taken a terrible turn," Griffin stared down at Wyatt, who slept peacefully in his crib.

"Brenten, what are you talking about?" Amara stared at her mate.

"I didn't bother *Looking* for all the *Possibilities*. I was afraid to go down those paths," Griffin sighed. "And now, Belen has removed my ability to *Look* into Wyatt's future. Since Lissa wouldn't punish me, he chose to do this in her stead. I've been *Looking* into the paths of others, now, and I don't know what to do. Deaths will come and there's no way for me to stop them."

"Tell me these deaths won't affect your daughter," Amara frowned at Griffin.

"I can't say that, Amara. I can't lie, so don't ask me."

# Chapter 13

"You just answered my question, Brenten. Whether you intended to or not. How many deaths will come?"
"Many," Griffin muttered before folding away.

# Chapter 14

*N*emizan
*Lissa*
"Any legitimate religion should welcome an investigation into their background." I'd stood when my turn came to speak. "Not only should the world in question have approval, but that approval should also come from the Alliance itself. The Charter Members look carefully into each world before it is admitted to the Alliance; why can't each religion bear the same scrutiny?"

"Many religions have bloody beginnings, but are now widely accepted and serve the people," someone else across the room stood up to have his say. He was right about that—the Inquisition came to mind, among other things.

"Then put a time limit on that," I countered. "If they've changed and haven't engaged in unlawful practices for the past two hundred years, then the older stuff can be ignored. I don't see Solar Red giving up their torture and sacrifice anytime soon, do you? Red Hand is right behind them on that front, and Black Mist, if they decide to declare themselves a religion—well, let's hope we're all spared that."

"You think Black Mist will go that far?" Someone else stood and asked.

"How far do you think they've gone already?" I demanded. "They move about freely outside the Alliance worlds and would love to gain a legitimate foothold in the Alliance itself. Believe me when I say that there's something else there besides a group of bloodthirsty assassins who'd happily kill you, along with the one you'd paid them to kill."

I looked about me. My argument was falling on deaf ears; the Ra'Ak had seen to that. I felt compelled to make the argument anyway—to get my objections on record, at least.

"Therefore," I went on, "you have to ask yourselves what it is that these religions want. Is it control? Do they wish to take your worlds from you by treachery and assassination? If so, what comes after that? What will happen when they have those worlds and only their own live upon them? Will they then war among themselves? I see no end to it. The time to stop Black Mist, Solar Red and Red Hand is now. While we have the opportunity and they only have a slight presence in the Alliance. If we wait, then we fall."

"You only say that because Black Mist has a price on your head." Tamaritha of Twylec stood to give her two cents.

"So, you know for certain that it's Black Mist that has a price on my head? Until now, that has only been a rumor," I shot back. "I'd like to know how you came by that information. What would you do, if Black Mist had placed the price on your head? I haven't heard you speak up before, Queen Tamaritha, even though you have what you think to be Solar Red

# Chapter 14

sycophants following you around like lapdogs. If you knew what they truly are, you'd run screaming from this hall instead of standing there, defending a caste of assassins in front of the entire Alliance."

I know—I shouldn't have let that last part slip past my lips, but just as I was always taught—words, once said, are impossible to take back. Looks like I hadn't learned that lesson yet. And when all three Ra'Ak changed inside the meeting hall and were immediately joined by their two remaining brothers, all hell broke loose.

Alliance members were shouting and backing away, and some began screaming when the lengthy, coppery serpents gulped down Tamaritha of Twylec and her six guards and assistants with barely any effort.

Alliance guards began shooting at the monsters while Alliance Heads of State fled the meeting hall amid screaming, shouting and chaos. Only a few members stayed—some were shapeshifters and had gone to their animal shapes.

They may have thought to help combat the Ra'Ak. I sent mindspeech, telling them to stay back—these had been full Dark Elemaiya before their turn to Ra'Ak, and all had le'meruh. We didn't need anybody else under the influence of these Ra'Ak.

"Lissa, more are coming, and they plan to destroy Nemizan," Thurlow whispered next to me. Garde, Erland and Reemagar were all for getting us off the planet, but stayed because I did. Six more Ra'Ak dropped in and went after anyone else left inside the meeting hall. As a second wave of Alliance guards and soldiers were killed and/or eaten by the Ra'Ak, I decided it was time to do something about them.

* * *

*Solar Red Headquarters*

"Yes, I see them." Prylvis was on his communicator, watching the events on Nemizan through tiny cameras placed in one of his Ra'Ak servant's eyes. They all had them—Ringolar had seen to it. Viregruz hadn't wanted to call in a few of Prylvis' Ra'Ak, but had them on standby anyway. They'd left Prylvis' side quickly, when the call came from Ringolar.

"Yours will provide the distraction while mine handle the destruction," Viregruz replied. "The Alliance is within our grasp, Tetsurna."

* * *

*Nemizan*

*Lissa*

The first five disappeared while I was busy causing the last six to explode by misting inside their brains. That was certainly different—I didn't expect them to run like that. Coming back to corporeality, I looked about me, wondering if the five were planning to return and attack me.

Thurlow was beside me, as were Erland, Garde, Rigo and Reemagar. Erland sent Grant and Heathe outside the building with the others, after asking them to help the wounded if they could. Now we had five missing Ra'Ak and no idea whether they were going to return with backup.

"I cannot interfere, unless it is to save your life," Reemagar informed me softly, as more Alliance guards came forward to examine chunks of Ra'Ak dust. These chunks were bigger than their fists and someone in my group—either Erland or Reemagar—had shielded anyone left inside the meeting hall when the last two I'd killed had dusted. The chunks were nudged with laser rifles or boots as Alliance troops stared at them and then at me. I just shrugged at them, stalling for time.

# Chapter 14

"What do you think they're going to do now?" I asked quietly.

"I do not know, avilepha, but I think we should leave," Garde whispered back. "I do not think we are safe, although it is quiet, now." He hadn't turned Thifilathi—the Alliance cameras were still recording and we didn't need to see images of a High Demon on the rampage scattered across the Alliance—that was trouble waiting to be exploited.

"Yeah, I get that idea, too," I muttered. My skin was itching like crazy and I had no idea what to do.

Who knew that together—five of them—would have that much power? Had any of them ever pooled their energy before, to cause that much harm? I had the briefest moment to think about asking Kifirin if this was what he'd intended when he'd created them, but there wasn't any time to pursue that train of thought.

When Thurlow said they'd intended to destroy the planet, I'd thought it would be a direct attack. It wasn't. Three inhabited worlds revolved around Nemizan's sun, all belonging to the Alliance. I knew what they planned the moment everything went dark.

The Ra'Ak meant to destroy everything in that sun's orbit, by destroying the sun itself. Planets, moons, lives, everything. I had a shield around Nemizan, but not around anything else and certainly not its sun.

Even if my shield remained in place around Nemizan, without sunlight, the planet would freeze and die. It might take a week for the whole thing to freeze up, but it would.

I also had only a few minutes to do something—it would take little more than eight minutes for the blast caused by the Ra'Ak to hit Nemizan and its sister planets. Eight minutes to save billions of lives.

# Blood War

No pressure.

*Connegar and I will place shields around the other two planets*, Reemagar sent to me. *We dare not interfere beyond that. You must find a way past this or come with us and leave the others here to their fate.*

What was I supposed to do? Five powerful Ra'Ak, who'd combined their power and destroyed a sun with it, had one major objective in mind—killing me. In order to accomplish that, they were about to kill billions. In doing so, they still wouldn't get what they wanted—I could fold away with my small party and live comfortably on my own world. And then wallow in depression and misery afterward, knowing that I'd caused billions—including children—to die. Could I live with that?

The short answer was no. I didn't have much time to fix things, either. What do you do when you're faced with three orphaned planets and the billions of lives that exist upon them?

*I'll help*, he offered. Well, why wasn't I expecting him to show up?

*What are they supposed to do?* I grumped mentally. *File a change of address at the post office?*

*We don't have much time*, he warned. *Look for a suitable sun. The placement of these worlds is critical and we have to move them before the blast from their destroyed sun hits them.*

He was right. The placement was critical if we expected to maintain climate, polar positions and a multitude of other things.

* * *

"Where did she go?" Erland shouted as Lissa's body went limp and dropped to the floor.

296

# Chapter 14

"She has gone to energy, warlock," Reemagar replied. "That is not the least of our worries, however. Nemizan's sun is now dead and the blast from its destruction is coming our way. And we have these." He nodded toward fifty Ra'Ak who'd appeared from nothing. "I will protect her body," Reemagar went on. "But be prepared when we," he was unable to finish his sentence; the planet lurched beneath their feet.

"What the fuck?" Erland shouted as the grinding noise began. Wood and marble floors buckled and split beneath their feet, windows cracked and shattered in the walls around them.

"High Demon, the cameras are no longer recording," Connegar folded in. "Reemagar and I are protecting Nemizan's sister planets. Might you slow down these Ra'Ak? They think to destroy Lissa, then feed and fold away at the last moment."

"I'll most certainly slow them down," Garde muttered and went Full Thifilathi. His roar caused more glass to fall from shattered windows and the wind created when he flapped huge, leathery black wings caused Alliance guards to lose their footing. Roaring again, Garde launched his black-scaled Thifilathi toward waiting Ra'Ak.

"I can help with this," Erland strode forward as the planet lurched again. It barely slowed the spell Erland hurled against the first of many charging Ra'Ak. Gardevik Rath had already twisted heads from three coppery bodies and was now chasing after others. His deafening roar created new cracks in the ceiling overhead.

"They're running outside," Heathe shouted as he slid to a spot beside Erland. "They're eating people out there."

"I won't mind if it's only politicians," Erland snarled and leveled another blast at fleeing Ra'Ak. He was thankful that

# Blood War

Gardevik's Thifilathi negated a Ra'Ak's considerable power—these were racing away from the High Demon in an effort to regain their folding ability.

A High Demon in full Thifilathi could neutralize a Ra'Ak's power for a hundred yards, and these Ra'Ak were only beginning to discover that fact. They could either run to regain their ability or turn and fight with the strength in their scaled bodies.

"I'll help those outside," Rigo rushed toward the doors and the Ra'Ak who were killing in the courtyard. Rigo moved swiftly as he attacked the first two Ra'Ak he reached. They screamed in pain, too, from the deep slices dealt by his claws.

"Oh, no," Heathe murmured as twenty-five Ra'Ak turned to attack Garde's Thifilathi.

"No worries, young vampire," Erland said. "I've been saving this one." The blast that erupted beneath twenty-five huge, scaled serpents blew them upward and through the meeting hall ceiling.

* * *

*We must hurry,* he urged me on. *I don't have the ability to change What Was. At this moment, only the Larentii Wise Ones hold that talent, and they may only use it to affect individuals or isolated incidents. For this, their power is terribly insufficient.*

I knew—in some way—what he meant by *What Was.* It didn't involve bending time or interference. It involved standing in the present and changing what had already happened. Somehow, those who wielded that ability had the talent for reversing any negative impact on the timeline. The Larentii Wise Ones were called that because they were wise enough to recognize when their talent was required and when it wasn't. They didn't use it often.

# Chapter 14

Grace was alive because of the Larentii Wise Ones—she'd died when Graegar was born. Even as a newborn, Graegar held a great deal of power and he'd combined his talent with that of the others and brought his mother back. It was something I wasn't supposed to know, but I did. Connegar had told me.

*Here*, I shouted.

*Yes. This is good*, he agreed. We'd found a suitable sun. Now, all we had to do was move three planets—in less than two minutes.

*Lissa, you must hurry—the blast is arriving*, Connegar sent. Oh, lord. He sent images, too—the five Ra'Ak who'd pooled their power to destroy Nemizan's sun weren't finished; they were speeding up the blast, somehow.

Fuck. We didn't have as much time as we thought. I turned to the one helping me. If I'd been corporeal, I would have wept. *Think of the planets as tennis balls*, he shouted inside my head, pulling me away from my mental dismay.

* * *

*Nemizan*

"Where the hell is Lissa? The fucking planet is breaking apart!" Erland shouted.

"There are dead people all over the courtyard outside," Grant panted as he came to stand with Erland and Heathe. "Either poisoned or crushed by Ra'Ak. Rigo is doing what he can and some people got away, but Ra'Ak are chasing them, now. There's just too many of them."

"They'd better fold away soon, before everything is blown to the void," Erland hissed, shooting another blasting spell toward a Ra'Ak threatening Gardevik's back. The Ra'Ak was thrown against a wall with a resounding boom, causing the wall to collapse in a pile of dust.

# Blood War

"I think we should fold away soon, warlock," Thurlow said as he coalesced beside Grant. "We will take Lissa's body. I have been energy outside the planet; things are not going well, my friend." The planet lurched again and they watched in horror as Garde's Thifilathi lost his footing and fell beneath a horde of attacking Ra'Ak.

* * *

*Lissa*

*Lissa, no!* he shouted. What was I supposed to do—dally with three tennis balls until their equators fell at exactly the right spot? I wasn't about to do that while my High Demon mate was attacked by Ra'Ak. Three worlds were slapped haphazardly into place before I refocused on Nemizan, my mates and the Ra'Ak.

I'm sorry to say that I ignored the shouting (and a little cursing) as he yelled for me to place three worlds in better spots. Garde would die if I didn't do something. Ra'Ak lives popped out of existence as I directed power into their brains. My High Demon's Thifilathi was slowly rising from a cracked and broken floor, his wings torn and black scales ruptured and broken in many places. He was alive and that's all I cared about.

Then, ignoring pleas to go back and fix the rotations of three planets, I went looking for the five who'd done this to begin with. Did they think to hide from me? I laughed at their petty plans and small minds. I was powerful as energy, and the fragile tether that held me to the worlds and my corporeal existence was ignored as I searched them out. Did they truly think to hide from me? The tether loosened.

* * *

*Nemizan*

300

# Chapter 14

"I'm fine, stop fussing," Garde wanted to brush Karzac aside. That wouldn't do. The curmudgeonly physician would only return, with help from Jayd and three other High Demons, if necessary.

Garde chose to ignore the healing and allowed his eyes to stray to Lissa's body instead. It lay on a table where Reemagar had placed it, appearing lifeless except for the random, occasional breath that lifted her chest. Garde turned away—it was difficult seeing her like that.

Rigo received medical care as well—he'd been clawed by two Ra'Ak while trying to slow them down. Jeff, Shane and Franklin worked on the ancient vampire's wounds. He, too, often turned his gaze to Lissa's body.

Erland had sailed through the fray without a scratch, although he now sat on the floor, breathing heavily from exhaustion. If the battle had lasted any longer, he would have drained every bit of his reserves.

The meeting hall was roofless and crumbling with only three walls standing. The rest of Nemizan looked much the same. At least a sun's light was shining down—even if it wasn't the sun Nemizan recognized.

"She should be back by now," Grant whispered. He'd come to stand next to Garde and blatantly stared at Lissa's body in fear. Garde blinked in alarm at Lissa's vampire assistant.

* * *

*Lissa*

So many things went through my consciousness as I flew through the universe. All the things that troubled me in my corporeal form weren't so troubling while I was energy. In fact, they weren't troubling at all.

# Blood War

All my cares and worries, left behind to trouble small lives on tiny planets. My body remained on a world the inhabitants named Nemizan. I barely gave it a thought as I flew free. I was of the Nameless Ones, after all.

Yes, I knew our name, but it wasn't something any of us could repeat, except to one another. I felt good as energy. Better than I'd ever felt before. I had no pain. No price on my head or stolen child. No father who'd betrayed me, time and again. No loved ones dying or deserting me. No beatings, deaths or near-deaths.

The universe was feeding me as I raced through it. I realized, then, that I didn't have to search them out. As energy, I could call them to me. The tether broke and five Ra'Ak died with barely a flick of my power.

* * *

"I was afraid of this." Kifirin reached out to touch Lissa's cheek, stroking it lightly. "She has discovered her true identity and is now flying unfettered through the universes, merely for the pleasure of it."

"But she's still breathing," Erland growled softly. Reemagar held Lissa's body in his arms, and even the power of the Larentii, great as it was, couldn't bring Lissa's spirit back to it.

They all stood inside the meeting hall as members of the Alliance stole back inside. Few realized how closely they'd come to annihilation. Many had died, but many more survived. Lissa had done that for them. Now, Lissa no longer inhabited her body.

"She has a decision to make, now," Kifirin replied. "To return to her body or stay as she is. I warn you, if she does not come back to her body voluntarily within four weeks, I will allow this body to die. If she does not return within that time,

# Chapter 14

she will not return. You may keep her body alive until then."
Kifirin folded away.

* * *

*Le-Ath Veronis*

"Rigo, Heathe and Grant stayed at the Conclave, but Rigo won't have a voice, he can only take notes," Erland paced inside Lissa's library at the palace. "Kifirin says he'll let Lissa's body die if she doesn't come back within four weeks."

Dragon and Devin had come to be with Drake and Drew, who were having difficulty understanding any of it. "She just flexed her power and suddenly forgot about us?" Drew was extremely upset.

"That isn't how things happen, young one," Belen appeared in a flash of light. "We have many cares and we hear and see many things. I have to place a Focus upon the Saa Thalarr and their doings, similar to placing a bookmark inside a book, so I can find that place easily when it is needed. Lissa has not placed any Focus, yet. She will, in all probability, but that could happen tomorrow or in a thousand years. Time has no meaning to my kind, when we are in our natural state."

"We have no way of getting a message to her—to ask her to come back?" Gavin sat beside Aurelius. Aurelius had an unobtrusive grip on Gavin's arm.

"Send out mindspeech, she may pick it up," Belen answered and disappeared.

"May pick it up? What the hell does that mean?" Tony almost exploded.

"You do not understand," Kifirin appeared in Belen's place. "As she is now, she has no pain. Think of what that means. She has had pain all her life and now she is free of it. I beg you not to be angry with her. If anything brings her back,

303

it will be your love for her and nothing else." Kifirin also disappeared.

Roff, who sat next to Flavio, began to weep.

* * *

*Black Mist Headquarters*

"Withdraw the reward on the Queen of Le-Ath Veronis," Viregruz, the creator and head of Black Mist demanded of his underlings. He glared at them angrily, toying with the idea of killing a few of them.

His brothers—all six of them, had died somehow at the Queen's hand. This had become personal for him. He wanted her death for himself, and intended to bring about that death as swiftly as possible. "I am declaring war—on the Queen of Le-Ath Veronis," he breathed. His minions cowered in alarm.

The End

www.ingramcontent.com/pod-product-compliance
Lightning Source LLC
Chambersburg PA
CBHW071725190726
48292CB00003B/622